Advance Praise for *Lavender Secrets*

"*Lavender Secrets* is a romantic's romance. My only complaint? It ends too soon."

~ **Joan Opyr**, author of *Idaho Code*

"Relationships are complex. They can be nurturing and supportive or the most destructive aspect in a person's life. They shape how a person thinks and reacts to situations and other people. Learning how to deal with them, especially if the relationship isn't positive, can be the most difficult part of living.

At first, *Lavender Secrets* appears to be another romance, but, as the story unfolds, it is clear that much more is developing. These people are trying to learn how they fit into each other's lives. They are also struggling to understand what they want from those lives and the people who are involved in them. It is about making connections, altering some connections, and learning to sever others. The book is about learning how to put the pieces of your puzzle together so that you get the best fit possible between all of your relationships to create the most satisfying life that you can. And the bonus in this book is that everything takes place in what is a plain good story. *Lavender Secrets* is well worth the time you will spend reading it."

~ **Lynne Pierce**, reviewer for JustAboutWrite.com

Lavender Secrets

Sandra Barret

Yellow Rose Books

Nederland, Texas

ISBN 978-1-932300-73-4

First Printing 2007

9 8 7 6 5 4 3 2 1

Cover design by Donna Pawlowski

Published by:

Regal Crest Enterprises, LLC
4700 Hwy 365, Ste A
PMB 210
Port Arthur, Texas 77642

Find us on the World Wide Web at
http://www.regalcrest.biz

Printed in the United States of America

Acknowledgments

My thanks to the following people, for helping to pull a story out of the incoherent dribble of my first drafts: Miriam English, Arlene (Skip) Germain, Matthew Hagan, Gail (Kali) Ludwig, Ilene Siegel, and editors Ruta Skujins, and Kathleen A. Torpy. Thanks to the many folks on www.livejournal.com, who made suggestions, listened to me babble, and cheered me on the whole way.

And a special thanks to author Lynn Viehl, for her constant support of new and aspiring authors.

For Shula. All of the good, all of the time.

"There is no lighter burden, nor more agreeable, than a pen."
~Petrarch

Chapter
One

EMMA LEVANTEUR WASN'T sure why she agreed to a night on the town. Even if it was Saturday night, and she didn't have a good excuse like college classes the next morning, she could have thought up an excuse to stay home, if she tried.

She took a swig from her bottle of beer and eyed her roommate who was leaning against the wall next to her. Jasmine Holly was short, her head barely reaching Emma's shoulders.

"Like what you see, Babe?" Jasmine asked.

Emma graced her with a fake smile and took another swig. This was a bad idea. Going dancing with the girl who broke up with her four years ago was definitely not one of her brighter decisions.

"Come on, Brainiac." Jasmine tugged at Emma's belt. "Let's dance."

Jasmine dragged her to the crowded dance floor. The DJ spun a jarring mix of hip hop and oldies with a heavy emphasis on the bass. Emma moved to the rhythm pulsating from massive speakers hiding in the corners of the darkened room. Other people around them danced to the beat. All of them were women, most of them drunk.

After downing the dregs of her beer, Emma set her bottle on a table before the next song started. Pointer Sisters. Where did the DJ dig up her music? Jasmine was oblivious to the DJ's decade of choice, her hips swaying and arms waving above her head. She shouted in Emma's ear, "What happened to that dance queen, Girl?"

Emma groaned. "Don't dredge that up again." Some things were better left in the past. Like drunk karaoke and ex-girlfriends who occasionally forgot the ex- part of that expression. The song segued abruptly into a slow dance. Jasmine's arms wrapped around her, pulling her close. Emma stiffened. Closing her eyes, she felt Jasmine's small, warm body pressed against her and breathed in Jasmine's perfume. This really was a bad idea.

"Jasmine," she said.

"Shush, you'll ruin the mood."

That was the idea, lover-girl. There was a time, a year or so after Jasmine broke up with her, when Emma would have given herself over completely if Jasmine had flirted with her as she was doing now. But after months of forcing herself to remain friends with Jasmine — that's what lesbians were supposed to do after a break-up, right? — Emma could now accept their occasional flirtations without risking another broken heart. Falling in love was a mistake she hadn't made since Jasmine and wouldn't make again any time soon. She and Jasmine were best friends, but the pain of their break-up had left a permanent mark in Emma's soul.

Emma pulled away at the end of the song. "I need another beer. How about you?"

"Sure, if you're buying."

Working her way through the mass of women on the dance floor, Emma searched for the bar. The flashing dance lights overhead exacerbated her general disorientation. She found the bar tucked into a corner beyond a dozen or more crowded tables. A swarm of women flirted with the lone bartender as Emma pushed her way to the front, holding a twenty in her hand. The combination of Jasmine's intentions and Emma's relatively celibate lifestyle was a volatile mix. A beer, a bit of distance, and she'd get through the night without making any big mistakes.

HOURS LATER THEY staggered through the dark streets of Cambridge, holding each other up and giggling at everyone they passed. Jasmine was in rare form. She pushed Emma up against the glass doors of their apartment building. The fluorescent lights illuminated Jasmine's elfin features as her hands wandered up under Emma's t-shirt, exploring, teasing. Emma bit back a moan. All her earlier worries were forgotten as she lowered her head, sinking into a warm, wet kiss.

She pulled out of the kiss and fumbled in her pocket for her keys. Jasmine pulled Emma's hand out of the pocket and slid her own in. Emma felt Jasmine's teasing hand slide across her inner thigh, only the thin fabric of her pocket separating their skin.

"We've got to get inside," Emma said. She looked at Jasmine through half-closed eyes.

"I'm trying, girl, I'm trying," Jasmine said.

Emma eased her back and found her key chain. They made their way into the elevator, arms wrapped around each other. The elevator started its journey to the ninth floor. Jasmine pressed her hip between Emma's legs and covered her neck with tiny nibbles.

Emma ran her fingers across Jasmine's back. She lifted Jasmine's chin and sank into another warm, inviting kiss. Emma's pants were unzipped before the elevator chimed their arrival at the ninth floor and the doors opened.

Jasmine took the keys from Emma's hands. "Allow me." She pulled Emma along the corridor, running her tongue across her deep red lips as she kept her gaze fixed on Emma. She opened their apartment and tossed the keys down the dark hallway. Emma heard them rattle as they landed on the linoleum.

"The lights," Emma said, feeling for the switch.

Jasmine pulled her into the dark front room. "Not tonight."

Emma let herself be led past the sofa to Jasmine's room. A streetlight glowed through the open window that looked down on Massachusetts Avenue, sending a pattern of light and shadow across Jasmine's unmade, queen-size bed. The sounds of cars drifted up from the street below.

"Jasmine. Maybe we..."

Soft lips pressing on hers ended Emma's half-hearted protest. She opened her lips to the pressure of Jasmine's tongue. Jasmine tugged at her pants, pushing them down and out of the way. Then she led Emma across the room. Emma stumbled as she walked, getting a low chuckle from Jasmine. She felt the edge of the bed against the back of her knees and sat back on the mattress, her jeans and panties gathered at her ankles. Jasmine knelt beside her at the side of the bed, pulling off Emma's clothes. Emma's ability to think disappeared as Jasmine's lips and tongue worked their magic up her legs. Jasmine's hands caressed Emma's taut stomach as Emma brushed her fingers through Jasmine's hair. Jasmine's hands moved down her stomach, one sliding to her back while the other worked its way across her inner thighs.

Jasmine separated her folds, and Emma's lips formed a silent "oh". An eager tongue licked and teased her until she was on the verge of begging Jasmine to go further. Then she felt Jasmine slip inside her. She rocked into the pressure of Jasmine's fingers. It felt so good. It had been ages, and this was so good.

She played with Jasmine's short black hair, urging her deeper. Thrilling currents of excitement grew from the focus of Jasmine's attention, where tongue and fingers worked in harmony. She clawed at Jasmine's thin shoulders as she rose to a rippling climax.

Emma lay back in a dreamy daze, feeling her own pulse throbbing against Jasmine's hand. She felt Jasmine slip out and opened her eyes. Jasmine stood up in the silvery light from the street and stripped off her top and skirt. She wore no bra or panties. Typical Jasmine style. Emma pulled off the rest of her own clothes and shifted on the bed to make room. Jasmine's scent mingled with her own as Emma wrapped herself around the smaller woman.

"Did I do you good, Babe?" Jasmine asked, her voice deep and husky.

Emma laughed. "You always did. Now I get to return the favor." She nudged Jasmine back on the sheets. Jasmine complied, stretching out beside her.

She pressed herself against the hard curves of Jasmine's toned body and sucked hard on Jasmine's swollen nipple, extracting a soft moan. Emma ran short nails in a trail along Jasmine's thighs, feeling the other woman arch into her. She rolled Jasmine onto her side so that she could spoon her from behind. Emma cupped a small breast with one hand and traced her other hand down Jasmine's side and across her thigh. She felt Jasmine shift toward that free hand as she stroked her inner thigh, then along the edges of Jasmine's black, curly mound. When she'd teased her enough, feeling the light body squirm toward her, Emma pushed two fingers into Jasmine, hard and fast. Jasmine's deep groan sent a thrill through Emma as she slipped in and out, her thumb brushing across Jasmine's swollen clitoris. Jasmine moaned as she pushed in time with Emma's thrusts. Her wetness dampened Emma's palm and Emma quickened her pace to match Jasmine's growing need. She could smell Jasmine's scent and wanted to taste her, but didn't dare shift positions. With one final thrust, Jasmine held Emma's hand in place, and Emma felt Jasmine's pulsing climax. She slipped her fingers out, and Jasmine rolled to face her, her dark eyes full of mischief. Emma felt herself grow moist again. This would be some night.

HARSH SUNLIGHT GLARED down on Emma. She groaned and pulled the bed sheet up over her head. Someone pulled it back off.

"Come on, Lazy Girl. Get up."

Emma rolled away from the offending light and mumbled obscenities into her pillow. Something poked her in the ribs.

"I'm serious," Jasmine said. "Alicia's coming over for brunch, and I need you out of my room before I bring her in."

Emma stifled a snide remark. Of course. Alicia. Date of the week. She peeled one eye open. Jasmine stood before her, showered, dressed, and ready for the next girl. Emma wasn't surprised. "Okay, I'm moving." She pulled herself upright and pushed back the jumble of sheet and blanket that she'd pulled up to cover them both sometime in the night. The coolness of the room hardened her exposed nipples, but it was far too late for modesty.

Jasmine planted a soft kiss on Emma's brow. "Thanks, Babe."

She whispered in Emma's ear, "You were great last night. Next time don't wait so long between sex-capades. It's not good for the soul." Jasmine gave her a wink and skipped out of the room.

Emma rubbed the sleep out of her eyes. Her head throbbed from too much beer. She looked around Jasmine's room, searching for her clothes. She found her jeans under the bed and her t-shirt draped over Jasmine's bureau. Her bra hid under the covers at the base of the bed, and her panties must have escaped into another dimension. Definitely too much beer and not enough common sense, she thought.

So what if she seldom had sex since Jasmine broke up with her. She had lived 18 years without sex before Jasmine. Four years sex-free afterward wasn't so bad, was it? In that time, she'd managed to get over her romantic feelings for Jasmine and develop a solid friendship with her ex-girlfriend. Occasionally, Emma developed crushes on other women, but she wouldn't let it get any further than that. After all, she'd let her feelings for Jasmine go beyond that, and what did that get her but months of unbearable pain when it all ended. Nope, she'd rather stay focused on graduate studies. Math was a safe haven for her.

She tossed her pile of clothes into her bedroom, grabbed a bathrobe to cover her naked body in case Alicia showed up early, and staggered into the bathroom. Her pounding head demanded attention as she tried to focus on the disheveled mess staring back at her in the mirror. Her pale brown eyes were barely visible through her tangled, chestnut-brown hair. She heard the doorbell ring. Alicia must be the prompt type. Emma stared at the claw-foot porcelain bathtub. Yes, that would be a good place to spend the rest of the morning. She turned on the hot water and let the steam fill the small bathroom. Now if only she'd brought in her English Literature book for tomorrow's class, then life would be perfect. Sort of.

PROFESSOR DAVIS LEANED forward on the old oak lectern, facing the class. "Sonnet 18. 'Shall I compare thee to a summer's day?' Who can tell me where the change occurs in this sonnet?"

Emma watched three hands shoot up in the front of the class. The front always answered. That's why Emma sat in the back. Volta, line nine, 'But thy eternal summer shall not fade', she thought to herself. Online Cliff Notes were a gift from God. English was not her best subject by any measure. But an hour and a half to stare at the professor three times a week was worth every minute of plot, theme, and symbolism torture.

She shifted in her hard metal chair to get a better view of

Davis. The tall British woman moved to the chalkboard as Emma studied her lean form. Tan slacks and a blue cardigan led up to the professor's shoulder-length hair, brown with golden highlights. Emma knew the highlights were a recent addition, but she approved of the change. Not that Davis cared if she approved or not, since Emma was just auditing the class. Emma suffered through these lectures, surrounded by English majors, Liberal Arts types, and who knows who else. All so she could sit in the back and bask in the beautiful British accent of Professor Nicole Davis. And beautiful British smile, and British hips, and British backside.

"Excellent," Davis said, jarring Emma back to the present. One of the over-achieving front-row types must have given the correct answer. "Now which of Shakespeare's favorite themes appears in this sonnet?"

Love, changing of the seasons, use of time, Emma thought. She didn't volunteer the answer, though. Her photographic memory, which knew every word of the Shakespeare Cliff Notes, was an unfair advantage over her classmates. So she kept quiet. Of course, the fact that she turned into a complete idiot whenever Davis spoke to her also helped to keep her mouth shut. She was probably the only Harvard graduate student in Mathematics who obsessed over Shakespeare and other early poets this semester.

Her thoughts wandered, remembering how she had bumped into Davis at the bookstore during winter break. She'd heard her voice first, arguing with one of the student drones who worked at the store. Emma had glanced around a pile of first-year Physics books to see who was telling the clerk off in such polite but scorching terms. She wasn't prepared for the sudden arousal that had swept over her at the first sight of Professor Davis. She'd waited to pump the frazzled clerk to find out who she was. Emma had already given herself over to a hopeless infatuation when she signed up to audit one of Davis's classes. It wasn't until later that she realized she'd committed herself to studying her least favorite subject, Shakespeare's English.

Davis's rich accent filled Emma's thoughts. She paced down the aisles as she lectured. Her tan slacks clung to long legs with a hint of strong thighs just beneath the curves of a well-exercised backside. Emma sank back into her chair when Davis came down her aisle. Her soft brown eyes met Emma's for an instant and then moved on to the next student. Emma studied her notebook just long enough for her flushed face to regain its natural color. This is why she came to class every day, she thought. Pathetic, but true. After weeks of auditing the class, Davis had noticed her, even if it was only a passing glance during class.

"Next week's assignment will be to read aloud and analyze a

sonnet of your choice."

Emma joined the class in a group groan. Davis had one of these open readings every month, and Emma hated it. The room became a shuffle of backpacks and papers as the class readied to leave. Emma lingered at her desk as the rest of the class got up.

"If you need help, you know my office hours," Davis said over the heads of the departing class.

Emma stuffed her notebook in her pack and made her way up the aisle to the exit. She managed to be the last one at the door when Davis called. "Sorry, could you hold that open for me?"

Emma stood with her mouth hanging open. Nice impression, she thought. She shut her trap and waited as Davis hoisted a box from under the lectern and walked out the door that Emma held open.

"Cheers," Davis said, and stepped past Emma.

Emma felt her face burn as Davis passed by. She caught the scent of the professor's perfume and struggled to recognize it. She regained an inch of sanity and followed Davis down the hallway, close enough to watch, but far enough to not be an obvious stalker. She hoped.

NICOLE DAVIS CAUGHT a glimpse of one of her students behind her as she walked out of the classroom building. She recognized the lanky, chestnut-haired woman from her last lecture, the quiet one who sat in the back of the class. She shifted the box of decorations into her left hand as she tried to adjust the drooping strap of her over-stuffed satchel with her right. The satchel chose to fight back, falling off her shoulder and hanging over the bend of her elbow. Exasperated, Nicole rested the box on the ground and readjusted her satchel to cross over her neck and shoulder. Not entirely fashionable, she thought, but who on the Harvard campus would care? She glanced around, searching for her quiet follower, but the woman was nowhere to be seen. Too bad. She could have used the help to her office.

With the heavy satchel firmly in place, she grabbed up the box and continued down the shady path toward the Humanities Building. As she walked past the open quad, she heard a voice calling her. She turned to see a rail-thin woman, impeccably dressed, emerge from the classroom building she'd just left.

"Katie, I'm so sorry," Nicole said, waiting for her friend to catch up with her. "I forgot that we were meeting after class today."

"I guess so," Katie said, pushing a loose tendril of her reddish-blonde hair back in place. Her pale blue eyes scanned Nicole. "Give me the box," she said. "And do something with that bag you insist on carrying around before someone notices."

Nicole obliged, ignoring Katie's jibe. Katie was her best friend and sister to her future husband. And Katie insisted on being Nicole's personal fashion critic. The worn leather satchel was a present from her parents when she left England seven years ago, and she wouldn't part with it. Not even to soothe Katie's jarred fashion nerves.

"These are the decorations I ordered," Nicole said, pointing to the box now tucked under Katie's thin arm.

Katie glanced at the package. "Still insisting on running your own wedding, then?"

Nicole shrugged. "If I didn't, your mother would run it for me, wouldn't she?"

Katie laughed. "I guess you're right. Mother's pushy at times."

Nicole would have used a few more choice words for her future mother-in-law, but Katie enjoyed her mother's company, so Nicole kept her thoughts private.

"But you should get my brother to help, you know," Katie said. "It is his wedding, too."

Nicole hid her exasperated sigh as they walked up the stone steps to the Humanities Building. "Adam is too preoccupied with Neo-Tech. I barely see him once a week." And she didn't think he'd be too pleased to spend that time organizing their wedding. Nicole could have done without the added burden herself. Her side of the wedding party consisted of her parents, Katie as her maid of honor, and her handful of friends. The rest of the wedding'would be flooded with the politicians and socialites that Adam's mother would invite to be a part of her son's grand event.

"HOW'D CLASSES GO, Brainiac?" Jasmine asked.

Emma moved her Numbers Theory book out of the way on the kitchen table before Jasmine could plant her coffee mug on it. "Lectures bite," Emma said, tapping her pencil over a particularly nasty problem.

Jasmine sat down, putting her sandwich on Emma's backpack. "Hey, I told you to quit with the Bachelor's degree, but do you listen to me?" Jasmine gave her a mock wounded look.

"How different life would be if I listened to you," Emma said. She tried to focus on her math problem, but her roommate seemed in need of entertainment.

Jasmine flipped open Emma's backpack as she munched on her sandwich. She pulled out the Sonnets book. "Still feeding the infatuation?"

Emma grabbed the book and stuffed it back in her pack. "I like to study English."

Jasmine choked on her food. "You like to study *her* English, you mean."

Emma gave Jasmine a practiced evil stare that was completely lost on her.

"You need to get out more," Jasmine said between mouthfuls of her sandwich. When she got no response, she slammed a hand down on Emma's notebook.

"Hey!" Emma glared at her.

"I'm serious. If you're not going to bust a move on this woman, then you need to move on, Girl."

"Yeah, because I do that so well."

More crumbs landed on Emma's homework as Jasmine finished off her sandwich. Emma could have done without the nagging and messy eating habits. She brushed off the crumbs and turned back to her book.

Jasmine stood up. "I know just the thing for this."

Emma didn't like the sound of that. She didn't like the look of it, either, when Jasmine grabbed her phone book and shut herself in her bedroom.

JASMINE CAME BACK out about a half hour later. Emma had finished her homework and was contemplating calling her mother. Jasmine plopped into a chair and started in the middle of a conversation that Emma wasn't sure she'd been a party to.

"Okay, she'll be here by eight o'clock, so you better get changed," Jasmine said.

Emma glowered at her. All her best looks were lost on this woman. "Who will be here, and why should I care?"

"Your date, Stephanie. Stephanie something, I can't remember. But she's hot and, trust me, she's easy."

"Jasmine."

She closed Emma's books. "You can thank me later. Up, dressed, chop chop."

Emma sat back and folded her arms. "I'm so not doing this."

Jasmine gave her an exasperated sigh. "Well, you get to answer the door then, when she shows up, and explain why you won't go out with her. I'm out of here."

Before Emma could grab hold of her, she was out the door with a wave and a laugh.

"I'll get you for this," Emma hollered at the disappearing form.

"You're welcome," came the sly response.

Emma dropped her head in her hands. A blind date. Great.

How pathetic are you when your ex-girlfriend starts setting you up on blind dates? She glanced at the clock. She had less than an hour to go before Stephanie Something showed up. Long enough for a shower, she wondered? She gave herself a sniff-test. Yes, definitely a shower.

If she was quick, she'd have enough time to see if hit-men advertised in the Yellow Pages. If this date turned into a nightmare, a certain roommate might need to be taken out.

"SO YOU'RE A graduate student at Harvard?" Stephanie asked.

"Yes. I've still got a year to go." Emma sipped her wine. The white zinfandel cleansed her palate as she waited for dinner. She hoped it would also settle the nervous knot in her stomach. There was a good reason she avoided blind dates.

Stephanie sighed. "That's a lot of math. I hated math."

Emma gave a wan smile. Where was dinner? No tip for the waiter if he didn't speed things up here. Two other waiters wove their way through the maze of tables around Emma and Stephanie. The scents of Mandarin Chinese food teased her as she tried to engage her date in some semblance of interesting conversation. "So where did you meet Jasmine?"

Stephanie sighed again. She sighed a lot. "My company hired her to design our website. You know, when she called, I thought she was finally asking me out again."

Emma cracked a bread stick and munched. This was going well. Her mind cataloged a series of punishments that she considered appropriate retribution for Jasmine setting her up. Stephanie tilted her head so she was looking at Emma through half-closed eyelids. Was that an attempt at being sexy?

"But I'm glad I'm here with you instead, Emma."

Definitely an attempt at something, Emma thought.

The waiter interrupted their moment with hot plates of Kung Pao chicken and broccoli beef. Emma focused on her food as if she hadn't eaten a big ham and cheese sub just two hours ago. Anything to speed up the date.

Stephanie played with her food, pushing the broccoli away. She nibbled on the beef, and then grabbed a glass of water. "That's too spicy."

Should have given her the Kung Pao, then. Emma felt bad. Maybe she just wasn't giving it a chance. Stephanie was definitely attractive. Her curly blonde hair and hazel eyes held a certain allure, when the woman wasn't being coy or sighing.

"What do you like to do, I mean outside of work?" Emma asked.

Stephanie tilted her head again. Obviously this was a nervous tick of some kind. "Women mostly," she said.

Yeah, definitely Jasmine's idea of a fun date. Emma gave up on polite conversation and dedicated herself to the plate of delicious food in front of her. At least the night wouldn't be a total loss.

After dinner and an extra twenty minutes waiting to pay the bill, they made their way outside the restaurant as a light drizzle fell on them. It cooled off the warm spring night. Emma almost regretted not bringing a heavier jacket as she zipped up her navy blue windbreaker. Stephanie pulled a thick poncho over her head. Where she managed to find an adult-sized poncho in this millennium was a deep mystery. The multicolored garment from a by-gone era hung below Stephanie's waist, with just the right tangled mess of tassels to perfect the image.

She slipped an arm around Emma's waist. "Would you like to come see where I live?"

Now there's a line Emma couldn't use on Stephanie. She was sure that Stephanie had already been to where Emma lived. Possibly more than once, knowing Jasmine. Emma extricated herself from the arm. "Sorry, not tonight. I still have a lot of homework to do."

Stephanie sighed. Emma winced.

She held out her hand. "It was nice to meet you, Stephanie."

The other woman brought Emma's hand up to her lips, kissing her open palm. What was obviously meant to be seductive felt instead like a cat was about to do something unmentionable in the palm of Emma's hand. She rescued her hand and placed it in her pocket for safe keeping "Well, bye," she said.

Stephanie frowned. "Okay, bye."

Emma didn't wait for Stephanie to rethink her strategy. She turned and walked down the wet sidewalk, heading for the nearest train station. Two blocks away, Emma saw the glowing T marking the station entrance. She trotted down the steps to the Green Line station, taking them two at a time. It wasn't that she was in a rush to get away from the miserable evening. Not much. She felt the warm rush of air that preceded the train. She pushed her way onto the train with a dozen other late-night travelers and settled into a rear-facing seat. She had five stops to go. She let her eyes drift shut as she dreamed about legal forms of torture she could use on Jasmine as payback for tonight's pain.

JASMINE BANGED ON her bedroom door. "Pick up the phone. It's your mother."

Emma managed one more sit-up, and then pulled herself off

the floor to grab the phone.

"Hey, Ma. How are you?"

"Fine. I'm not interrupting anything, am I?"

"No, not doing anything." Emma wiped the sweat off her temple. "How's business?"

"It's picking up. I've got three new weddings to plan this month."

"That's great."

"How about you, dear?"

Emma sat on her bed. "I've got one graduation bash to plan, that's about it."

"Well, maybe you should advertise more? I got two weddings from that wedding planner ad I put in the Malden paper."

Emma remembered reading that ad. Event Planning by Margaret LeVanteur. She couldn't imagine putting her own name out there like her mother had. "That's okay, Ma. I'm just a part-time party planner. I can only handle one event at a time anyway. This one will be over in May."

"Well you can always come and help me over the summer. It's the busy season for me."

Emma laughed. "Yeah, maybe."

"Your cousin Patty dropped by the other day. You remember her, right? Anyway..."

Emma sank back into her pillows. Sunday mornings were her mother's time to bond with her for the week, and she knew the conversation would work its way through most of her relatives in the Greater Boston area and then some before it was over.

JASMINE WAS SITTING at the kitchen table, munching a donut when Emma emerged from her room.

"Want one?" Jasmine asked, pointing at a Dunkin' Donuts bag.

"No thanks. I'm going for a jog."

"Okay," Jasmine said between bites. "But don't overdo it. Maya will be here at noon."

Emma paused at the door. Just go out, she told herself. Don't ask, just go out and jog. She clenched the doorknob and looked over her shoulder. "Who's Maya?"

A smug smile painted itself across Jasmine's face. "Trust me; you'll like this one better."

"Jasmine."

Her roommate held up her hands. "Easy. She's fun. And it's not a date. We're all going ice skating."

Emma banged her head against the door frame. "Why me? Why me?" she mumbled.

"Maya's cool. And she's new. Even I haven't slept with her yet."

Now there's a high recommendation, Emma thought. She left the apartment, letting the door swing shut on its own. There must be some form of legal recourse to deal with this particular kind of roommate abuse.

IT TOOK JASMINE a dozen phone calls to find a rink open this late in the spring. That left Emma responsible for entertaining Maya while they waited.

"So, the tattoo," Emma said. "Bet that hurt a lot, eh?"

Maya flexed her biceps to make the Celtic knot pattern dance. "Like a son of a bitch, it hurt. You got any tattoos?"

She shook her head. "Not much for pain."

Maya eyed her up and down. "Too bad."

Jasmine, where are you? Emma asked silently. She straightened her jeans as she sat on the sofa. Maya sat on the arm of the sofa, her black army boots crossed at the ankles. Emma pondered why Jasmine thought this would be her dream date. Maya's one-inch long, bleached hair crowned her round head like a thorny white thistle. She had three studs in each ear and one in the nose for good measure. Emma gave a sidelong glance at Maya. Possibly a belly piercing too, and who knows where else if the woman liked pain.

Jasmine skipped into the room with a flourish of waving arms. "I found one in the North End. It'll take us maybe a half-hour on the T."

Emma stood up and pulled off the long sleeve shirt she wore over her t-shirt. She found Maya smiling at her and nodding when her head poked out the top of the shirt. Emma flushed and pulled down her disheveled t-shirt. Nice. Flash the flesh for the new girlie, leave an impression. Emma gave a half-grin back as she grabbed a heavy sweatshirt, anticipating a cold ice rink. She followed the other two women out of the apartment door.

THE ICE RINK in the North End had seen better times. So had the rental skates. Emma glided around a puddle covering the faint pattern of a goalie's crease and tried not to lose an edge on her cross-over turns. Maya skated up hard beside her and dusted her with ice shavings from an expert stop. Just what every girl wanted, skate slush up the pant leg.

"You like hockey?" Maya asked.

"When the Bruins are having a good season, yeah," said Emma, trying to maintain her balance as she dodged a pair of five year old figure skaters.

"Ever play?"

Emma watched Maya's stride. Of course, a hockey player. "Not me. I guess you do?"

Maya nodded. "Defense. No one messes with my goalie."

"I'm sure."

Jasmine caught up and pushed herself between them, threading an arm through each of theirs. "Whoa. Hard to stay vertical on this slush," Jasmine said, smiling up at Maya.

Maya soaked up the attention, looping an arm around Jasmine. "It's not so bad. I've played on worse."

Jasmine, one hundred percent lesbian flirt. Emma slowed her pace. "I need to hit the restroom," she lied.

Maya and Jasmine skated away as Emma glided to a stop at the exit. She hopped on the rubber matted floor and found herself a bench to sit on. She could have gone to the movies or done the laundry. Hell, she could have worked on her sonnet for class this week, instead of coming to a rink to watch Jasmine in action. Not that Emma minded, really. Maya was a little on the scary side. A bit more bravado than Emma liked in her dating choices. Not that she had much for dating choices lately. She blew on her cold hands as she watched Maya and Jasmine circle by. Yep, Maya would be spending the night. Emma would bet on that.

"SO YOU'RE SURE you're not mad at me?" Jasmine asked. She blew on her morning coffee.

"Not at all." Emma packed her books in her backpack. "It's not like Maya and I hit it off or anything."

Jasmine smiled. "Good. The woman's a beast in the sack."

"T.M.I, Jasmine."

"Yadda, Yadda. You're too squeamish. Nothing wrong with good clean loving."

Emma laughed. "So sayeth the lesbian poster girl for sex."

Jasmine stuck her tongue out. "At least I go for what I want. Can't say the same for you."

Emma stuffed her sonnet book into her backpack and sank into a chair. "I wish I had half your nerve."

"Well, why don't you just go for it then? With this professor lady."

"Wish I could." Emma stared out the window. "I wouldn't even know how to begin."

Jasmine pulled Emma's sonnet book out again. "Well, what's all this about?" she asked, waving the book. "Even I know Shakespeare was a love freak in his sonnets. Don't tell me you can't make up an excuse to go to her office hours." Jasmine flipped through the book. "'Sin of self-love possesseth all mine eye; and all my soul, and all my every part; and for this sin there is no remedy.'"

Jasmine held the book to her chest and batted her eyelashes. She pitched her voice sugary sweet. "Professor, whatever can he mean? Is he really talking about masturbation? Do you masturbate?"

Emma grabbed the book from Jasmine and swatted her on the shoulder.

"You never know. She might love it," Jasmine said. She ducked and laughed when Emma took another swat at her.

Emma thought a moment. "We do have to recite a sonnet this week."

"See? There's your chance. Pick a nice lewd one and read it just to her. See if she reacts."

"Maybe not a lewd one," Emma said.

"Chicken."

"I prefer cautious."

"Cautious chicken."

She grumbled at Jasmine and put the book back in her pack. But the idea did have merit. And if she could get a reaction out of Davis, it would be worth it.

Her thoughts were interrupted by noise coming from Jasmine's bedroom. "Is Maya still in there?" she asked, nodding her head toward the bedroom.

"Yeah. She doesn't have to get to work until later. She'll lock herself out."

Emma frowned but kept quiet. Jasmine's revolving bedroom door was none of her business, but it tweaked her when she left virtual strangers alone in their apartment. She swung her backpack over her shoulder and headed out the door. Maybe there was something she could do with a sonnet. Anything would be better than another weekend of blind-date hell, compliments of Jasmine.

Chapter
Two

"EXCELLENT, MR. HARRIS. Your analysis brought out the themes of death and discontent in Shakespeare's later sonnets." Professor Davis read from her class list. "Okay, my next victim is Emma LeVanteur."

Davis looked directly at Emma where she sat in her choice seat at the back of the room. Emma felt a room full of eyes shift in her direction, but only the soft brown pair at the front of the room mattered. Now or never, cautious chicken, she thought. She looped her long, chestnut hair into a ponytail and stood. Grasping her paper in sweaty palms, she walked up to the lectern. She passed a blur of disinterested faces. Her own face was already bright red, for sure.

Why do I ever listen to Jasmine, she wondered as she took her place in the front. Emma had spent more hours on this sonnet assignment in the past week than on her own thesis work. If the gambit didn't work, she would slither back under the rock she came from. She could picture herself explaining to the Admission's office why she had to drop a class she was auditing. Well, you see, I made a pass at the professor, and it went bust.

She turned to look at Davis, who sat in a chair by the wall to Emma's right. As usual, Davis was impeccably dressed in tan slacks and a hunter green pullover. Her blonde-streaked hair curled at the edge of her collar, and she played with a lock of it while Emma straightened her papers.

Davis gave her an encouraging wink. "And which sonnet did you choose?"

"I chose poem 264, from Petrarch's Canzoniere." Emma cleared her throat. Somehow, the plan didn't seem as brilliant now that she had to unveil it in front of Davis and thirty-three of her classmates.

Davis raised her eyebrows and smiled. "Not exactly the assignment, Ms. LeVanteur."

Emma returned the smile. She had caught the professor's attention with that. Maybe the plan would be worth the hours of study. "The assignment was for a sonnet. I chose a more liberal interpretation, reaching back to Shakespeare's predecessor, Francesco Petrarch."

Who happens to be the topic of your Ph.D. dissertation, she thought, glad she had spent the time to dig up Davis's background online.

Davis nodded. "Touché."

Emma read Petrarch's sonnet, which she had memorized. She looked at Davis, not at the class. Davis signaled with a nod of her head that Emma should be looking at the entire class. Emma ignored the hint. The poem was for Davis only.

"'You know well what sweetness came
to your eyes at the sight of her
who I might still wish,
for our peace, had never been born.
Remember clearly, as you must,
how her image ran to your heart,
there where perhaps the flame
of no other torch could enter,
she kindled you.'"

Her cheeks blazed with heat as she recited the love poem by heart. She had Davis's full attention, their gazes locked on each other. Had Davis's cheeks reddened as well? She might be imagining that. Nothing else existed in the room except her voice, and the brown eyes that held her transfixed.

"'So that writing of her does not calm me:
and the light of lovely eyes that melts me
gently in their serene warmth
controls me with a rein
against which no wit or force avails.'"

Emma's voice held true, deep and clear, as she finished the poem. Her pulse pounded in her ears, the only thing she heard in the quiet room. Davis's eyes remained locked on hers, her lips parted, while Emma waited for some sign or response.

Then Davis shook her head as if coming out of a dream. "That," she said, "that was well recited. And what do you think the poem is about?"

"Unrequited love," Emma replied. Davis's gaze stayed on Emma, and it seemed as if the rest of the class had melted away and it was just the two of them. "It reflects Petrarch's long unfulfilled love for a woman he could never have. He lived to be caressed by her warm brown eyes."

Davis licked her lips. This time, she blushed for sure, but a smile curved her moistened lips. "Now that's poetic license, Ms. LeVanteur. Petrarch never described the woman he loved as having brown eyes, warm or otherwise."

Emma flinched, and she diverted her gaze to the paper she'd ignored on the lectern. She'd slipped up with that last statement. Did Davis notice? Had she been too obvious? Emma risked a furtive glance back at her but the magic of the moment had faded away.

Davis looked at her watch. "That's all the time we have today. Next class we'll start with," she shuffled her class list, "James McPherson."

Emma's heart hammered in her chest. She'd gone too far. She grabbed her paper and slithered back under her rock in the back of the classroom. What she wouldn't give for a second exit to the room. She rammed her notebook and papers into her pack and shuffled her way to the front door with the rest of her class. With luck, she could find a nice friendly bus to jump in front of and end her embarrassment.

"Ms. LeVanteur, if you have a moment?"

Her stomach lurched. Could she pretend she hadn't heard Davis call her? No. Her classmates gave her a look as she paused in the doorway. Face the music, LeVanteur, she thought. You wanted her attention and now you have it. She slouched and turned back into the classroom, ready to accept her deserved dose of rejection and embarrassment.

Davis gathered up her lecture notes. "Interesting choice, Ms. LeVanteur." She glanced up at Emma. "And an impassioned delivery."

Emma recognized the teasing tone in Davis's voice, and her pulse quickened. She hadn't blown it. "Call me Emma," she said. "Ms. LeVanteur is my mother's business name."

"Emma, then." Davis held out her hand. "And I'm Nicole."

Emma surreptitiously wiped her sweaty palm on her pant leg and shook the offered hand. Nicole's long tapered fingers wrapped around Emma's hand in a firm grasp. Emma hoped the tremors she felt inside didn't extend down her arm. "Sorry," she said, making up an excuse just in case. "I'm still a bit nervous from the recitation." She licked her lips.

Nicole's intense gaze held Emma transfixed. "Well, nervous wasn't the emotion I'd have said was clearly pronounced in your poem," Nicole said, her voice low and quiet.

She's flirting with me, Emma thought, as Nicole let go of her hand. She felt a pang of regret when the warm touch of Nicole was replaced by emptiness.

Nicole averted her gaze. "Would you like to join me for a cup of tea in my office?"

Would I? she thought. "Um, yeah, sure." To keep her hands from visibly shaking, Emma shoved her hands into the pockets of her jeans. Inside, her mind danced between smug congratulations that her gambit might have paid off and quiet fear that she didn't know what move to make next, if any. Standing beside Nicole, Emma realized for the first time that they were nearly the same height, something new for the Nicole Davis Fact Book. She waited while Davis slid her notes and class book into a black leather satchel.

Nicole swung the satchel over her shoulder. "Do you drink tea?" she asked.

Sort of. Sometimes. Never. "Yes." Tea? She could handle tea.

"Good," Nicole said. She graced Emma with a warm smile. "So few Americans do."

Emma walked beside her out of the classroom and down the stairs. She scrambled to think of something to say as they walked across the grassy quad to the red brick building that housed the Humanities Department. Being this close to Davis, to Nicole, filled her mind with fantasies that threatened to overwhelm her. Don't mess up now, LeVanteur, she thought. Keep it cool. "How long have you been here?" she asked. "In America, I mean."

A wayward Frisbee buzzed by Nicole's head from a game of Ultimate that they walked through. Nicole ducked to avoid being hit. "Sometimes I think I've been here too long."

"Really?" Unexpected panic edged Emma's voice. Would Nicole go back to Britain? Emma had never considered the possibility, and it left her with an odd, hollow feeling in her stomach.

"Not really," said Nicole, to Emma's instant relief. "I like it here, especially Boston. But I do miss my family. I've been here for seven years now."

They walked up the steps of the Humanities Building in silence. The brick façade, dotted with newly painted white shutters surrounding each window, loomed before them. Emma looked around with interest as they entered the bustling foyer. Unlike the Math and Sciences Building, this one was lined with paintings and sculptures from different eras. She recognized one Da Vinci replica hanging opposite the doors they'd just entered through. The rest of the classic works were beyond her limited artistic knowledge.

"I'm just around the corner here," Nicole said as she dug in her bag, presumably for keys. She led Emma down a corridor to the left of the main foyer. Doors lined either side of the hallway, each with frosted glass windows and wooden frames that bore the marks of a century of student abuse.

Emma kept her gaze averted, looking around the hallway. She didn't want to stare at Nicole. Didn't want to be caught at it anyway. Her hands remained in her pockets, keeping her from fidgeting too much, or reaching out to pull back a loose strand of Nicole's hair as it dangled into her eyes. They stopped in front of the door to office 119. She stood close enough to Nicole to smell the other woman's faint perfume. Emma's mind struggled to identify the scent as she waited nervously beside Nicole.

"There," said Nicole as she opened the old wooden door. "Welcome to Professor Davis's office hours," she added with a flourish. She pouted. "It's a lonely time. No visitors."

Emma smiled. "Maybe you should advertise more. 'Tea and poetry, 1:30 to 3:00 p.m.'"

"Now, now. I don't invite just anyone for tea," Nicole teased. "Have a seat."

Definitely flirting, Emma thought. Now if only she knew how to flirt back. What would Jasmine do? Emma mentally shook herself. She wouldn't do what Jasmine would do. That would involve locking the door and clearing off the desk in front of them. She didn't have that kind of bravado.

Emma looked around, and then chose a worn, wooden chair in front of the tidy oak desk. Two other chairs squeezed into the small space. Nicole opened the lone window to let in some of the clean spring air. The office was nothing like Emma imagined it would be. It had the requisite floor to ceiling bookcases full of authors she'd never heard of. But it also had a shelf dedicated to graphic novels. And sheep. A dozen or more little black sheep in various sizes, even a black sheep pillow, were scattered throughout the office.

She picked up the nearest sheep, a miniature one covered in black fluffy fur. "A sheep collection?"

"Yes," Nicole said as she stood in front of the small shelf that held an electric kettle and a set of teal tea cups. "My mum gave me one every Christmas when I was little."

"Cute. I prefer the LEGO I got at Christmas."

"And thus we stand, two nations divided." Nicole waited for the water to boil.

"And graphic novels?" Emma asked.

"Don't mock a form of literature until you've thoroughly experienced it."

"Does 'Batman' count?"

"Hmm. Well, I was thinking more in terms of European and Japanese graphic novels. Did you know Japan's 'Barefoot Gen' has been compared to Hemingway? Or that Art Spiegelman won the Pulitzer Prize for 'Maus', retelling the Holocaust in comic-book style?"

Emma ducked her head. "No. I guess I haven't paid much attention to it."

"You're forgiven," Nicole said, brushing a free hand across Emma's shoulder as she brought over a steaming cup of tea. Nicole's touch left a trail of fire across Emma's body. Emma waited, breathless, as Nicole prepared a second cup of tea for herself.

Emma dropped her gaze, afraid that her sudden arousal would be too obvious to Nicole. She blew on her tea and sipped. Milk, no sugar. Obviously, there weren't options when it came to tea in Nicole Davis's office. "You're office is nice. Homier than I imagined," Emma managed to say finally.

"Well, if you'd used my office hours anytime this semester, you'd know." Nicole watched her from over the rim of her tea cup, the rising steam swirling around her pale, beautiful face.

Emma's shaking hands rattled the tea cup and saucer. She put them down on the desk. The intensity of Nicole's gaze mesmerized her. She knew now what that deer felt when it looked into the approaching headlights.

"You've quite an active mind for literature," Nicole continued as she absently trailed a finger around the damp rim of her tea cup. Emma followed that finger as Nicole lifted it to her lips and licked the dewy moisture off it.

Heat trailed from Emma's chest, centering much lower on her body. She swallowed hard. "Thanks," she muttered.

"Have you considered majoring in it?"

Emma blinked, trying to fathom Nicole's question. Literature? Was that the reason for the invitation, because Nicole thought she wanted to major in Literature? "I'm working on my master's already," she said. "In Mathematics."

Nicole raised an elegantly shaped eyebrow. "Really? Well, I wouldn't have guessed. You've done so well in my class so far."

"It's not like the two can't mix," Emma said more defensively than she intended.

"But they don't very often, do they?"

She shrugged. "I'm an enigma."

"Yes, you are." Nicole's lips curled in a sensuous smile that pulled at her.

This enigma needs to move the conversation in a safer direction, Emma thought, before she combusts. "So, what do you do besides English and collecting sheep?" Smooth, real smooth.

"Well, I write, but I suppose that's part of the English category, isn't it? I also play racquetball."

"Really? Me too."

"Well, something in common. What other hobbies do you have?" Nicole asked.

"Besides math until I puke?" And making a minor fool of myself, she thought.

Nicole snorted. "Besides math until you puke."

"I work part time as a party planner."

Nicole leaned over her desk. "Really?"

"Yep." Emma warmed up under Nicole's gaze. "My mom's a professional organizer. She does weddings mostly, sometimes company functions."

Nicole put down her tea, staring at Emma. "Do you do weddings as well?"

"Sometimes," Emma said, confused by the shift in conversation. "Mostly small affairs, like college students getting married."

"Any chance you have time in your schedule for an event I'm planning?"

Emma's eyes widened. She tried to keep a grin from plastering itself across her face. This could work. They'd work side by side for a while, get to know each other better, and then who knows what.

"I'm getting married this summer," Nicole announced.

And then, I can beat myself with a bat, Emma thought. "Married? Um, when?" She tried to ignore the hollow feeling growing inside her chest.

"June 28th" Nicole straightened up. "It should be a small house wedding, if I can get my future mother-in-law to agree that is."

Smile, act natural, and act like this is good news, Emma thought. "Congratulations." The congenial reply didn't extend beyond the fake smile splitting her frozen expression.

Nicole returned the smile. "Thanks. We just had an engagement party that I organized myself. I think it went well, but I'm told it wasn't up to the Chandler standards."

Emma nodded, unable to formulate any further small talk. Had she read Nicole's signals so poorly? She studied the other woman. Nicole's demeanor had shifted when the topic of her nuptials came up. She avoided eye contact with Emma, and crossed her arms as she spoke.

"I really do want a small wedding, but Adam's mum is pushing for a country-club affair." Nicole said. "It would be nice to have a friend and professional on my side to convince her that a house wedding can be just as elegant without the excess pomp of a country club."

A friend, just a friend, Emma thought as she fidgeted in her chair. She had two months left to get her thesis proposal approved and plan the graduation bash she'd already agreed to. She really didn't have time for a wedding. "I think I can help you," spilled past her lips before she had a chance to convince herself it was a bad idea.

"Marvelous." Nicole reached across the desk and clasped Emma's hand in hers. Emma's entire body focused on that one warm hand as it sent a tingle of excitement coursing through her. This was definitely a bad idea.

"Can you give me your number?" Nicole asked, letting go of Emma's hand. Her eyes held Emma under their sway.

Emma fought to control her emotions. It was ridiculous to be so attracted to a straight, nearly married woman. "Yeah, give me a minute." She dug in her backpack. "My mother made these for me last year," she said, pulling out a business card and giving it to Nicole.

"Very professional," Nicole said, reading the card. "Pam will be impressed."

"Pam?"

"My future mother-in-law."

Mother-in-law. Emma clamped down on her frustration. She took a gamble, and it failed. No reason to take it out on Nicole or her future family. She painted a smile on her face and listened with feigned interest as Nicole described in detail her plans for a house wedding.

NICOLE LEANED AGAINST her open office door as she watched Emma walking down the hallway. Emma walked through patches of sunlight from the corridor windows, highlighting the rich hues of her chestnut-brown hair. She should wear it loose, Nicole thought, such gorgeous hair. She watched her until Emma entered the front foyer and disappeared from view. Then, Nicole shook her head and closed the door, feeling at odds.

She looked down at the business card she still held in her hand and smiled. Emma would be back. She walked to her desk and sat in her chair, still lost in her own thoughts. The vision of Emma sitting in her office filtered through her reverie. She had an infectious smile and casual friendliness that Nicole enjoyed. And the chemistry between them flooded Nicole with an odd warmth. They got on well.

The easy teasing and flirting she'd shared with Emma brought a smile to her lips. Emma would be her secret weapon against her future mother-in-law. She tapped the business card against her lips as she considered how she would present this new idea to Adam's mother. Maybe she would start with Katie. Get her best friend on her side, and then they could both tackle Pam.

"GETTING MARRIED?" JASMINE tumbled onto the sofa next to her, fighting back hysterical laughter. Not fighting hard enough in Emma's opinion.

"Comedy hour is over," Emma grumbled. "At least I'll get some extra money for the summer." And she would get to spend more time with Nicole, which was good in a pathetic sort of way.

"Look on the bright side." Jasmine dried a tear from her eye. "You still have a couple of months to convince her she's batting for the wrong team."

Emma threw a pillow at her. "Not helping."

Jasmine settled down. "Well, I'm proud of you. At least you tried. So what if it didn't work?"

So what if she still tingled when she thought of Nicole's hand on hers, Emma thought.

"Hey," Jasmine said, "Maya's coming over later tonight. Any chance you can, you know..." She tilted her head toward the door.

Emma sighed. "Yes, I can make myself scarce for a few hours. My crowded social life is eating away at my thesis work anyway."

"Cool. And if you want, I have a few more names in my little magic book."

Emma held up her hands. "No, thank you. Two blind dates and a failed take-me-now proposal is enough for one semester."

"That's no way to talk." Jasmine pulled Emma up off the sofa. "You've got to jump right back on that horse."

"Fine," Emma said, heading to her room. "But I get to choose the next horse I jump on, ok?"

Jasmine whooped. "And you'll just ride that wild pony."

Emma shook her head. Hopeless, just hopeless. She knew she wouldn't be jumping on anything soon. The sting of rejection just reinforced her instinct that she should stay on her own and not get involved. The pain and frustration just weren't worth it. Back to the safety of Math, she thought, as she grabbed her notebook and sprawled across her bed.

NICOLE DAVIS STOOD outside the Humanities Building, waiting in the dark for Adam. She checked her watch. She hated it when he was late, especially when he was late by forty minutes or more and never bothered to contact her by cell phone. She scanned her surroundings. Finally she saw a familiar burly man dressed in a gray, pressed suit, deep blue tie and tailored shirt stroll around the corner of the building, towering above the handful of undergraduates who'd just passed Nicole.

"Hey, I made it." Adam wrapped his arms around Nicole and pulled her in.

She grazed him with a kiss, and then pushed him off. "You're late."

"Sorry. Neo-Tech is like that. Life at a start-up."

She looked up into his brilliant blue eyes. "You're not sorry, are you? You could have at least called me. I could have been waiting in my office instead of out here."

"Come on, let's not get into that." Nicole let Adam lead her to his double-parked BMW.

"How's your day been?" he asked.

"Actually, my day went rather well," she said as she waited for him to unlock the car door. "I hired a wedding planner." Nicole buckled into the car as Adam put the BMW in gear and merged into traffic.

"Do we need a wedding planner?" he asked, his eyes staying on the road.

"I do. A wedding is more difficult than the engagement party was." And she'd enjoy Emma's company. Thoughts of Emma had drifted through her mind most of the afternoon.

"Mom would help you."

She sighed. "Yes, but she doesn't want the same sort of wedding we want, does she?"

Adam shrugged. "Small or big, I don't mind." He gave her hand a squeeze. "So long as you're with me."

Nicole returned the smile. "Well, I'd like small. If we were in England, we'd use my aunt's house. She has the most beautiful garden." She hadn't even bothered pushing for an English wedding. Some battles were hopeless with Adam's family.

A car cut them off at the intersection. Adam leaned on his horn. "So who'd you hire?"

"Emma, Emma something French. I have her business card in my bag somewhere." She dug through her satchel in earnest, angry with herself for forgetting Emma's last name. She remembered every other detail about their time together with brilliant clarity; the way Emma's pale brown eyes crinkled when she laughed, the tightness of her firm grip. Nicole marveled that hands that appeared so strong could feel so soft and warm when she'd held them in hers.

"Great. Emma Something French can handle the details. Feel better now?" Adam stole a glance at Nicole as he drove, but she turned away, afraid that he'd catch a glimpse of the blush she felt creeping up her cheeks.

"Yes," she said. "Tired though. Any chance we can skip dinner with your parents tonight?"

He laughed. "Not a chance in hell. Mom's best friend is coming over to meet you."

Nicole sank back in the leather bucket seat. A light sprinkle began outside, wetting the windshield and blurring her view of Cambridge at night. So much for having an early evening.

EMMA STUDIED AT the library until they booted her out. Then she moved to Café Brio, just off Harvard Square. When they shooed her out the door as well, she decided Jasmine had enough one-on-one time with Maya, and Emma headed for home. Light drizzle turned into a hard, steady rain. She pulled her coat over her head. Stylish and yet practical, she thought. She ignored the cluster of smirking teenagers who lingered by the liquor store she passed a block from the café. Ten minutes at a half-run, and she was finally at the train station. It was nearly midnight by the time she got back to her apartment building. Jasmine better have moved her escapades into the bedroom by now, she thought.

She shook off her wet coat and backpack in the elevator as it rose to her floor. She unlocked the door to her apartment and peeked in. Dark and quiet. Good. She kicked off her soaked sneakers and padded across the living room to her bedroom. Light flickered from under Jasmine's door. Candles, how romantic.

Emma changed into flannels, flicked off her light and climbed into bed. She'd nearly drifted off to sleep when she heard a yelp. She frowned, listening harder, and then she heard it again. This time she got up and went into the dark living room. Candlelight still flickered from under Jasmine's door. She could hear them talking now. Jasmine's voice came out, muffled. "No. It hurts. Stop it."

Emma heard another voice, Maya's, but she couldn't make out the words. She stood motionless for a moment. Then she looked down at herself. Grey striped flannels, bare feet, standing in the dark and eavesdropping on her ex-girlfriend's foreplay. Nice. She shook her head and went back to bed. Whatever was going on, Jasmine was a big girl and could take care of herself. Emma rolled onto her stomach and shoved her head under the pillow. No more interruptions.

Chapter
Three

EMMA UNLOCKED THE door to her apartment and ran in, nearly barreling over Jasmine on her way.

"What's the rush?" Jasmine asked, planting herself against the wall as Emma ran past her.

"Nicole asked me to meet her at her place this afternoon. Wedding stuff."

Jasmine followed Emma into her bedroom. "Ooh, this sounds interesting."

Emma paused long enough to give Jasmine her best disdainful stare. No affect, again.

"So, what are you going to wear?" Jasmine asked. She plopped down on Emma's bed.

"Nothing."

"Ooo."

"No, I mean nothing different, gutter mind."

Jasmine gave her a shocked look. "Going to meet the woman of your dreams, and you're not even changing that rag of a sweatshirt?"

"It's not that bad, is it?" Emma asked as she looked down at her maroon school sweatshirt. So what if she'd bought it her freshman year at Harvard?

"Give me a break. The cuffs are frayed, and you've got bleach spots across the back."

Emma caved in. Jasmine had better fashion sense than she had. Two sweater changes and a jean swap later, Jasmine was satisfied.

"Okay, I have to go," Emma said. "Wait, where's my planner catalog?" She rummaged through the pile of notebooks and papers on her desk. "Here it is."

"One more thing," Jasmine said, running to her room. She came back with two bottles of perfume. "You want sexy," she held up one bottle, "or sweet", the other.

Emma shook her head. "No way. It's not a date, it's a business appointment."

"Yeah, right. You're wearing your best sweater, and you haven't yanked your hair back into a sloppy ponytail. Some business appointment."

Emma dropped her pack, whipped a scrunchy out of her back pocket and pulled back her hair. "Satisfied?"

Jasmine shrugged. "You look hotter with it down."

A HALF HOUR later, Emma stood in front of Nicole's apartment building, forcing herself to calm down. She scanned the list of names on the intercom, then buzzed Nicole's apartment. Her palms were sweating again. Why couldn't she just focus on the business at hand?

Nicole's British accent came over the intercom. "Come on up, love, number 302."

That's why she couldn't focus. She was a sucker for that accent. She walked up to the third floor. Focus on the task, she told herself. Nicole's practically a married woman, and she was organizing her wedding. She pulled the scrunchy out of her ponytail, smoothed out her chestnut hair, and stuffed the scrunchy back into her pocket. Nothing wrong with looking her best for a business appointment. Then she knocked on Nicole's door.

A NERVOUS THRILL ran through Nicole when the buzzer rang. She'd spent half the morning tidying her small apartment before Emma's visit. That she wanted to make a good impression was obvious; but more than that, she wanted Emma to feel welcome. She paced the small front hallway, waiting for Emma. Despite her preparations, she still jumped at the sound of Emma knocking on her door. She brushed back her hair and opened the door.

Emma stood before her, and the first thing that caught Nicole's eye was the long chestnut hair cascading over Emma's broad shoulders. Her mouth felt dry as her eyes continued to study Emma. A light gray sweater stretched across the soft curves of Emma's chest and then hung loose over a pair of dark blue jeans. When Nicole looked up again, somewhat embarrassed by the way she'd just checked her out, she saw a faint redness in Emma's cheeks. Had she just embarrassed Emma with her blatant appraisal?

Nicole looked down at her own sweats and t-shirt, wishing she'd dressed better. "You look great," she said, stepping aside to let Emma through the door. As Emma stepped into the room, Nicole noticed how well the jeans molded to Emma's legs. Nicole blushed.

"I brought some sample menus," Emma said. Her voice sounded deeper, sexier than Nicole remembered.

Nicole led her through the cleaned apartment. She had decorated with an old world flair that she hoped Emma wouldn't find too stodgy. A tapestry hung along the wall behind the stereo, the gold and green hues picking up the colors of the rugs that covered most of the natural hardwood floors. She led Emma to the small parlor, and they sat on the French provincial sofa, sinking into the deep gold cushions. She faltered a moment as Emma placed a binder on her lap. Nicole considered placing it on the cherry-wood coffee table in front of them, but the thought disappeared the moment Emma reached across her to flip open the binder. Nicole breathed in Emma's lilac perfume and tried to calm her nervousness.

"About how many guests are you expecting?" Emma asked.

"Well, my parents will fly in from Oxford. And let's see." Nicole counted on her fingers. "Maybe six of my friends who are local."

"Singles or couples?"

"Couples mostly, I guess."

Emma scribbled the information into a notebook. "And your fiancé's side?"

"Well, if he keeps his mum under control, probably twenty or so."

Emma smirked. "And if he doesn't?"

"If he doesn't, then he's in trouble." Nicole frowned. "Sorry, his mum's a bit pushy." She put a finger to her lips. "Don't tell Adam, but I hired you to keep his mum from running the whole event."

Did Emma flinch at the mention of Adam? Nicole brushed the thought aside. Her imagination was really out of control today.

"I take it you don't see eye to eye with your future mother-in-law?" Emma asked.

"Hardly. If she had her way, there would be a hundred guests, and we'd be at some golf club function hall."

"Sounds expensive."

"Oh, they can afford it." Nicole folded her hands in her lap and gazed out the window. It looked out onto a tree-lined street, the brilliant green leaves waving in the spring breeze. "It's not what I want, though."

Emma put down her pen. "What do you want," she asked.

"I wanted a small family wedding." Nicole looked down at her hands. "I always dreamed it would be at my aunt's house in Sutton Courtney. She has a country house that looks out onto the Thames Valley. We'd have it in the garden when the lavender was in full bloom. My cousins would all be there." Nicole turned back to Emma, embarrassed by her revelation. She hadn't even shared this wayward dream with Katie. "Silly isn't it? It sounds so very school-girlish when I hear myself explain it."

"Not at all," Emma said softly. "Did you ask Adam about this? Sounds like his family can afford to fly out to England."

Nicole laughed half-heartedly. "No, I never really asked him. His mum would never go for it. I only won out on the small wedding when we agreed to have it at her house in Newton. I shouldn't complain, I suppose. It's only eight miles from Boston, so I could have my choice of caterer."

"Did you spend a lot of time at your aunt's house?"

"Oh yes. We lived about ten minutes away. It's my mum's sister. We spent half of summer holiday there every year. My cousins and I would make lavender bags after they bloomed."

Emma frowned. "Lavender bags?"

"I suppose you've never heard of them." Nicole felt a sudden wave of homesickness. She hadn't thought of England so much until recently. She wanted to share more of her home and family with Emma.

Emma shook her head. "The only other place I ever lived was with my Mother in Malden, fifteen minutes from here. And she never made lavender bags."

"Well, you take a stem of lavender and dry it out. Then take a soft cloth that you like, put in some dried blooms and seeds, and tie it up with a ribbon. Then we'd put it in a sock drawer or something. It would make it smell of lavender." Nicole loved making the delicate flowery bags. "Sorry," she sighed. "I'm indulging in old memories, probably boring you to tears."

"Not at all," Emma said.

Nicole smiled. "You're sweet." She lost herself in Emma's gaze, feeling heat rising in her cheeks. Why did she blush so much in front of her? Nicole coughed and turned back to the planning binder to hide her growing flush.

"Um, so, the wedding," Emma said. "It sounds like fewer than forty people. Let me show you some small party ideas." She shifted closer to Nicole, their forearms just touching. Nicole's cheeks felt warmer, and she kept her eyes glued to the binder.

"Lavender," Emma said, barely above a whisper.

Nicole looked into Emma's brown eyes. She could feel the warm puffs of breath as Emma exhaled. "Lavender?" she asked, amazed that her voice didn't crack.

"Um, yes," Emma looked away, breaking the trance that held Nicole. "You're wearing lavender perfume. I just recognized it."

"Oh, yes," Nicole let out a nervous laugh. "It's my favorite. I'm a little obsessive, aren't I?"

"No, not at all," Emma said. Her gaze turned back to Nicole. "Anyway, if you have the wedding in the early afternoon, you can get away with a light meal. Maybe this one." Emma pulled out one caterer's menu. "Or this," she said, pulling out another menu. "And if you haven't picked a florist or baker yet, I've got a couple of good recommendations."

Emma dug more pamphlets out of the binder on Nicole's lap. Nicole scanned the papers, but her mind refused to focus on more than Emma's strong hands as she pointed to the pamphlets and talked on about caterers, bakers, and florists.

"I recommend this florist." Emma looked up at Nicole as she passed her a pamphlet. "I've worked with her before, and she'd make sure there was lavender in your flower arrangements, if you'd like."

Nicole's eyes widened. "Yes, I'd like that very much." She wrapped her arms around Emma. "I just knew you'd be great," she whispered into Emma's ear. She felt a tremble through Emma's warm body that matched her own and pulled back, unsure of herself. Emma's eyes studied her, but a smile lightened her intense gaze.

Nicole finally broke the silence. "Can I get you anything? Soda or biscuits?"

"Soda would be nice, thanks," Emma said. Nicole sensed the other woman's eyes on her as she walked into the small kitchen beyond the dining area. She found Emma's attentiveness alluring. She returned a moment later and handed Emma a drink. "I've gone on and on about me. Let's talk about you, if that's okay."

Emma gulped her drink. "Ah, okay. Not much to tell."

"You lived here your whole life?"

"In Malden, yeah. My mom and I. I got a partial scholarship to Harvard. Then I applied for the graduate program in mathematics and got accepted. Now I'm here."

She has the most charming smile, Nicole thought. "And a very succinct summary of your life," she teased.

"Sorry, I don't talk much about myself."

Nicole folded her legs up on the sofa, sipping her own drink and trying to maintain an appropriate distance from Emma. Maybe she was pushing herself on the other woman too much. She didn't want to upset the delicate start of their friendship. "Well, how did you get interested in literature, then?"

Emma drank slowly before she spoke. "Well, I never really got into Shakespeare in undergrad classes," she said.

"What made you start now?" Nicole asked.

"Well, you're a good teacher, and the class is fun."

Nicole's cheeks grew warm. "Thank you," she said. "But why my class?" She wasn't sure what she was searching for. After all, theirs was a chance meeting. What did she want to hear from Emma?

"Well, Shakespeare read in an English accent," Emma said. "Can't beat that for authenticity."

Nicole laughed. "Maybe I need to add that to my CV." She returned Emma's smile. The phone rang, cutting off their discussion. "Excuse me." Nicole walked to the kitchen to get the phone.

"Hello? Oh, hello, Adam."

Nicole surreptitiously watched as Emma got up and wandered around the room, picking up one knickknack after another. She returned her attention to the phone conversation.

"Maybe you can talk to Mom. She really is pushing the country club wedding," he said.

"No, really. She's your mother." She hoped Emma couldn't hear her arguing with her fiancé. "Can we talk about this later? Emma LeVanteur is here with me right now."

Emma turned to her, a bemused smile on her face when she heard her name.

"LeVanteur?" Adam repeated.

"Yes, the wedding planner." Nicole heard the impatience in her own voice, but knew it would be lost on Adam.

"My manager's name is Paul LeVanteur. Ask her if she's got relatives in Cambridge," he said.

"Just a moment." Nicole sighed and lowered the phone. "Emma," she called, "Do you have any relatives in Cambridge?"

Emma looked up from her paperwork, frowning. "No, just my Mom's family in Malden."

Nicole picked up the phone again. "No, no relation."

"All right," he said. "See you tonight. Love you."

Nicole hung up and came back to the room. "Sorry about that. Adam's mum is giving us grief."

Nicole settled back on the sofa. She wished that they could sit closer, but with no binder to share anymore, she remained at one edge of the sofa and Emma at the other.

"Adam mentioned he works with another LeVanteur. Small world, I suppose," Nicole said.

"I guess." Emma picked up her drink.

"What did he say was the man's first name? Paul I think."

The glass Emma was holding slipped out of her hands, spilling on the dark green rug.

"Oh, my." Nicole grabbed a napkin to dab up the spill. When she looked up, she saw that Emma sat frozen, her cheeks pale.

"Are you all right?" Nicole asked.

"Yes, sorry." Emma said. "Let me help." She bent down and retrieved the ice cubes and glass, which hadn't shattered when it bounced off the rug.

Nicole grabbed a towel from the kitchen to mop up the rest of the spill.

"Will it stain?" Emma's hands shook as she sat back on the sofa.

"Oh, these rugs have seen better days," Nicole said as she sat back on the sofa. She left the wet towel on the coffee table. "Are you sure you're all right?" She put her hand on Emma's arm. "You're shaking." The feel of Emma's silent tremble triggered a matching ache that welled up inside Nicole. She didn't understand what went wrong, but she wished she could lift the shadow that clouded Emma's dark eyes.

Emma stood up. "Yes, I'm fine. I should probably be going though. Lots of homework. Besides," she added with a faint smile, "I have an English professor who loves to pile on the essays."

Nicole sat dumbfounded, but smiled. "Well, thank you for coming over. I'll get back to you on these caterers." She didn't know what else to say as Emma gathered her binder, leaving behind only a handful of pamphlets for Nicole to study. When Emma rushed out the door, Nicole watched her tense form disappear down the stairwell. Emma's behavior changed after the phone call. Was Paul someone Emma knew after all? Or had Nicole crossed a line with her eagerness to befriend her? Maybe Emma thought that they needed to maintain the boundaries of a student/teacher relationship, even though Emma was just auditing. Nicole sank back down on the sofa, absently piling the pamphlets in one corner as her mind struggled to figure out what she'd done to hurt Emma.

EMMA WALKED AS if in a dream. Her mind did not register her surroundings as she wandered down the street, past the closest train station. Her long stride took her along the busy sidewalk, but her mind struggled against unwanted memories. Paul LeVanteur. The name stabbed at her heart, reawakening an old, buried pain. Maybe it wasn't her father. After all, he'd been gone for over a decade. Maybe it was just coincidence.

Yeah right, she thought. Like the name LeVanteur was popular anywhere outside southwestern Louisiana where her dad's family came from. A family she had no contact with after her father deserted her and her mother. The memories of an abandoned, confused child rattled around in her mind until a blaring horn brought Emma back to the present. She looked past the driver who had stopped short to avoid hitting her. She stepped back onto the sidewalk, barely registering that she'd nearly gotten hit. She kicked the stoplight, willing it to change in her favor.

Well, it didn't matter, she told herself. Maybe it was her father, maybe it wasn't. He hadn't tried to contact her in over ten years, so why should she care now? She didn't need him. She hadn't needed him all through high school and college. She didn't need him now.

She crossed the street and focused on the next train station three blocks ahead. A black T on a white circle background became her marker to sanity, to forgetting, repressing the heartache of so long ago. She forced herself to think of something else, anything else but Paul LeVanteur. Anyway, it's not like he wanted to see her or anything. Just coincidence. Serendipity.

Emma realized that she had left Nicole's apartment in a rush, using a blatantly weak excuse. Her shoulders slumped as she took a seat on the train. So much for making an impression. She closed her eyes, shutting out the world around her. She focused on the memory of Nicole's hand on her arm and the accompanying look of concern. The afternoon had been going so well—as well as a lesbian wedding planner infatuated with her client could expect, anyway. Someone pushed into the seat next to her, elbowing Emma in the process. She swore under her breath.

When she got home, she found Jasmine sprawled out on the sofa, looking paler than when Emma had left earlier. "What's your beef?" Emma asked, dropping her backpack beside the sofa.

"Didn't sleep well last night," Jasmine said, avoiding eye contact.

Emma saw dark circles under Jasmine's eyes that she hadn't noticed that morning. "Are you sure? You look like you're getting sick," she said.

"It's none of your damn business, anyway." Jasmine stood up and stomped off to her room, slamming the door.

Emma stared at the closed door. "Excuse the hell out of me for caring," she mumbled.

She picked up her bag and sat on the sofa to start some homework. She needed something to occupy her mind and block out old memories. She flipped past her English books. No Shakespeare, not today. She pulled out her thesis proposal instead.

EMMA MET NICOLE at the end of the next lecture. She lingered after the rest of the class had left the room, standing by the front, but not able to break the awkward silence.

Nicole gave her a timid smile. "Feeling any better today?" she asked.

Emma's mind went blank for a moment, trying to comprehend what Nicole was referring to. Then she realized that her abrupt departure from Nicole's apartment probably looked like she'd been getting sick. Emma accepted the ready excuse, relieved that she didn't have to explain what had happened, and no mention was made of Paul LeVanteur.

"Did you want to continue some of the wedding plans?" Emma asked.

Nicole shook her head. "Can we do it another day? I spent half the night arguing with Adam's mother about the color scheme. I think I'm all planned out for the moment."

"Okay," Emma said, hoping her disappointment didn't show in her voice or expression. She'd wasted half the lecture trying to figure out how to approach Nicole afterward and how to explain her odd behavior. Even though it had been resolved so easily, she felt her shyness return and didn't know what else to talk to Nicole about if not the wedding. She shifted awkwardly from foot to foot, watching Nicole pack up her bag.

"Would you like to go for a walk instead? It's finally sunny, and I'm tired of being cooped up inside," Nicole said as she grabbed her leather bag and looped it over one shoulder.

"Um, sure," Emma said, thankful that she wouldn't have to leave Nicole's company right away.

Emma led Nicole on a wandering trail around the campus, taking her as far from the Humanities Building as possible. Their arms brushed lightly against each other as they walked.

"You're very quiet today." Nicole stopped to look at Emma. "Is everything all right?"

"Yes, just tired."

Nicole brushed her hand along Emma's arm. Emma's heart raced. How could she feel so much for a straight woman? Did Nicole even realize the affect she had on Emma or was she oblivious to it all? She saw sadness in Nicole's eyes and hoped she wasn't the cause.

"I'm okay, really," Emma said, forcing herself to smile. When Nicole relaxed and returned her smile, Emma's grin became genuine. Emma felt a closeness growing between them as they continued their walk, but she wondered if it was just platonic on Nicole's side. Sometimes, she swore that Nicole felt their physical chemistry, but she brushed away such thoughts as wishful thinking.

They slowed to a stop as they neared the Humanities Building. Nicole reached out and held Emma's hands in hers. "Can we meet again, early next week?" she asked. "We can settle some of the wedding details then."

"Sounds good." Emma held onto Nicole's hand for a moment longer, then let go and waved goodbye. She trotted back toward the street leading to her apartment. Each step that took her away from Nicole increased her conviction that what she thought of as Nicole's flirtatious actions was just a figment of her oversexed imagination.

LATE TUESDAY AFTERNOON, Emma sat in Nicole's small office in a comfortable silence as Nicole graded the latest round of essays from class. Emma worked on details for each step of Nicole's wedding. Nicole caught herself staring at her on more than one occasion, just admiring Emma's concentration as she scribbled notes or made corrections. Emma didn't seem to notice her stare. Nicole turned away, watching as rain dripped down the one window behind her desk. She gave an involuntary shiver as she turned back.

"Unseasonably cold for May, isn't it?" Nicole asked.

Emma blinked as if she'd been deep in thought and looked up at Nicole. "Welcome to New England," she said. "It was in the 80's and sunny yesterday."

"And it's 55 degrees and pissing it down today."

"Excuse me?" Emma asked with a grin. "'Pissing it down?'"

Nicole blushed. "Sorry, a bit common of me to use that expression, but it really does match the weather you have here."

"And now I've learned another fine English expression," Emma said. "Who knew there was so much more to the English language than Shakespeare and Chaucer?"

Nicole whipped a small, fluffy, black sheep at Emma's head, but Emma caught it and whipped it back at her.

"Good reflexes." Nicole smoothed out her returned sheep and put it back in its place of honor by her gray desk lamp.

"Thanks. I play softball," Emma said with some pride in her voice.

"Really, what position do you play?"

"Third base."

Nicole raised one eyebrow. "Third base, eh?"

Emma blushed, catching the innuendo. "How's the grading going?" she asked.

Nicole sighed and stretched, her purple sweater pulling across her chest. She heard a muffled gasp from Emma and locked her gaze on a pair of dilating brown eyes. Nicole knew that she was the cause, and that realization both thrilled and frightened her.

"Well enough," she said, trying to control her reckless flirtations. "I only have a half dozen left. Then maybe we can get out of this damp office and go find some dinner someplace. Unless you have other plans?" She felt a warm blush flood her cheeks as she waited for Emma's answer. Maybe she shouldn't have assumed that Emma wanted to spend any more time with her. She studied Emma's face, looking for a hint of her feelings. Emma moistened her red lips. Nicole's eyes traced the progress of Emma's tongue, unable to focus on anything else.

"No," Emma said, a wide grin spreading itself across her face. "I'm plan-free today."

"It's a date then," Nicole said, releasing a long, slow, breath as she accepted that maybe Emma did enjoy her company as much as she enjoyed spending time with Emma.

EMMA SAT IN her usual spot in the back of the class, listening to Nicole's lecture. Nicole had given her a quick smile at the start of the class, and the feeling of warmth still lingered for Emma. She felt a bit smug as she let her gaze wander over her classmates. She was Nicole's friend. Okay, it would never lead to anything, but still. Me special, you not. Chah!

At the end of the lecture, Nicole called Emma to the front of the classroom. Yeah, special had its privileges. Nicole waited until the class emptied, her eyes dancing with some untold secret. Something good must be up, Emma thought. She grinned in anticipation as she mentally urged her classmates to leave the room faster.

Nicole grabbed her wrist when the last student left. "You won't believe this," she began at a whisper.

"What?" Emma asked, stifling a laugh. Nicole's mood was contagious.

"Adam spoke to that man at work, Paul. He says he knows you."

Emma's mind roiled as Nicole's words echoed in her head. She looked away.

"I told Adam you were from Malden," Nicole continued, seemingly oblivious to Emma's state. "Paul is sure he knows you and your mum."

"Yeah, I bet he does." Emma pulled her arm free. She wanted to be away from here and Nicole's revelation.

"But, do you know him then?"

Damn him for coming back like this, Emma raged silently. She crossed her arms, trying to stop them from shaking. "It doesn't matter."

"Sorry, I don't understand."

Emma turned her back to Nicole, not wanting her to see that she was so affected by the news. "He's my father," she said, barely above a whisper. Her palms felt cold against her sides.

Nicole stepped around to face Emma. A frown creased her brow. "But the other day you said you didn't know him."

"I don't know him anymore," Emma said. "He's my father, but I haven't seen him in ten years. End of story."

Nicole stepped back. "I'm sorry, I didn't mean to intrude."

"Can we just drop it?" Emma asked, staring at the floor. Her hands shook.

"Yes, I'm sorry." Nicole said, her voice subdued.

Emma reached out to stroke Nicole's arm. "No, I'm sorry. It's just, it's not something I like to talk about."

Nicole covered Emma's hand with her own, sending a rush of heat to Emma's cheeks. "Would you like to go for a walk or get a snack?"

"Or get drunk maybe?" Emma asked, curling her lips in an unconvincing grin.

Nicole didn't smile.

"Sorry," she said. "I'll be fine, really. A walk would be nice."

They walked together in silence across the campus, along paths that divided the green lawns of Harvard's campus from the patches of blooming flowers. Clusters of students lay sprawled across the grass, socializing between classes. The sun broke through the billowing white clouds that drifted slowly overhead. They remained quiet for a time, an awkward silence that Emma knew she needed to end. But, how to start? Her thoughts were muddled and clouded by the fears and loneliness of her younger self, resurfacing when she thought she'd long since gotten over her childhood pain.

"He left us when I was ten," she began. "I never saw him after that." She looked into Nicole's worried face. "I guess it's been more like thirteen years since I last saw him."

Nicole held Emma's hand. "That's horrid."

Emma's rattled mind calmed at Nicole's gentle touch. "I don't even really know why they separated. I guess maybe he just didn't want a family anymore."

"Your mother never talked about why he left?"

"Never. She hates him."

Nicole slowed to a stop, letting her hand drop from Emma's. "What about you? Do you hate him?"

Emma shrugged, feeling alone again in her turmoil. She stuffed her hands in her pockets, wishing she could bury her old heartache. "I don't know. Sometimes. I try not to think about it."

"Do you want to meet him?"

"No." Her jaw clenched. "Definitely, no. If he ever wanted to see me, he knew where I lived." And he never did, not once in thirteen years, she thought.

They walked in a silent loop as they headed back to the Humanities Building. Emma was lost in her thoughts and unsure how Nicole was reacting to her messed up family life. Maybe she shouldn't have admitted that Paul was her father. She could have pretended that he was some sick uncle with deep personal problems. Or that she'd never heard of him and he was delusional. Her mood lifted at the thought of maligning his character, but one look at Nicole told her that she could never really lie to her.

Nicole stopped at the steps to her building. "I've got some questions on the wedding plans, if you have time. But if you'd rather not right now, I understand."

"I have time," Emma replied, pushing down the memories of her father. She followed Nicole into the noisy building. Focus on the project, she thought, and forget about him.

"NICOLE? ARE YOU paying any attention?"

Katie's voice interrupted Nicole's worried musings. "Sorry," Nicole said, unsure how long she'd been staring at the shoe display without focusing.

"What's up with you today?" Katie asked as she stuffed her narrow feet into another pair of black pumps.

"Just preoccupied." She had been thinking about Emma and her father, trying to imagine what Emma must be going through. Nicole was blessed with two loving parents and never had to deal with the kind of abandonment issues that must be plaguing Emma.

Katie modeled the pumps to herself in the mirror. "Wedding plans getting you stressed out?"

"No, they've been going smoothly now that Emma's taken over," Nicole said, trying to bring her attention back to Katie.

"So what's on your mind, then?" Katie asked as she kicked off another pair of rejected shoes and slipped on her own.

"Emma's father works with Adam," Nicole said.

"So?"

"So, he left her when she was about ten. She hasn't seen him since then."

"Oh, that is nasty," Katie said, pulling out a pair of midnight blue high heels. Nicole studied her friend's face, looking for any real sympathy. All she saw was an increasing frown as Katie grew frustrated with her shopping. Nicole sat on the nearest bench, folding her arms across her chest. Katie finally noticed her after picking and discarding yet another pair of shoes. "You are in a funk today, aren't you?"

"And you're being incredibly unsympathetic. How would you feel if one of your parents left and never came back?"

Katie walked back to Nicole and put her hands on Nicole's shoulders. "Sorry. I'm all ears now. Tell me about your friend."

Nicole described how hurt Emma was. Katie's expression mimicked concern, but Nicole knew her well enough to recognize when Katie was presenting the politically correct response. Nicole took a deep breath. What did she expect? Katie was very loyal to her friends, but strangers meant nothing to her.

Nicole tried to relax. "I'm just tired," she said. She wouldn't tell Katie that she'd been sleeping fitfully the past couple of nights. Emma appeared in a number of her dreams, and she wasn't sure how she felt about that. She certainly wouldn't share that detail with her fiancé's sister, best friend or not. It was something she'd work out on her own.

EMMA RIFLED THROUGH the folders piled on her bureau. Where had she put the details for that graduation party? Someday she'd be organized. Someday. Meanwhile she had two weeks left to get the event settled, and she'd only managed to book the hall and DJ.

"Jasmine, have you seen a blue folder anywhere?" she called out from her bedroom. The muffled reply was unintelligible. Emma stuck her head out of her room. "What did you say?"

Maya shouted back, "She said no!"

Emma caught just a glimpse of Maya dragging Jasmine back into the bedroom. Did that woman ever go home? And since when did Jasmine let someone else push her around? Emma ducked back into her own room, ignoring the pod-person who had replaced her roommate.

She padded out of her bedroom half an hour later, after she'd booked a caterer and verified the venue with the students throwing the party. She heard muffled voices and then watched Maya leave the bathroom and saunter out of the apartment. Jasmine was in the bathroom, heaving her guts out by the sound of it.

Emma knocked on the bathroom door. "Are you okay in there?"

Another hurl. "Do I sound it, Brainiac?" A cough followed.

"Can I get you anything?" Nice girlfriend, Emma thought, to leave when Jasmine probably needed her.

"Just leave me alone."

Emma leaned against the door. She didn't like seeing Jasmine sick. And her attitude lately? Just unpleasant. Maybe it was hormones. "Well, knock if you need anything," she said. The reply, if there was one, was drowned out by the sound of the toilet flushing. Emma backed up as Jasmine emerged from the bathroom, draped only in a towel. Her face was colorless, if you ignored the black circles under her eyes. "You look like death warmed over."

Jasmine ignored her and shuffled back into her room, kicking the door shut behind her. Emma paused outside the door. Something was up. Jasmine was never one to suffer in silence when she was sick. She was the 'sprawl on the sofa and moan for attention' type. Why was she hiding in her room this time? Emma contemplated knocking on the door, but considering her roommate's earlier reaction, she dropped the idea. Emma returned to her own room. If pod-person Jasmine wanted to be alone, who was she to butt in?

Chapter
Four

"DID YOU IV caffeine at work today?" Emma asked as she watched Jasmine wiggle out of her work dress and into a tight black top and white corduroy pants. "You were sick as a dog all last night, and now you're so hyped up your hands are twitching."

"No caffeine," Jasmine said as she bustled out of her bedroom and into their shared bathroom. "Have you seen my eyeliner?"

Emma guffawed. "Eyeliner? Yeah, like maybe two years ago. Didn't we use it on those Halloween masks that one time?"

Jasmine gave Emma's shoulder a smack as she buzzed back into her bedroom. "If you can't be helpful, then be somewhere else."

"Seriously," Emma said, following Jasmine into the bedroom. "You're extra frantic. I can't believe this isn't from a coffee overdose."

Jasmine's hands flew through her close-cropped hair, applying some kind of light gel that Emma never knew she owned. The result created patches of spiked hair surrounded by patches of flat black. Cute, but kind of retro.

"What's all the fuss about anyway?" Emma asked, examining a bottle of perfume on Jasmine's bureau.

Jasmine snatched the perfume out of Emma's hands and gave herself a short spray down the front of her top. "No fuss. Just a date."

Emma bit back a snide remark about Maya. She didn't much like Jasmine's latest girlfriend, but she chose not to emphasize that fact. It was not like she approved of most of Jasmine's girlfriends, but she refused to believe it was all some latent form of jealousy. Maya was just the latest in a series of women that Emma would never have chosen to associate with. She supposed the date meant that Maya would yet again be staying the night and then remaining in the apartment after Jasmine left for work the next morning. She wasn't sure which bothered her more, Maya hanging around when Jasmine was gone, or how Jasmine seemed to be changing so much since she started dating that woman. And whatever they were getting up to, Jasmine was not getting enough sleep. She'd been sick three times in the past two weeks, and that was three more times than Jasmine had been sick in the past year.

"So what big plans do you have, Brainiac?" Jasmine asked. "Going to recreate the universe as a mathematical point of singularity?"

Emma cocked an eyebrow. "You know what a singularity is?"

"Hardly." Jasmine brushed past Emma. "But I've vegged out to enough Star Trek repeats to almost sound like you."

"And, hypothetically speaking, which is worse—being a Trekkie or understanding the underlying principles they bastardized on that show?"

Jasmine paused by the front door. "Good point. Later, Girlie."

Emma checked the time after Jasmine left. She had a good hour before her mother was due to stop by. With luck, her mother would bring some cake samples from the new bakery she was working with. Sampling the food was a definite perk in their line of work.

MARGARET SPREAD OUT the contents of her canvas bag on Emma's kitchen table, creating a hodgepodge of baskets, ribbons, and small, mesh packets that smelled of honeysuckle and lilac. She pushed back an unruly strand of her wiry gray hair and sat at the table.

"How many of these do we have to make?" Emma asked.

"Only forty." Her mother finished organizing the pieces in front of them. "We've made these wedding favors before. Do you remember how?"

"Wrap the two ribbons around the little basket handles and tie one of the potpourri packets in each."

Margaret picked up the first basket and got to work. Emma grumbled about disorganization and put some of the wedding favor parts in an assembly-line order across the kitchen table in front of her, little wicker baskets first, potpourri second, ribbons third. When she was satisfied, she sat down opposite her mother and picked up her first basket.

"Are exams over?" Margaret asked, ignoring Emma's organizational fit.

"Not yet. I have one final essay left, but that's not due for another two days."

Her mother eyed her over rectangular reading glasses. "Shouldn't you be writing then, instead of helping me with these baskets?"

"It's all right, Ma. The essay is already done." Emma wrapped the yellow and blue ribbon strands around her basket and tied a bow on the top.

"That's good. Read it over once more before you turn it in."

"Yes, Ma." Emma masked her snicker with a cough as she started her next basket. For all Emma's insistence on organizing her piles, her mother had already completed three baskets and was working on her fourth.

NIGHT SETTLED AROUND them as they finished the final baskets. Her mother had continued her rapid pace, easily doubling Emma's output. Forty-three potpourri wedding favors lined the kitchen table, and her mother insisted on taking a photograph of them for her sample brochure. Then their night's work was carefully placed back in the canvas bag, and Emma stood up to stretch.

"Well, thank you, dear. Another pair of hands always makes the work go faster," Margaret said.

"No problem. I didn't have any other plans tonight anyway."

"Nothing new on the dating horizon?"

Emma shrugged. "Nothing much."

"One of the women in the gardening club has a gay daughter. Would you like to meet her?"

"Ma. Sometimes you take the understanding parent routine a bit too far." And who wanted to have blind dates arranged by their mother, anyway, gay or straight?

"Just trying to help." Her mother stretched and stood up to get herself a drink of water. Emma joined her at the sink. When the apartment door banged open, they both looked down the hallway. Jasmine skipped in like a school girl in a playground.

"Hey Margie!" she shouted. She came to a stop in the kitchen and gave Emma a kiss on the cheek.

Emma frowned and pushed her off.

Margaret gave Jasmine a bemused look. "You seem chipper this evening," she said.

"Chip chip chipper," Jasmine echoed. Then she succumbed to a fit of giggles as she continued her skip into her bedroom and collapsed onto the bed.

"Sorry, she's a little odd these days," Emma said as she shut the door to Jasmine's bedroom.

"I'd say. How long has she been like this?"

Emma shrugged. "Since she started dating her latest girlfriend."

She was surprised to see her mother frown, but she didn't question her reaction. Her mother knew that she and Jasmine had been lovers for a time, and was fond of Jasmine. She had never commented on Jasmine's loose morals, but something in Jasmine's behavior had definitely hit a disapproving chord tonight.

"I should be going," Margaret said. She swung the canvas bag of wedding favors over her shoulder. "Don't forget your Uncle Philly's barbeque is the Sunday of Memorial Day weekend."

Emma hugged her at the door. "I wrote it on the calendar," she said as her mother waved goodbye and walked down the hallway to the elevator. Emma closed the door and then meandered back to her bedroom. She still needed to study for Nicole's class the next day.

THE NEXT SATURDAY, Emma ran around her apartment, cleaning up piles of books and papers. There was no sign of Jasmine, and she thanked her lucky stars for that small blessing. She loved her roommate and best friend, but lately Jasmine had been just too bizarre for words. And tonight was not the night for freaky ex-girlfriends. She glanced at the clock on the VCR as she ran a sock over it to clean off the dust. She had less than an hour before Nicole showed up. They wouldn't be in the apartment for more than a few minutes before they left for Emma's softball game, but Emma still wanted the place spotless.

She rammed a stray lock of hair back into her ponytail and surveyed the small living room. She walked around one last time and placed the books back on the shelves, then ran down the hallway to stuff the newspapers and magazines in paper recycling. When she returned, she spied dried up water marks on the coffee table. She whipped out her makeshift dust rag, grabbed the cleaner and tackled the coffee table.

Just as she finished obsessing over dishes in the strainer by the sink, the doorbell rang. Her gaze darted to the wall clock. Seven-thirty. She cursed as she ran to the buzzer.

"Nicole?" she asked over the intercom.

"Yes. What floor are you on?"

Emma's stomach flip-flopped. "Ninth floor. I'll meet you in the hallway."

She turned back to her apartment. It was spotless, but she was an odorous mix of Pine-sol and Windex. She grimaced, but there was no time to change with Nicole on her way up in the elevator by now. She opened her apartment door and waited, her eyes fixed on the mechanical doors at the end of the hallway. When the elevator pinged in the distance, her heart skipped a beat.

Nicole stepped from the elevator, dressed in blue jeans and a white sleeveless shirt. Emma waved, and then concentrated on reestablishing her ability to breathe as Nicole approached. She was mesmerized by the rhythm in Nicole's long stride. There was strength in that stride, which suggested a firm body underneath the casual clothes. Emma felt a lump in her throat as Nicole paused in front of her, the other woman's faint scent of lavender wrapping itself around her.

"Come on in," she managed to say with a voice steadier than she felt. She led Nicole back into her apartment.

"Not much for the grand tour," she said, pointing as she walked along. "This is the living room and kitchen area."

Nicole smiled as she looked around. "It's nice."

"It's not really, but thanks," Emma said, grinning. "It's home for now." She pointed to the two closed doors. "That's my room on the left and my roommate's room on the right."

"I didn't know you had a roommate," Nicole said.

Emma shrugged. "She hasn't been around much lately. Anyway, have a seat. I just need to change and grab my gear. Then we're ready to go."

She popped into her bedroom, opening the door as little as possible to hide the cyclone-like mess inside her room. She changed into her softball team shirt, pulled a pair of sweatpants over her shorts, and then stood in front of her bureau mirror, obsessing over her hair. She raked a brush through it and yanked it into a semi-neat ponytail, then rammed it into her team baseball cap. Time to go.

Nicole watched her as she emerged from her bedroom. Emma felt herself blush under Nicole's intense stare.

"Giovanni's Beer Brats?" Nicole asked, raising an eyebrow.

"Yeah." Emma looked down at the lettering on her green team shirt. "Giovanni's Pub sponsored our uniforms." She glanced sidelong at Nicole. "Are you sure you're up for this? My softball team is a little rough around the edges."

"I'm looking forward to it," Nicole said as she stood.

"Cool." Emma grinned. "Let me grab my glove and bat and we can head out."

"You bring your own bat?"

"Oh yeah. Makes me feel all macho and professional." She heard Nicole laugh as she dug through the debris in the hall closet to find her softball equipment. "Okay," she said, emerging from the mess with a bat and duffel bag.

"Can I help carry anything?" Nicole asked as she walked toward Emma.

"Ah, sure. You want the bat or the bag?"

Nicole watched her with a sly grin. "If I take the bat, will I look all butch and professional?"

Emma's voice caught in her throat as she tried to answer. Nicole just laughed, oblivious to Emma's fumbling reaction. She lifted the duffle bag off of Emma's shoulder, her fingers just brushing the edge of Emma's t-shirt and creating a jolt of excitement where her fingers touched Emma's bare arm.

"Maybe I'll stick with the bag," Nicole said.

Emma nodded as she tried in vain to stop the flush creeping up her cheeks. Nothing attracted her more than a feminine woman willing to put on a little butch now and then, and the thought of Nicole in that role threatened to turn her into Jell-O. Mentally reining in her wayward thoughts, Emma led Nicole out of the apartment with the bat slung over her shoulder.

"At least we'll get some respect on the subway," she said when her ability to speak finally returned.

EMMA SAT ON the bench with her teammates, watching the game through the chain link fence that separated her team from the field. Her legs twitched nervously, not because she was third in the batting order this inning, but because she knew Nicole was watching from the cement stands behind her.

The catcher, nicknamed Pag, sat beside Emma. "So, who's the new girl?" she asked.

"A friend from college," Emma replied, glancing back to catch a glimpse of Nicole in the stands.

"Just a friend?" Pag's black eyebrows bounced up and down.

Emma slapped her with a glove before standing to stretch.

"Well, if you're not interested, introduce her to me," Pag said.

"You want another smack?" asked Emma.

"My, my. Protective of someone who's just a friend, ain't you?"

Pag ducked when Emma tried to swat her with a baseball cap. Emma didn't have time for a second try as she was next in line to bat. She gave Pag one dirty glare, then grabbed her batting glove and left the dugout. The harsh night-lights cast an unnatural brilliance on the baseball diamond, and Emma lowered her cap to cut out some of the glare. She wiped a sweaty palm across her shorts as she took her spot in front of home plate. She had a good batting average, but still she prayed that she'd get a solid hit this inning. Her last two at-bats were pop flies. Not quite what she wanted Nicole to see of her softball skills. Then again, the double-play she got the prior inning should be enough to impress Nicole. Should be.

Emma crouched and waited for the first pitch. It came in fast and high, for a ball. She loosened her shoulders and prepared for the next one. It was straight down the middle, and she heard a satisfying crack as her bat met the ball in the sweet spot for a line drive past third base and into left field. She rounded first base and was waved on to second. She saw the outfielder's throw as she slid safely into second. She stood up and brushed the dust off her legs. Finally, she was having a game worthy of a personal spectator.

NICOLE SAT IN the stands, surrounded by the family members of Emma's teammates. She'd struck up a conversation with the short-haired woman to her right, surprised to discover that she was the pitcher's girlfriend. By the end of the game, Emma had another hit, but her team lost in the end. Not that anyone on the team seemed to notice, Nicole thought, with all the hi-fives and cheers. She waited outside the dugout, and Emma trotted over to see her.

"Did you like your first softball game?" Emma asked. Sweat dampened her forehead, a light sheen that glistened under the bright lights.

"Yes, and you looked good out there. Well, from what I could tell of the game in one viewing. I'm impressed." The light summer breeze lifted loose tendrils of Emma's chestnut hair. Nicole lifted a hand and brushed it back behind Emma's ear. Someone slapped an arm around Emma's shoulder, and Nicole dropped her hand in a rush.

"So, you up for a beer?" the woman asked.

"I don't think so," Emma said, turning to Nicole.

"Sounds like fun," Nicole said. She was unsure who this other woman was, but wanted to stick around and find out what her relationship to Emma was.

"Great." The woman stuck out her hand to Nicole. "I'm Pag, by the way, since our mutual friend here has lost all manners."

Nicole forced a smile. "Nice to meet you, Peg. I'm Nicole."

"It's Pag, P-A-G," Pag corrected. "Short for Paglioni."

It was a short walk to Giovanni's Pub from the softball field. Emma and Nicole, with Pag tailing along, walked with the team through the active streets of the North End of Boston. A group of teenagers battled half-court games in a sunken basketball court that captured Nicole's attention. But what made her comment was the patchwork of open windows from the brick apartment buildings that overlooked the court.

"Do they do that frequently?" she asked, pointing up at a couple of round, elderly women chatting in rapid Italian, their plump arms resting on bed pillows that they'd hung over the window sill.

"Always," Pag answered. "My mother lives three blocks from here, but I swear I can hear her going at it from Giovanni's some nights. Past midnight if it's a hot night."

Nicole couldn't imagine what growing up in the city was like. Her home in England wasn't much more than a stable working class community, but at least most people had a back garden and a private area to sit out on. They walked around a group of neighbors who'd taken their beach chairs out and set them up on the sidewalk. The glare of the streetlamp cast grey and white patches across the sidewalk as they passed.

Voices drifted out from Giovanni's Pub as Pag graciously held the door open for Emma and Nicole. She bounced her eyebrows as Emma passed her, eliciting a low growl from Emma. Nicole passed by, giving Pag a cool stare. She didn't trust the dark, Italian woman and wanted her to know it. Pag just smiled at her and followed her into the pub. The cluster of players piled around a worn oak table in the back of the bar. Nicole sat down first and then Emma sat beside her on the bench. Pag joined them as well, forcing Nicole to slide further along the bench. She felt a growing frustration as Pag dominated Emma's attention while they ordered drinks.

Before their pitchers of beer showed up, Ezio Giovanni came out to greet them. The round, balding owner with a thick accent wrapped his arm around the team captain, chatting with her, and telling the waitress that the first pitcher was on the house for his team. Nicole surmised that the team would drink through a good half dozen more pitchers before splitting up and heading home on the T.

"Do you play softball?" Pag asked, leaning over Emma to talk to Nicole.

"I played rounders for a time in sixth form." She replied. "It's something like softball."

"Was it a co-ed team?" Pag asked, shifting forward on the bench. Nicole clenched her jaw, wishing Pag would quiet down. Her idea of a good evening with Emma didn't include random chatter with an overly friendly teammate.

"Oh no," she said. "I went to an all-girl school. But my girlfriends and I were considered the more tom-boyish of our form. We had quite the reputation."

Pag raised her eyebrows, glancing at Emma. "Really? Your girlfriends, eh?"

"So were you a troublemaker or something?" Emma asked, interrupting Pag.

Nicole laughed. "Sort of. Nothing that got us in major trouble. Well, except the time we wrapped cellophane over the toilets in the teachers' lounge."

"No, you didn't?" Emma's eyes widened.

"Well, we didn't get caught, or I'm sure I'd never have been allowed back to the school."

"And you hang around with Miss straight-laced Emma?" Pag asked between foamy sips from her beer.

"Hey," Emma objected. "I've gotten into my fair share of trouble."

"Such as?" Pag asked. Nicole turned to Emma, waiting for an interesting tale.

"Such as the time Jazzie and I made that fake arrest," Emma began.

"Oh yeah," Pag said. "Jasmine your ex-..."

"Roommate," Emma interrupted. Nicole felt somewhat lost as Pag masked a snicker behind her glass of beer, while Emma continued. "We were coming home from a Halloween party, when we came across these two teenagers trying to break into an ATM machine. Jasmine was wearing a police outfit, and those kids took her for the real thing."

"Thick as bricks," Pag added.

Emma nodded. "No doubt. Anyway, we handcuffed one kid to the nearest street sign, and told the other one that he had to stay there with his buddy until the police car came for them."

"And he did?" Nicole asked.

"As far as we know, yeah. We didn't hang around. We ran down the block, laughing our butts off."

Pag laughed. "I bet Jasmine misses those handcuffs."

"I got her another pair," Emma said. "Um, as a gag gift," she added. Nicole studied her with a bemused smile, not sure what had just transpired between Emma and Pag. Emma took an extra long gulp of her beer and pulled her baseball cap low over her head. Pag reached over and grabbed the hat, exposing Emma's flushed cheeks.

"No hiding," Pag said, putting on the green hat. The way that Emma glared at Pag told Nicole that Emma didn't approve of Pag's antics. Neither did she.

"And no stealing." Nicole picked the hat off Pag. She placed it back on Emma, letting her fingers touch Emma's soft chestnut hair. The wide grin that spread across Emma's face made her smile in return.

"We should probably head out," Emma said, lowering her voice so that only Nicole could hear her.

Nicole looked at her watch, realizing it was nearing eleven o'clock. "It is late," she said. She'd be glad to be away from Pag. The other woman's attentiveness to Emma bothered her.

They stood and said goodbye to the team. Pag gave Emma a

big hug and winked at Nicole, but Nicole just glared at her for a moment before leaving with Emma. At the train station, Nicole considered inviting Emma to stay the night so that she wouldn't have to go home alone, but she felt too self-conscious to ask as they stepped onto the Green Line train. They rode the T together until they reached Nicole's station. She wrapped her arms around Emma for a moment, sending a rush of heat through her as the train pulled to a stop. Nicole got off and watched in a daze as Emma smiled from the train. She felt a pang of sadness as the train started, waving from the platform before Emma was carried away into the tunnel.

Chapter
Five

FINAL EXAM WEEK ended with the graduation party over the Memorial Day weekend. After a couple of frantic days pulling together the last minute changes for the Friday night party, Emma could finally relax. The last business on her plate was Nicole's wedding. After the initial revelation about Emma's father, they both ignored the topic. Emma never mentioned it to her mother. She already knew how her mother felt in that regard.

She slouched on the sofa, flipping TV channels. She still had thesis work to do over the summer, but the lack of real classes, especially Nicole's class, had her in a funk. That, and she'd barely spoken a word to Jasmine in weeks. Either her roommate was absent or hanging around with Maya hovering over her shoulder. And when Maya was around, Jasmine wasn't worth talking to anyway. She acted like a Stepford bride, letting Maya take over any conversation. Emma shivered at the thought, even as the warm, late spring breeze blew in the open window. Something about Maya just unnerved her. She thanked her lucky stars that Maya never took an interest in her. Good luck to Jasmine.

She turned off the TV. Daytime shows, yeesh. She stretched out on the sofa, determined to take a mid-afternoon nap. She'd done a fair amount of moping around, and a rest seemed in order.

The ringing phone ended her lethargy.

Emma picked up the phone and heard Nicole's voice. Her breath quickened. She closed her eyes and let Nicole's voice wrap around her as she listened.

"I know it's a bit late, but have you any plans for this weekend?" Nicole asked.

Laundry, thesis work, a party at her uncle Philly's. "No, nothing much, why?"

"Well, Adam's mum is having some folks over for a barbeque on Monday. I'd like you to come."

It didn't collide with her family's party on Sunday. Emma's

pulse thudded in her ears. "I'd love to come. Should I bring anything?"

"No, it's all taken care of. It'll be a great chance for you to see where the wedding will be, too."

The wedding. Emma opened her eyes, trying to ignore the dull pain that formed in the pit of her stomach. "Yes. I suppose I'll get to meet Adam as well."

"And his mum. Try not to be scared, too much," Nicole said with a laugh.

"Does she bite?"

"Excuse me?"

"You know, like the heads off bunnies? Um, never mind."

She listened to Nicole describe the house and the backyard. She sat up and scribbled notes when Nicole gave her the time and place for the barbeque.

"Do you have a car?" Nicole asked.

"No, but the Green Line train goes to Newton."

"Nonsense. Adam and I can pick you up."

Great, she thought. A cozy ride for three. "Are you sure? I can make it by train."

"I'm sure. It's on our way." Nicole's voice held a note of eagerness in it. "See you on Monday, then?"

"Yes, and thanks." Emma hoped her voice didn't reflect her nervous excitement. She hung up the phone. Two days and she'd see Nicole again. Okay, Adam would be there, too, but she could ignore that, couldn't she? She no longer wanted to slouch on the sofa for the day. She changed into shorts and a tank top. It seemed like a good day to go for a run.

EMMA WAITED OUTSIDE her apartment building for Nicole and Adam. Jasmine wasn't around to critique her outfit, but she thought she'd chosen well. A pair of tan shorts to highlight her jogger's legs and a light blue t-shirt for the biceps. And after two days' effort in the limited New England sunshine, she'd managed a reasonable early tan as well.

A warm breeze blew her loose hair off her shoulders, but she resisted the urge to pull it all back into a ponytail. Looking her best for a soon-to-be married woman might not make a lot of sense, but she couldn't help but dress up when she was meeting Nicole.

She played a game as she waited. Spot the car likely to be Adam's. She'd sat through enough chats with Nicole to have an idea what kind of guy her fiancé was. Three Cadillacs and a Camry later, a metallic blue BMW screeched into an abrupt stop in front of her. She should have guessed. The passenger door opened, and

Nicole stepped out, wearing denim capris and a sleeveless off-white blouse. She swept Emma up in an affectionate hug. "Sorry if we kept you waiting."

"I've only been here a minute," Emma lied as she crawled into the back seat, hoping her new tan hid her flushed cheeks. She noticed the driver, a large man with close-cut blond hair. His eyes hid behind reflective sunglasses, but his smile seemed genuine.

"Emma, this is Adam," Nicole said.

"Hey." He waved at her in the rear view mirror.

"Hi," Emma said, buckling in. In one quick move, Adam pulled the car into traffic.

It took them a quarter of an hour to get to Adam's parents' house in Newton. Any hope of conversation during the brief drive was drowned out by the stereo blasting Foo Fighters from four expensive speakers. Or was it six? It wasn't Emma's favorite musical style, but she hoped that it belonged to Adam and not Nicole. She still held a glimmer of hope that Nicole owned something more interesting, like Melissa Etheridge.

They pulled up in front of a sprawling, white colonial house surrounded by a pristine, moss-covered stone wall. It was suburban New England at its best, with dual sentinel oak trees in the front lawn and neatly trimmed hedges bordering the driveway. Cars filled the driveway, and Adam parked on the street. Emma could hear at least a few children in the back yard as she crawled out of the back seat. A tall woman with short, gray hair came out of the front door to greet them. Her smooth, tanned face was offset by the creases of a permanent frown.

"Finally made it," she said, giving Adam a perfunctory hug.

Nicole waited for Emma to join them on the front steps. "Pam, this is my friend Emma. Emma, this is Pam, Adam's mother."

Emma felt the heat of Pam's scrutiny as the older woman's steel-blue eyes scanned and dismissed her without so much as a blink. "Nice to meet you, Emma," Pam said, her cool demeanor giving Emma little confidence that she'd met Pam's exacting standards. Standards for what, Emma didn't know, but she knew in her heart that she hadn't measured up. Emma shook the offered hand, a cool but firm grasp. Pam turned away from them the instant that Emma let go. Pam's arm looped around her son, and she walked into the house without a backward glance at Emma and Nicole.

"Sorry," Nicole whispered as they followed mother and son into the house. "She's always like that, stand-offish."

Emma smiled. "At least it wasn't something I said."

They walked through a large marble-tiled entry. An elegant stairway on the left wound up to the second story. A mahogany banister followed the stairs up, where it wrapped around the second story hallway that bordered the open living room to their right. Emma stared up at the wide-beamed cathedral ceiling above the living room. Sunlight streamed in from immaculately clean windows, and down across a matched set of cream-colored chairs and sofa.

"Would you like a tour?" Nicole asked.

"If they won't miss us," Emma replied, glad to have some time alone with Nicole before joining the party.

"Not likely. Adam's got some of his work friends here as well as his family."

Emma wanted to ask whom else Nicole had invited, but she thought that might be rude. Instead, she let Nicole lead her from room to room, the grand tour. Nicole started in the living room, which led to a middle room dominated by a massive, wide-screen television and an entertainment system that could fill in as a work of art in any modern art museum. Nicole pointed out the six well-hidden speakers that gave the system its surround sound effects.

"This is the largest room," Nicole said as they entered the third room on the tour. "It gets a lot of sunlight."

The south-facing room sported a polished, light oak wood floor and a long dining table that held a dozen yellow roses in a crystal vase. Emma scrutinized the space and lighting in the room, contemplating how the sun would overwhelm the room by the time of the wedding. "If it's not too hot a day, we could serve the cake in here, but I'm not sure we'd want to have the buffet set up in this room. The sun would be too much."

"Oh, they'll have the air conditioning going by then, I'm sure," Nicole said.

They detoured to the left, past the study and family room, then into the kitchen. Nicole's heels clicked across the gray tile floor as they entered the room. A central black-marble island split the room in half, with a double row of glimmering copper pans hanging from some complicated structure over it. The oven, dishwasher and refrigerator were all polished steel

"Your future mother-in-law cooks a lot?" Emma asked.

"She entertains a lot." Nicole walked past the island and into the back end of the dining room they'd looked at earlier. She paused at the patio doors leading to the backyard. The sound of voices drifted through the closed glass door as they stood there.

"'Once more into the breach, dear friend'." She smiled at Emma as she slid open the glass door.

The voices of the dozen or more guests grew louder. The backyard was a square well-kept lawn with a black, stone pool and bubbling fountain at the far side, surrounded by a wide tiled sunning area. A large grassy expanse to the left was wide enough to hold a tennis court with space to spare. Already, people were splashing about in the elegant pool, including a few children by the diving board. Emma smiled as she watched the kids playing. "If I'd known there was a pool, I'd have brought my swimsuit."

Nicole flushed. "Sorry, I didn't think to mention it." She left for a moment, slipping between three guests chatting in front of the drinks table, and requested two sodas from the young man mixing drinks. She returned and offered one to Emma.

"You don't swim?" Emma asked. She let the coolness of the glass counter her sweating palms.

"Not really. I don't much like how I look in a swimsuit."

Emma laughed. "You can't be serious. With your legs?"

"You haven't really seen my legs." Nicole lowered her voice. "I have a scar on my thigh. I think it makes my legs look awful."

Emma couldn't stop her eyes from drifting down to Nicole's legs. Now the longer capris on such a hot day made more sense. "Still," she said, "this'll be your family soon. You should feel comfortable with them."

Nicole snorted. "These events aren't for family. They're mostly business parties. Pam's an avid socialite and Henry's on the boards of at least four corporations."

Emma frowned. "Henry?"

"Sorry, Adam's dad. They're all highly ambitious."

Emma looked around. Most of the crowd did seem very stiff, chatting in small clusters around the yard. The party had none of the boisterous antics that her uncle's barbeque had yesterday. They stepped off the large wood porch and onto the lush green lawn. When Nicole didn't attempt to join any of the clustered groups of guests, Emma finally asked, "Do you know anyone here?"

Nicole surveyed the group. "Not really. Katie's not here yet. That cluster over there, I think, is from Neo-Tech, Adam's company." She pointed back to the porch. "Henry's the shorter, bald man over there just getting more wine at the table."

"Who's Katie?" Emma asked.

"Adam's sister. She introduced me to Adam."

Nicole slipped her hand into Emma's, wrapping her elegant fingers loosely around Emma's hand. "I asked you here under false pretenses," she said, feigning guilt. "Adam's family tends to dominate my social life, but I wanted someone here I knew I could talk to without worrying about the political ramifications of what I say."

"Glad to be of service," Emma said with a bow, warming to Nicole's gentle touch. "So, I take it Katie carries on the family's socialite leanings?"

"Oh yes." Nicole let go of Emma's hand. "So, what do you think of the yard for the wedding?" she asked.

Emma estimated the size of the grassy area between sprawling maple trees that marked what she assumed to be the limits of the back yard. "Definitely enough shade in there," she said, pointing to the trees. "If you keep it under fifty, you should be able to sit everyone in two sets of rows." She spread her arms wide as she spoke, "Make an aisle from the porch to the back bushes, and that could be where you walk down."

"Yes, that's what I thought, too, if the weather's on our side."

Emma nodded, ignoring the growing knot in her stomach. "If not, there's enough room to put up an open tent. You might want it anyway, just to extend the shade over your guests."

"I hadn't thought of that."

A tall woman, over-dressed for a backyard barbeque, paced toward them in quick, measured steps. She wrapped an arm around Nicole and gave her a perfunctory peck on the cheek that caused Emma to clench her teeth.

"Katie," Nicole said, returning the hug. "When did you get here?"

"I've been here for an hour. I was over there trying to get your attention, but you've been otherwise occupied," she said, her voice lacking anything akin to humor as she eyed Emma.

"Oh sorry," Nicole apologized. "This is Emma LeVanteur, the wedding planner."

Katie raised one perfectly shaped eyebrow as her icy gaze examined Emma. "So nice to meet you finally," Katie said, holding out her hand.

Emma shook the offered hand, wondering how anyone could have cold hands on such a warm day. "Nice to meet you, too." Should she be worried or flattered that Nicole had spoken about her to Katie? Her short introduction was interrupted when Pam waved for Nicole and Katie to join her, and Emma thought it best to limit her exposure to Adam's family. She wandered over to sit by the side of the pool. Sunlight glinted off the many ripples in the water, creating a soothing rhythm of light and shadow so that Emma hardly noticed when a teen-age girl swam up to the side.

"Coming in?" the girl asked.

Emma blinked, and then looked at her visitor. The teenager had tightly curled, dark brown hair pulled back into a ponytail and hazel eyes on a light caramel face. She'll get some attention when she's older, Emma thought. Much older.

"No thanks," Emma answered finally. "I didn't bring a suit."

The girl looked at her with the uncomprehending stare that only a teenager can manage. "So what? Kick off your sneaks and come on in."

Emma laughed. "How about if I just sit on the edge?"

The girl shrugged with a look that said 'adults, who ever gets them?'

Emma pulled off her sneakers and socks. She dangled her legs over the side of the pool. The water lapped against her calves, providing cooling relief from the hot sun that beat down on her. "I'm Emma, by the way," she said.

"Annah," the girl replied, holding out her dripping hand.

Emma shook the wet hand. "Nice to meet you. Are you related to Adam?"

"No. My dad works with him. That's my brother on the diving board."

Emma watched a boy of about eight or nine do a cannon-ball jump into the deep end. A wave of water crashed over the two other kids floating nearby. "Impressive."

"Yeah, he's a show off. That's my mother by the barbeque grill, the black lady."

Emma glanced at the tall, dark woman who was engaged in lively conversation with the chef tending the grill.

"Who are you here with?" Annah hung onto the side of the pool beside Emma, propped up on her elbows.

"Nicole. I'm helping out with the wedding."

Annah pulled herself out of the pool and sat, dripping, on the edge by Emma. "You don't look old enough to be a caterer or anything."

Emma cocked an eyebrow. "You don't think so? Well, I'm twenty-three, but I'm not a caterer. I just help with the planning, making preparations with the caterers and minister and the like. My mother's a professional wedding planner, and she's trying to pass on the family business to me I guess."

"Tell me about it. My mum's got the same crazy notions about passing on the family business," Annah said, shaking water out of her ear. "I turn sixteen in a month, but am I allowed to make my own decisions about my future? Nope. I have to seriously consider an engineering degree and then work for her at Neo-Tech."

"Congratulations on being sixteen." Emma smiled, steering clear of the hot button of Annah's mother. "Practically an adult."

"Yeah, tell my mother that."

"Mothers are like that. It's their job." Emma kicked at the water. It certainly was tempting to go for a swim. Too bad she had no suit.

Annah's brother paddled over. He had a darker complexion, but the same hazel eyes peering out from under dark eyebrows. "Getting out already?" he asked, splashing his sister.

Annah retaliated with rapid-fire kicking, and a full out water war ensued between the siblings. Emma didn't stay dry for long.

"Hey, you two," she said when the battle came to her turf in the form of repeated sprays of water. She grinned at the shocked expressions on both young faces.

Annah stopped immediately. Her brother stopped one splash later. "Oh, sorry, Miss," he said, his eyes wide.

Emma looked at him with a frown, planning her counter-attack. "Sure you are." She sprayed him with a hard double-kick splash. He ducked under the water and resurfaced with a laugh. He splashed a wave of water that drenched Emma's legs and shorts.

Annah laughed beside her. "You might as well go swimming, now."

"Yeah, maybe you're right," Emma looked at her soaking shorts and shirt. No sooner had she said it than two firm hands pushed her off the pool side from behind. She sank into the cool water, hearing the muffled echo of laughter around her. She resurfaced and turned to discover her silent assailant. Nicole squatted beside Annah at the pool side, laughing. Emma leaned forward on the warm tiled edge of the pool.

"Think it's funny, eh?" Emma asked.

"Oh yes," Nicole said, looking down at Emma with a mischievous grin.

Emma gave a subtle wink to Annah, and the girl was her instant accomplice. A moment later, Nicole resurfaced in the pool, sputtering and claiming righteous indignation.

"A conspiracy," Nicole said as she flipped her bangs out of her eyes. She grinned at Emma, and Emma was glad she was floating in the pool, as it kept her nervousness hidden under the cool water. She had only a moment to admire the way Nicole's damp hair clung to her forehead, and then Nicole renewed the battle, splashing at her. She returned the attack with interest. Annah jumped back in the pool and with her brother, it turned into a four-way water war. When they finally let up, a small crowd had gathered by the side of the pool, most of them laughing at the antics. Emma looked up to see the stern face of Pam standing in the group, her arms crossed. Beside her stood Katie, her cool expression unreadable. Emma worried more about Katie's inscrutable gaze than Pam's openly hostile reaction.

Adam crouched by the side of the pool, smiling. "Cooled off now, dear?"

Nicole's smile waned as she swam to the side. Emma gave a shrug to the two kids and made her own way out of the pool as well. Adam hoisted Nicole out of the pool. Her light, wet blouse clung to her, revealing round firm breasts under a lace bra. Emma's eyes burned that image of Nicole into her mind. She stood transfixed as she dripped by the pool side. Katie came into view, pushing a towel at Nicole. Emma's eyes shot up to meet the growing frown creasing Katie's forehead as she watched Emma.

"Cover yourself, Nicole," Katie ordered, her piercing eyes fixed on Emma. "People are staring."

Emma looked away, her face burning, but the image of Nicole's chest clung to her thoughts as tightly as her own wet clothes against her body. She squeezed out the excess water from her shirt, and then ballooned it out so she wouldn't be the next victim of the indecency police. Pam and Katie rushed Nicole off toward the house, leaving Emma alone to cool her burning desire for her friend.

The rest of the crowd moved on, except one: Annah's mother. She looked down at her two kids in the pool. "Did they start all this?"

Emma squeezed water out of her hair. "No, we were all in it together. We were just having some fun."

The woman smiled at her. "Hi, I'm Marina. And no need to defend my kids. If there's trouble afoot, I know who to blame," she said with a light-hearted grin.

The boy swam to the side. "What's the big deal? Everyone was having fun."

Marina pulled a chair up and sat down. "Yes, and what else is new?" She turned to Emma. "I take it you've met my delightful offspring?"

Emma nodded, "Annah and me, we go way back. But I didn't catch your son's name." She looked at the boy, who blushed instantly.

"He's Sam," Annah said, filling in for him.

"Samuel," he said indignantly.

Annah rolled her eyes. "Sorry. It's Samuel now."

Emma laughed. "Nice to meet you, Samuel."

He grinned and did a back flip, swimming away.

"He's shy," Marina said.

"He's a show off," Annah countered.

Marina leaned over and pulled up another chair for Emma. "Do you need a towel? I'm sure there's more in the house."

"No, I think I can drip-dry out here. It's keeping me cool, anyway."

"WHAT WERE YOU thinking?" Katie asked as she handed Nicole a light bathrobe from her mother's closet.

Nicole kicked the last of her wet clothes onto the master

bathroom floor and wrapped the bathrobe around her. Her face still felt warm as she remembered the way Emma had stared at her when they'd emerged from the pool. She didn't want to get into a debate with Katie on appropriate public etiquette. She just wanted to be left alone to bask in the memory of how Emma made her feel. But it seemed Katie would remain with her until Adam returned from her apartment with a fresh set of clothes. Katie had offered a pair of shorts from the clothes she'd left behind in her old bedroom, but Nicole refused. She wouldn't show the guests her scar. She certainly wouldn't show it to Emma.

Katie pulled out a comb and blow dryer from the master bedroom. "You can take care of your hair and makeup at least while we wait."

"My hair's fine," Nicole said, sounding more petulant than she'd intended.

Katie sat on the edge of her parent's cream-colored bed, crossing her arms. "What's gotten into you?"

"Nothing. I'm just tired of having to be perfect all the time around here."

"And that's all?" Katie asked. "Nothing to do with that wedding planner of yours?"

Nicole blanched. "Why would Emma have anything to do with, well, with anything?"

Katie studied her a moment, then shrugged. "No reason, I suppose. Still, you know what my mother is like. We'll be hearing about your little escapade for the rest of the summer, now."

Nicole walked to the open window overlooking the front lawn. She silently prayed that Adam would return soon, so she could get out of Katie's critical eye. She didn't like Katie second-guessing her friendship with Emma. And she didn't like the idea of leaving Emma alone with all those socialites.

EMMA SAT WITH Marina, chatting idly for an hour or so until Nicole came back. Nicole wore a more conservative, and dry, pair of slacks and short-sleeve top. Her hair was combed and dry as well. She half smiled at Emma, who had managed to stop dripping, but her clothes remained cool and damp.

"Sorry," Nicole began. "Adam drove back to my place for dry clothes."

Emma was frustrated with the way that Nicole let her future in-laws control her, but she managed to keep herself in check when Marina gave voice to her thoughts.

"Well, that was overkill," Marina said. "You could have soaked up the sun like your friend here and stayed cool for the rest of the party."

The tension in Nicole's shoulders loosened. "My sentiments exactly. I'm Nicole Davis, by the way."

Marina held out her hand, "I'm Marina LeVanteur. My husband works with Adam."

Emma's vision narrowed as her jaw locked shut. Her eyes bore into Marina as the woman continued talking.

"Paul's over there with the rest of the Neo-Tech gang. They never give up on the shop-talk."

The sun couldn't penetrate the cold that encased Emma's body as she resisted the urge to look where Marina pointed and instead stared at her father's current wife. Current wife. New family. Because his first family, his first daughter, wasn't good enough. A hand rested on her shoulder, momentarily stopping the downward spiral of her thoughts. Emma broke her stare and looked up into a pair of worried eyes.

"We should talk about the wedding," Nicole said. Her gaze held Emma's as she slipped her hand into Emma's. Emma's breath quickened as confused emotions collided within her. The cold, hollow revelation of her father's re-marriage battled with Nicole's caring touch.

Nicole turned to Marina, "Excuse us. Emma's planning my wedding, and we really should finalize a few things with Pam and Adam today."

Marina waved as they stood. "Nice meeting you both. Hope my kids behaved themselves."

Her kids, Annah and Samuel. Paul's kids. Emma turned away from the two kids splashing in the pool as Nicole held her hand and led her to a bench by the side of the house, away from everyone else.

"I'm so sorry," Nicole said, her voice filled with concern. "I had no idea."

Emma's hands clamped down on the edge of the bench, her knuckles turning white.

"Emma?"

"I don't want to talk about it," Emma said gruffly, cutting off any conversation about her father. If she didn't acknowledge it, or acknowledge him, maybe she could block it all out, lock it away in the depths of her heart where it could eat away at itself for all she cared.

Nicole sat beside her, her hands folding and unfolding in her lap as the silence between them seemed to swallow up the breathable air. Just as Emma felt the urge to bolt, Nicole broke the silence. "Have you eaten yet?"

"No." And she wouldn't now, not with the brick of truth

weighing down her stomach.

"Shall I get you a burger or something?"

"No, thanks."

"How about another soda?"

"Yeah, Okay." Anything to erase the lines of worry around Nicole's eyes.

Nicole waited a moment, and then left quietly.

Emma stared at the ground. How could he have a family, another family? She leaned forward, holding her head in her hands as the vision of Paul's new family swallowed all other thoughts. All her excuses for why he'd left were empty now. He had a wife, so he wasn't gay like she was. He had a family, so he wasn't just an incompetent father who couldn't handle the responsibility anymore. He even had a new daughter who wasn't Emma.

It was just her then, she thought, her and her mother who weren't good enough for him.

Nicole returned with two drinks, once again halting Emma's downward spiral. She put them down on the bench and knelt in front of Emma. Emma raised her head. Tears threatened to escape as she searched Nicole's worried face.

"I don't want to see him," she said in a whisper.

Nicole put her hands on Emma's knees. "You don't have to. Adam can take you home."

Adam. A stab of anger burned through Emma's mental fog. "Did he do this?" Emma asked. "Did he set this up?"

Shock and a faint reflection of anger passed over Nicole's fine features. "I don't know. I'd hope he would be more sensitive to your feelings than that."

Which meant he might have. Emma took a deep, steadying breath. It wasn't Nicole's fault. Maybe it was even a perverse coincidence, though she doubted that. She took Nicole's hands in hers, stroking small circles on each with her thumb. "I'm sorry. I know it's not your fault. I just, I'd like to go home." She had to get away before she broke down completely.

NICOLE FELT RESPONSIBLE for Emma's pain, but knew no way to help her. Then Katie's harsh voice interrupted them. Emma jumped, letting Nicole's hands drop. Nicole turned to face her best friend, wishing for once that Katie would mind her own business.

"There you are. Why are you skulking in the corner?" Katie's cold blue eyes left Nicole's face and bored into Emma. She didn't wait for either of them to answer. "Well, my mother would like to go over the wedding notes you gave Nicole. She doesn't agree with some of it."

Nicole stood up. "Can we do this another day? Emma's not feeling well. I'd like Adam to take her home."

Katie shook her head. "It'll only take a minute. And really, Adam's done enough driving already."

Emma squared her shoulders, returning Katie's icy stare. "I'd be glad to review my plans with your mother."

Katie turned away. "Fine. She'll meet you in the study if you are dry enough. And please, put on some shoes. Nicole, bring her a towel to sit on."

Nicole's face flushed in anger. It was bad enough that she had to deal with her mother-in-law putting on airs, but now she was getting it from Katie? She held Emma back when she started heading into the house. "I'm sorry that Katie's being so pissy. You don't have to do this."

"No, I'm fine. I'll leave when your future mother-in-law is satisfied with my work." Emma shrugged off Nicole's restraining hand and left to retrieve her shoes by the pool. Emma's quiet resolve in the face of her personal pain pulled at Nicole. She watched as Emma ignored the calls from Annah and marched toward the house. Nicole followed, grabbing a dry towel as they passed through the kitchen.

Pam waited for them in the dimly lit study. Sets of matched books lined the ornate bookshelves along each wall. A circle of well-padded chairs surrounded a central glass coffee table. Emma took the chair that Nicole encased in the dry towel. Pam immediately questioned each item on Emma's suggested wedding arrangement, forcing Emma to justify every decision she and Nicole had made over the past month. Nicole tried to speak up in defense of their decisions, but Pam only talked over her. Emma held her ground against the formidable older woman, but by the end, Pam remained unsatisfied.

"I still don't like the menu," Pam said in an exasperated tone. "These light sandwiches, they're very working-class."

Emma bristled. "The caterer is an excellent chef. He prepares these with his own bread and freshly cut meats."

"I'm sure that's all well and good where you come from." Pam turned to Nicole. "This is what I've been trying to tell you, dear. Your friend does an excellent job on her college functions, but this is just not the sort of event she's qualified to arrange."

"If you want a more traditional menu," Emma said through clenched teeth, "then I recommend the Beef Wellington with Yorkshire pudding."

Nicole marveled at Emma's composure and jumped to agree with her before Pam had a chance to argue further. "Excellent idea. My mother loves Yorkshire pudding."

Adam entered the room. "Why are you all hiding in here?"

"Wedding details," Pam answered. "Nothing you need to be involved in." She waved him off.

He turned to leave but Nicole reached out to him. "Stay, please."

He settled on the arm of Nicole's chair, his arm around her shoulder. Nicole rested her arm on his leg. Her fingers worked at knotting a napkin she'd picked up earlier. Maybe with Adam present, Pam would back off from her rigid stance. The woman doted on her son.

Pam huffed her displeasure, ignoring Adam. "What about this florist? She works out of her home?"

Emma glanced at Nicole. Their eyes locked for an instant as Emma's expression darkened. Nicole shifted away from Adam, self-conscious of his attention.

Emma turned her gaze away from Nicole and Adam. "Her uncle runs a wholesale flower business in the North End."

"Still, a more respectable florist is in order here," said Pam.

Nicole clenched her napkin. "I don't want to change the florist." Her voice sounded weak in her ears and when Pam ignored her, she repeated herself, raising her voice. Emma caught Nicole's eye, giving her an encouraging wink. This was the florist that Emma promised would add lavender to the arrangements, and Nicole would not use any other florist.

Emma turned to Pam. "Her work is excellent. I can give you her references if you want confirmation or you can interview her yourself, but I'm certain you'll be more than satisfied with her work. And more importantly, Nicole and Adam will be happy with it." She turned back to Nicole. "It's their wedding, after all."

Nicole relaxed, and Adam smiled. "Damn straight it is. If Nicole wants this florist then that's who she'll have." He leaned in and cupped Nicole's face in his large hands. He covered her lips with his wide thick mouth. Nicole pushed him away, uncomfortably aware that she didn't want Adam's affection in front of Emma.

Emma stood up. "If that's all, Mrs. Chandler?"

Pam nodded without looking up from the papers. "Yes, for now, thank you."

EMMA TURNED TO leave. Adam still held Nicole in his arms. Seeing them kiss proved too much for Emma to handle. She'd leave if she had to walk all the way back to Cambridge. On her way out of the room she collided in the hallway with a tall lean man, his chestnut hair just beginning to recede.

He held her up when she nearly fell, his brown eyes searching hers. "Emma?"

Father. The word came unbidden to her thoughts, and that angered her. "Yes." She pulled herself out of his grasp. "And you are?" She kept her expression cold and neutral.

His face fell. "Don't you recognize me? I know we haven't seen each other in years. I'm your father."

Emma sneered. This day had been too much. "Sorry, I have no father." She tried to push past him, but he held her arms.

"Emma, please." His deep voice plunged into the depths of her heart and back out again, yanking bittersweet memories of her childhood in its wake, memories that threatened to soften her anger at him.

"Go away!" she shouted, not wanting to remember anything about him. Not the way he taught her to catch, nor the stabbing pain when he'd left her for good. "Just go away. You've got your family. Just leave me the hell alone."

Emma turned as Nicole and Adam came out of the study behind her. Nicole's pale face mirrored her own. Adam only frowned, looking between Emma and Paul.

Emma pushed past her father and ran out the front door, letting the screen door slam shut behind her. She heard someone calling her as she sprinted down the block. Years of jogging made her legs strong. She ran. She ran to escape the nightmare of Nicole in Adam's arms. She ran to escape her father's face. She ran until the burning in her legs blocked out all other pain.

Chapter
Six

NICOLE PULLED AWAY from Adam when he prevented her from following Emma. "You can't just let her go like that!" she shouted. Adam moved in front of her, blocking her view of Emma's retreating form. She pushed him. "Move."

"No. Let her go," he said, holding her arms in his rough hands. "She can take care of herself." Nicole struggled in his arms, and he eventually let her go. She pushed past him, determined to catch up with Emma, but Katie came down the stairs and blocked her way.

"What's all the shouting about?" Katie asked, looking from person to person.

Paul spoke up from behind Nicole. "It was Emma. She didn't want to see me. I can't blame her after all these years."

Katie sighed. "Sorry about that, Paul. Who knew she'd go off the deep end?"

"It's okay. Thanks for trying to help," Paul said.

Nicole turned on Katie with a fury she'd never experienced before. "You did this? I told you she didn't want to meet him. And yet you invited him anyway, when you knew I wanted to invite Emma? And why didn't you tell me?" She felt betrayed.

Paul stepped in from behind her. "I'm so sorry, this is all my fault. I asked Katie to set this up when she told me that you were friends with my daughter."

Nicole turned her anger on Paul. Why did he have to show up? His penetrating, pale brown eyes and chestnut hair matched Emma's so much it made her heart skip. Emma, who'd just run away in tears, and it was all Nicole's fault for trusting Katie.

She couldn't just let her go. Nothing else mattered. Her wedding plans, Paul, Katie's betrayal. It all drifted away as she realized that she'd never be able to catch up with Emma. "I have to go after her," she said, feeling helpless because she wouldn't find Emma without a car.

Pam's harsh voice cut her off as she stepped out of the study. "You'll do no such thing. The girl's unstable, for all you seem to like her."

Paul glared at Pam. "You're talking about my daughter," he said, his voice deep and angry. "If she's upset, it's my fault."

For the first time ever, Nicole saw Pam back down. Her future mother-in-law lowered her head and mumbled an apology to Paul. Then she went back into the study as if something needed her attention in there.

Nicole fought back her tears. Katie and Paul had orchestrated a horribly painful confrontation with Emma and made Nicole an unwitting partner in it. Would Emma blame her for this? Nicole felt an icy stab of fear. Would Emma ever speak to her again? The thought of not seeing Emma again threatened to overwhelm her. She frantically tried to think of the right words to convince Adam that they had to search for Emma. Annah and Marina wandered in from the backyard as Nicole leaned against the wall, feeling numb and alone in her misery.

Marina approached them as they stood by the front door. "What's all the commotion?"

Paul reached for Marina's hands. "My daughter, Emma. She didn't want to see me."

"Maybe she'll come around. This wasn't the best way to meet up with her." Marina wrapped an arm around him. "Come on, let's go back outside."

Annah interrupted, "Emma? That was *the* Emma, your other daughter?"

Nicole watched Annah's expression twist in unsuppressed anger. She looked from Paul to Marina to Annah, realizing that Annah would be Emma's half-sister.

Paul nodded, his eyes glistening in the dim light.

Annah seemed oblivious to her father's distress. She turned on her mother, her hazel eyes blazing. "You knew I wanted to meet her today. Why didn't you tell me that was her?"

Marina held up her hand. "You knew Emma would be here, but she didn't know anything about you. I couldn't let you just pounce on the poor girl."

Annah's fists clenched at her side. "Well, where is she now?"

"She ran out the door," Nicole said, feeling a renewed sense of hope. Maybe she could recruit Annah to be her ally in this madness. "We need to go find her."

"I'm coming with you." Annah pushed her way out the front door, still wearing her damp top and surf shorts from the pool. "Let's go."

Nicole looked up at Adam. His hands fell to his sides. "Fine," he said. "I'll drive."

The three of them piled into Adam's car as Paul and Marina

watched from the doorway. Pam remained indoors, no longer interested in what was going on. Emma had a good ten minutes head start on them. Nicole bit her lip, hoping they would find her quickly, somewhere along the quiet streets of Newton.

EMMA SLUMPED INTO the plastic seat, which was sticky from the high humidity, as the Green Line train rattled along its tracks. Only a handful of people sat in the train car with her, a few other refugees from holiday parties. It had taken her over an hour to find the train station in Newton, after asking three separate times for directions. She didn't know how much of that time she'd spent randomly jogging through the town. The automatic pumping of her legs had kept her mind blissfully blank for that time.

She wanted to cry but she couldn't. She felt empty inside and alone. Why did so many things go wrong? Her eyes shut. She had visions of Adam kissing Nicole, his rough skin against Nicole's cheek. She tried to think of something else, but only thoughts of her father came to mind, his hands holding her up, the moment when she'd recognized him. A flood of childhood pain threatened to overwhelm her. She opened her eyes. Better to watch the trees whip past or count the light posts along the train tracks. Anything but remember the misery of the past couple of hours, or the pain and abandonment from years ago.

The sun was sinking low in the late spring sky when Emma finally made it home. Her muscles ached from running, and it felt as if heavy lead had replaced any remaining food in her stomach. She just wanted to sleep. She smelled something foul as she trudged down the hallway to her apartment. Someone's cooking experiment must have gone belly-up. She unlocked her apartment door and stepped inside.

The foul, undeniable smell was stronger. She nearly gagged on it. She'd only eaten breakfast, and that lead lump in her stomach threatened to make an unpleasant appearance. She walked down the hall and saw Jasmine sitting on Maya's lap on the sofa. One window was open, letting in the only breathable air in the apartment.

Emma's frustration exploded. "What the hell are you doing?"

Jasmine jumped up, looking for some place to hide her cigarette. Maya took it from her and sucked in a long, slow drag and exhaled.

"Got a problem?" Maya asked.

Hours of pent up anger crashed over Emma, destroying any semblance of civility she'd maintained with Maya. "Yeah, I do," she said. "Get the hell out of my apartment and take your damn pot with you." She stood behind the sofa glaring at Maya, her clenched fists hidden from the other two women.

"Sorry." Jasmine stood up. "I didn't think you'd be back until later."

Since when did Jasmine smoke pot? Emma wondered. She drank a few too many tequila shots at times, but Emma never knew her to dabble in drugs of any kind.

Maya stood up. "What are you apologizing to her for? It's your apartment, too. Tell her to go to hell."

Emma felt her fists tighten. One punch, just one punch to smash the arrogance off of that face. How could Jasmine stand this woman? She fawned over Maya, and Maya groped Jasmine in return, as if to prove who owned her. Emma thought she might still get sick on the rug. Their relationship bordered on disturbing, and she didn't want to witness any more of it.

"Let's go for a walk," Jasmine said, giving a long, nervous glance at Emma as she pulled Maya away.

Maya took one last long drag, licked her fingers, and then doused the joint with her fingers. Pain freak, Emma thought. As soon as the other two left, Emma pushed open all the windows and brought out the fans. The apartment reeked.

She slumped on the sofa, waiting for the fans to blow fresher air at her. Why couldn't Jasmine have been home alone? Emma needed someone to talk to. She missed confiding in Jasmine, but she'd be damned if she'd say anything in front of Maya. The woman was a walking freak of nature. What on earth did Jasmine see in her? Emma considered calling and telling her mother about her father and his shiny new family. But she didn't want a companion in her misery. She just wanted someone to console her, someone to just hold her.

She closed her eyes and tried to think of Nicole. She tried to remember Nicole not as she'd been with Adam, but as she'd been at the pool, with her blouse clinging to firm breasts and across a tight stomach. Tears spilled down her cheeks as she curled into a ball on the sofa.

THE PARTY GUESTS had dwindled until only Paul and his family remained, standing once again by the front door. Nicole's sense of betrayal had settled into a quiet, simmering anger directed at Katie, Pam, and anyone who'd ever slighted Emma. And that included the man standing in front of her who resembled Emma so much.

"You left her a message?" Paul asked.

Nicole nodded. "I hope she found her way back. I'll call as

soon as I hear from her." She would call for Annah, her mate in their unsuccessful search. Annah matched Nicole's anger and worry with an edgy fury that, for reasons Nicole couldn't quite follow, centered on the girl's mother. Nicole wished she felt as unworried as she sounded. She'd spent the rest of the party in a daze, staring at the bubbling fountain by the pool and wishing Emma would call. She'd kept her cell phone on, but it remained silent despite her frequent checks to see if she'd somehow missed a message.

Katie had kept her distance and eventually left the party. Nicole felt a certain satisfaction that Katie showed at least a semblance of guilt for having set up the awful situation. But now, the party was over, and Nicole could get home. If she could, she'd have shoved Paul and his family into their van herself. Adam wouldn't leave before Paul, no matter how much Nicole harassed him to take her home.

Marina shooed her kids out the door and into their minivan as Paul lingered.

"Thanks," Paul said, shaking Nicole's hand. She pulled away from him quicker than would be considered proper. She didn't care what he thought of her. He turned to Adam. "Sorry about all this."

"Not a problem. Hope it all works out for you," Adam said, the lightness in his voice expressing how little any of this had affected him. Nicole wanted to shake him out of his complacency. When she'd met him, she'd loved how easy-going he was, even in the midst of arguments between his parents. But now, that same trait frustrated her. Was there anything he truly cared about?

Paul walked in the dim dusk to his car. Nicole turned to Adam. "So he's your manager?"

"Yep. He was the CEO when they started Neo-Tech, but he stepped down when the venture capitalists came in for second-round financing. Now he's the VP of marketing, and Marina is the CTO."

Nicole felt too tired to be impressed. And the fact that Paul had misused his position to force himself on Emma grated on her. "We're leaving now," she announced. Maybe Emma had called her back at home instead of on her cell phone.

Adam kissed her on the top of her head. "Sure, let's go home."

Nicole remained silent for the drive home, trying not to imagine the terrible things that may have happened to Emma after she'd left. Would she have called a taxi from somewhere? She tried to convince herself that Emma was not wandering the streets of Newton, lost and alone. She considered asking Adam to search again, but gave up on the idea. They'd spent over an hour driving around earlier, and it was getting dark already. Emma must be home by now. She had to be home and safe, Nicole told herself.

Adam hummed to his music, oblivious to the day's tumultuous events. His indifference rankled on her. Sometimes she wished he could be more aware of her feelings, of anyone's feelings really. When they pulled up to her apartment building, she gave him a peck on the cheek and got out. As soon as he drove away, she ran up the three flights of stairs to her apartment, praying there would be a message from Emma waiting for her. When she got into her apartment, she saw that a light flashed on her answering machine, a welcome pinpoint of red in her dark apartment. Her heart pounded as she played the message back in the dark of her living room.

"Hi, it's me, Emma. I'm okay. I made it home. Sorry if I worried you."

The machine beeped to indicate the end of the message. Nicole leaned against the wall and replayed it. Emma's voice filled the quiet apartment, stirring an odd sadness within Nicole. She sounded so tired. Nicole reached out to touch the machine as Emma's voice ended the second time. Should she call her back? Maybe Emma didn't want to talk to her. Maybe she blamed Nicole for bringing Paul back into her life, for dredging up all that pain.

Nicole dug Paul's phone number out of her pocket. She'd promised Annah that she'd call. She flicked on the kitchen light and spread the crinkled paper out on the counter as she dialed.

"Hello, Annah? It's Nicole."

"Is she okay? Did you talk to her?"

Nicole had to smile. "I got a message from her. She made it home safe and sound, okay?"

Annah sighed on the other end. "Are you going to go see her tonight?"

"I don't know," Nicole answered. "Maybe it would be too late?" Maybe Emma wouldn't want to see her.

"No way, it's only eight-thirty."

Nicole warmed to the idea. "Well, I could go over and make sure she's all right." And see for herself if Emma was mad at her.

"Cool," Annah said, sounding excited now. "Can you give her a message for me?"

Nicole smiled. "Of course."

Annah's voice squeaked as she spoke. "Tell her I'll be taking my brother to his baseball game next Saturday. Ask her if she'll come."

Nicole couldn't mistake the eagerness in Annah's voice. "I'll ask. But Annah, don't take it personally if she doesn't show up. This has all been very sudden for her."

Annah was quiet for a moment. "Okay. But you'll tell her

anyway, right?"

"Yes. And tell your father that I called."

"Okay."

Nicole took down the directions and time for the ball game, and hung up. She walked into her bedroom and turned on a light. Looking down at the formal clothes Adam had chosen for her earlier, she decided a wardrobe change was in order. She walked over to her bureau and pulled out a pair of blue jeans and a maroon blouse, the match to the one she'd drenched in the pool. The one Emma had stared at when she'd gotten out of the water. Emma's intensity had stirred something inside her. She wanted to feel that attention from Emma again. She didn't think too much about it all, but it made her feel special. And it drew her to Emma, wanting to understand her, wanting to protect her.

Nicole dressed in the more casual clothes and put on a pair of trainers. She grabbed a yellow sweatshirt and tied it around her waist. She looked at herself in the mirror. No, that didn't match. She switched the sweatshirt for a gray pullover. She tied it over her shoulder. That looked too much like Pam's style to suit her. She settled for draping it over her arm. She tucked her wallet and keys into her pockets and walked out the door. She crossed her fingers and hoped that Emma would be home. She could call ahead, but fear of being turned away stopped her. If she showed up at Emma's door, at least she'd get to see her before being turned away. And seeing Emma was more important than anything else, even if she did get the door shut in her face. But the thought of that happening left a heaviness inside her that stayed with her all the way to Emma's apartment.

EMMA LAY ON her bed in the dark. She'd called her mother, but couldn't bring herself to talk about meeting her father. She knew that the hurt and betrayal that she felt would be worse for her mother. Moonlight filtered through the open window, casting a silver glow across her night stand and bureau. Her stomach growled, complaining over its empty state. She knew she should eat, but that required motivation, movement.

The doorbell rang. Emma rolled on her side. Whoever it was would go away. She played with the shadows of her hands on the bed until the doorbell rang a second, then a third time. Persistence will get you a kick in the chops, she thought as she rolled herself out of bed and shuffled to the intercom. "Take the hint, no one's here," she announced over the intercom.

"Emma? Emma, it's Nicole."

Emma's pulse quickened, oblivious to her despondent state.

She leaned her head on the intercom. Without a word, she buzzed down to the lobby to let Nicole in. She turned on the apartment lights and closed a few windows against the cool night breeze. She had enough time to wash her face before the knock on the door.

"Hey," she said, opening the door. Nicole stood at the threshold. Emma took in the casual jeans and sleeveless blouse in a glance. Nicole had changed her outfit. A faint scent of lavender drifted toward her.

"Come on in," she said, standing back. Her heart wanted to make something of the fact that Nicole wore a blouse that was a twin to the one she'd been soaked in earlier, but her mind refused to give her that much relief from her morbid state. Her own father didn't care about her, why should anyone else?

"Sorry to come so late," said Nicole, her voice shaking. "I just wanted to be sure you're okay."

Emma led her to the sofa and then curled into a ball at the other end. Her voice caught in her throat when she tried to speak. Nicole's eyes were locked on hers, but she didn't know what to say or how to recover from the nightmare the day had turned into.

"I wish you hadn't run like that," Nicole said.

"I had to get out of there." Emma's lips trembled, but she fought the urge to cry.

Nicole nodded, looking down at her hands. "We tried to find you."

We? Her and Adam? Her and Paul? Emma didn't want to know. "I found my way to the train station."

"I worried about you." Nicole's gentle voice tugged at Emma's numbed emotions.

Emma sighed, unfolding herself from the corner. "I'm sorry. I guess I shouldn't have left like that. I didn't mean to worry you." She held out her hand, and Nicole slipped her hand in Emma's. Their fingers entwined. Emma relaxed from the touch.

"I'm glad you came by," Emma said. Nicole's presence seemed to break the wall of ice that had formed around her.

Nicole looked up. "So am I. But, I did have strong encouragement to find you, at least from one rather assertive young teenager."

Emma didn't know what to make of Annah. She didn't want to hold her parentage against the girl, but then again, she did feel a certain jealousy that Annah had a father, and she didn't.

"Annah was very persuasive that I should check up on you."

"Oh? Is that the only reason you came over?" Emma asked, teasing.

Nicole's cheeks turned pink, "No. But it is my official excuse, and I'm sticking to it." She smiled.

Nicole's warmth drew Emma closer. She wanted to feel more of Nicole than just the warm hand holding hers. She wanted to feel Nicole in her arms, run her fingers through her hair, trace the outline of her red lips. For an instant, their eyes locked, and Emma felt her own burning desire threatening to overcome her.

Then Nicole looked away, breaking the spell. Emma swallowed hard. This wasn't right. She shouldn't be feeling like this for Nicole, for a straight woman. She didn't have the strength to pull her hand away, but then Nicole didn't make any effort to separate them, either.

"I was also asked to relay a message from Annah," Nicole said. "She would very much like to meet you again."

Emma studied the floor, pushing a discarded sock around with her toes. "She's a good kid." Her father's kid. Tears pooled around the edges of her eyes, and Emma brushed them away. She felt Nicole's arm around her shoulder, holding her. Emma's control dissolved as tear after tear rolled down her cheeks. Nicole pulled her closer, rocking her until the sobs faded into annoying hiccups. All the while, her head lay on Nicole's shoulder, her tears wetting the silky maroon blouse.

"I don't understand," Emma said between hiccups. "He must have lived near here all along. Why didn't he ever come see me?"

"I don't know." Nicole stroked Emma's hair as she rested her head on top of Emma's.

"Too busy with his new family," Emma said. She heard the bitterness in her own voice. "He just didn't want anything to do with the old one, I guess."

Emma's tears dried as she let Nicole console her. After a time, her sorrow gave way to something else. She felt Nicole's cheek on her head, then felt the warmth of a kiss placed lightly on the crown of her head. She closed her eyes while Nicole stroked her hair. She could rest there forever, but for her burning need for more from Nicole. The heat between her legs forced her to focus on something other than the way Nicole made her feel. Her body throbbed in places it shouldn't. Not for a soon to be married woman.

She sat up, and Nicole's arms slipped off her shoulders. "Thanks," she said, her voice deep, throaty.

Nicole clasped her own hands in her lap. "It's what friends are for," she said softly.

Emma stood up, needing to put some distance between them. "Sorry, I should have offered you something. Do you want a drink? Or chips and salsa?"

"A drink would be nice, please."

Emma went to the kitchen and came back with drinks and the chips and salsa. "I live for salsa," she explained as she sat, trying her best to quell her body's reaction to Nicole.

"What will you do now?" Nicole asked.

"I don't know. My mother's going to flip. And I don't know that I ever want to see my father again, thank you very much."

"Maybe you should start with neutral ground?"

Emma gave her a puzzled look.

"With Annah I mean," Nicole said, as she put her drink down and scooped up some salsa on a chip. "She's taking her brother to his baseball game at the Newton Centre field next Saturday. She really is a wonderful girl and somewhat eager to have a big sister. "

Emma smirked. "I'm not exactly big sister material." She sat back on the sofa. "Maybe. I don't have to decide right now, do I?"

"No, not right now, love."

Emma's eyes drifted shut. Her father was only part of the day's problems. Having Nicole here beside her was a poignant reminder of how strong her feelings had become for Nicole. Maybe she should tell her, confess that she was drawn to Nicole. But how could she? She hadn't even come out to Nicole, yet.

Keys rattled in the front door, and Emma's eyes shot open. Jasmine. Please don't let Maya be coming back with her, she prayed.

"My roommate," she said to Nicole as the door opened behind them.

Jasmine staggered in, with Maya in tow. Emma's jaw clenched as she watched Jasmine fumble with the lock, dropping her keys. Jasmine nearly fell over retrieving them, with Maya crouched over her as she stooped to get them. Drunk or worse; great, thought Emma. Jasmine bounced off two walls on her way into the living room. Maya had her hand tucked into Jasmine's waistband as they stood holding each other up in the hallway.

"Visitors," Jasmine slurred.

Of all the times Jasmine has been missing in action, why not tonight? "This is Nicole," Emma said, keeping her frustration in check. "Nicole, this is my roommate Jasmine and her friend Maya."

Maya whooped. "Oh, we're friends now, hear that, Baby?" She tried to pull Jasmine into her, but Jasmine gave her a shove.

"Nice to meet you, Nicole," Jasmine said.

Emma smiled her appreciation at Jasmine for trying to regain some dignity in her inebriated state. Maya tugged at Jasmine, trying to pull her toward the bedroom. When Jasmine resisted, Maya's expression darkened. She turned to Emma. "So, is this your English babe?"

Emma's mind froze. Jasmine had been sharing her confidence with this beast of a woman.

Maya leaned on the sofa, sticking her head between Nicole and

Emma. Her breath stank. "So, did you get past first base yet? I hear Emma's got some stamina in the sack."

Nicole pulled back, looking from Maya to Emma, frowning. "I'm not sure I understand."

Emma's temper flared. "Maya just needs to shut up, that's all."

Maya backed away with a laugh. "I guess not. Come on, Jazzie, we've got to show these kids how it's done." Maya forced Jasmine into the back of the sofa and slipped her hand under Jasmine's top to grope her breasts. Jasmine struggled against her, but her efforts didn't stop Maya. Nicole stood up, her face going pale. Emma stood as well, but no words would come out to explain all this. If thoughts could kill, Maya would be split into seven different pieces by now.

"I, I should be going," Nicole stammered, backing away.

Emma followed her to the door. "I'm sorry, they're drunk."

Nicole nodded. "It's fine. It's none of my business, really. Sorry, um, sorry, I need to go."

Emma stood at the doorway while Nicole rushed down the hallway. When Nicole disappeared into the elevator without even glancing back, Emma slumped to the floor. The apartment door stood wide open behind her. Her vision blurred. How did all this happen? Was Nicole running away from her now, too? Rejection and fear swirled inside her mind as she looked down the empty hallway.

Jasmine knelt behind her. "Come back inside. Please."

Emma slammed her fist into the wall, inches from Jasmine's face. "This is your fault!" she shouted.

Jasmine swayed back, unsteady. "Well, it's not like you'd ever get anywhere with her anyway."

Emma stood up, her back stiff. She glared at Jasmine. "I hate you. I hate you and that bitch you call a girlfriend. Get out of my face and get out of my life."

Emma stomped back into the apartment. When Maya planted her intoxicated self in front of her, Emma shoved the drunken sod into the kitchen table. She heard a satisfying thud behind her as she locked herself in her bedroom.

NICOLE STRUGGLED TO unlock her apartment door. Her fingers didn't want to follow the orders from her brain. She managed to get inside after a struggle, and tossed the offending keys on the floor. She'd worry about finding them in the morning. Her mind didn't want to deal with that right now. It didn't want to deal with anything. Her apartment smelled of stagnant air and the scent of cut flowers gone past their prime. She leaned against the

kitchen wall for a moment, staring at the play of light and shadow
from the moonlight shining through the trees. She moved to flick
on the kitchen light.

One message light still glowed on her answering machine,
reminding her of Emma's message that she hadn't yet erased.
Nicole laid her hand on the machine a moment and then moved off
to the living room. She sat on the edge of the sofa, unsure what she
should be doing. Her mind wouldn't focus. She tried not to think of
that awful woman in Emma's apartment. The stiff, bleached hair
and breath that smelled of who knows what. And the way she
treated Emma's roommate, it was almost predatory.

Nicole's thoughts bounced from Maya's evil stench to the
warmth of Emma's body in her arms as she quieted Emma's crying.
She felt a pang of guilt for having enjoyed holding Emma. She
closed her eyes and remembered the feel of Emma's long chestnut
hair sliding between her fingers. It was as soft as she'd imagined it
would be. She and Emma shared a bond, something precious that
outweighed any other friendship she'd ever had.

She wouldn't think about what that horrible woman said was
going on between them. Nicole guessed that Maya and Emma's
roommate were lovers. That was obvious, and she had no issues
with them. But she didn't want to think about Emma, not in the
way Maya insinuated. She'd made it sound so sullied, so dirty.
Even the way Maya treated her girlfriend was so disrespectful.
They weren't like that, she and Emma.

Their moments together rushed through Nicole's thoughts,
each shared glance or casual touch. She felt her body reacting to
thoughts of Emma, accepting for the first time the nature of her
own attraction to Emma. Was that what Maya sensed? Or had she
just jumped to conclusions to prove her dominance over everyone
present? What did Emma think? Nicole's cheeks flushed with
embarrassment. Was she letting herself flirt too much with Emma?
She didn't want to lose her like she'd lost female friends before, but
it seemed impossible to go back to a casual friendship. As she
thought back, she couldn't think of a time when there wasn't some
level of play between them. The tone of their interactions had been
flirtatious since the time that Emma had read the love poem so
passionately in class. And Emma seemed to enjoy it as much as
Nicole.

She picked up her remote control and turned the TV on to
distract her frazzled mind. She wouldn't think about it. The
implications were too far-reaching for Nicole to let her mind
wander down that dangerous path. Emma was a friend and a
business associate. If other people misinterpreted that, it was not
her worry.

Chapter
Seven

EMMA ARRIVED AT her mother's house just after lunch the following Saturday. She hadn't heard from Nicole all week and hadn't the guts to call her. Whatever fragile bond they shared had been shattered by Maya. Emma managed to be back on speaking terms with Jasmine, but she hated her girlfriend.

The long walk from the train station to her mother's house was punctuated by two active games of street hockey along the route and one adult game of stick-ball on the corner of her mother's block. Weeds blew in the warm breeze in the empty lot beside her mother's house as she walked up the stairs to the front door. Everyone seemed to be outside enjoying the late spring day. Emma watched the stickball game until she realized she didn't recognize any of the players. So much for coming back to the old neighborhood.

She opened the door to the screened-in front patio and unlocked the main door. "Ma, I'm home."

When no answer came, she guessed that her mother was busy in the backyard. She walked through the parlor and kitchen and shouted out the kitchen window. "Hey, I'm home."

Her mother stood up from her vegetable patch and pushed a fist into the small of her back to work out a kink. "Hi honey, didn't expect you this weekend." She came through the back door, kicking her gardening clogs off on the doorstep, and enveloped Emma in a sturdy hug.

"What brings you here?" she asked as she washed the mud off her hands.

Emma shrugged. "Just felt like coming home."

Her mother gave her a strange look. "Okay. Well there are some leftovers in the fridge if you're hungry."

Emma poked her head into the refrigerator, but nothing tempted her appetite, which had been missing since the previous week.

"Well, I need to finish the tomato plants, so help yourself to whatever." Her mother slipped her clogs back on and plodded out into the warm day.

Emma wandered around the first floor of the house, poking at knickknacks that had been in the same positions since she was a kid. She walked upstairs to her old bedroom. Her mother had left it unchanged since Emma moved out two years ago to share an apartment with Jasmine. A poster of k.d. lang hung on the wall over her old twin bed, staring across at, much to Emma's embarrassment, Britney Spears. So much for being the teen-aged lesbian's showcase bedroom.

She looked out of her bedroom window. It faced the backyard, where her mother still worked at the hard soil, digging in to add her fresh young plants to the small garden patch. The backyard hadn't changed either. The vegetable garden still dominated the left side of the yard and a small patch of grass took up the rest. She should convince her mother to replace the old chain-link fence that separated their yard from the neighbors'. Its rusted metal overshadowed the simple tidiness of the rest of the yard.

Emma left the windowsill and slid open her closet door. On tip-toes, she felt along the narrow shelf above the inside doorframe. Yes, they were still here. With a guilty jolt, Emma pulled out the pictures she had hidden in her room years before. She closed her bedroom door and locked it, just to be safe. Not that her mother would come check on her, but old habits die hard. Emma sprawled across her bed, kicking up a cloud of dust. Obviously no one came up here anymore. She spread the dozen worn pictures across her bed.

Emma and her dad at her eighth birthday party. His hair was fuller then, and longer, down below his ears. Another picture of her and her dad, shoveling snow. She looked about five or six in this one. He was smiling and waving at the camera. Emma turned over the last picture in her pile. She remembered this one the most. It was a Polaroid, taken with the camera she'd gotten for Christmas that year. Her dad stood by the front door, in his old denim jacket. He barely managed a smile. He had a suitcase in his hand and another at his feet. Tears flowed as Emma remembered begging her dad for one last picture. She was ten. She knew he was going away, but she didn't know until much later that he would never come back, not once. Not ever.

She heard the back door slam shut. Jumping up, she scooped up all the pictures and tucked them into her back pocket. Drying her eyes, Emma made her way back downstairs.

"Did you eat anything?" Margaret asked.

"Not really hungry."

Her mother turned to her, hands on her hips. "Since when are you not hungry?"

Emma sat in the kitchen, her elbows on the table and propped her head up with her hands. "Just not, that's all."

Margaret slid into the chair opposite her. "Emma Catherine, what's going on in that noggin of yours?"

Emma looked into her mother's patient eyes. "It's been kind of a bad week."

"Go on."

"Well, I told you about Nicole, the professor I've been working with, right?" Her mother nodded. "Well, she was over the other day, and Jasmine came home with her new girlfriend. They made some, well, some blatant suggestions about me and Nicole."

Her mother frowned. "That doesn't sound like Jasmine. I know she's pretty open about things, but you've never said she's outed you to anyone before."

"Well, it was more like her girlfriend did it. I hate this one."

"So," Margaret prodded Emma to continue.

"So Nicole left, and I haven't heard from her since."

"Well, was it true?"

Emma lifted her head. "Was what true? That Nicole and I are involved? She's getting married, Ma."

"Okay, maybe I should have asked, do you want it to be true?"

Emma dropped her head into her hands. "I don't know. I mean yeah, but then I know she's getting married, so I shouldn't feel this way."

Her mother rubbed Emma between the shoulders. "We can't always help how we feel."

"I guess."

"Well, that does sound like a bad week. "

It gets worse, Emma thought. She looked at her mother. Her long gray hair was braided down the back, and her face already showed signs of a summer tan. "Ma, has Dad ever called you? I mean since he left?"

Her mother pulled back, sitting up. "He's long since gone, Emma. No sense dragging that back up."

"I know."

Her mother stood up. "I need to walk down to the hardware store for some more plant spikes. Do you want to come?"

In other words, end of conversation, Emma thought. She glanced at her watch. She had three hours until she was supposed to meet Annah at Samuel's baseball game. "Yeah, okay. Let me get a drink of water first."

She guzzled down a glass of tap water and then followed her mother out the front door, giving up on the notion of getting any further information about her father.

THE MID-AFTERNOON SUN glared in Emma's eyes as she scanned the small crowd for Annah. She searched the benches along the side of the baseball field. There, along the far bench, she saw Annah, looking sullen and bored. Typical teenage posturing, Emma thought with a grin. She paused by the side of the field for a time. Was she ready for meeting Annah again, for being a big sister? She'd spent most of the past week just moping about her father and the mess she'd made of things with Nicole. But she wanted to come to meet Annah today, not just because Nicole had suggested it, but because it was a connection to her father. No matter how rejected she felt by him, she still wanted to know his new family. Emma walked around behind home plate and hopped onto the metal bleachers where Annah sat. There were a dozen or so people cheering the teams on either side. Emma had no idea what inning it was. She walked up next to Annah.

"This seat taken?" she asked.

Annah looked up, and her expression changed from bored to excited. "Emma!" She jumped up and threw her arms around Emma, giving her a tight squeeze.

"Hey, nice to see you, too," Emma said.

Annah gave a quick look around like she wanted to be sure no one that mattered saw her un-teenage-like outburst. "Glad you could come," she said more sedately, though her eyes still held a sparkle.

"Glad you invited me." Emma gave her a pat on the back. "Now, which team is Sam on?"

"Samuel," Annah corrected with an exasperated sigh. "He's number 7, shortstop, in blue."

Emma blocked the sun from her eyes to see Samuel. He crouched between second and third base, shifting from foot to foot.

"Did I miss anything good?" she asked.

Annah rolled her eyes. "As if. I get to baby sit him at every game because Mom and Dad think Samuel and I don't spend enough time together anymore."

Emma flinched at the mention of her father.

"Sorry," Annah covered her mouth, her face paling. "I guess I shouldn't mention them, huh?"

"No, it's okay. They're your parents." Emma would have laughed, if it didn't hurt so much. They sat quietly for a time, watching the game. The inning changed but Samuel's turn at bat didn't come.

"So, do you play sports too?" Emma asked.

"I do track at school. 200 meter sprints and the hurdles."

Emma gave her best 'I'm-impressed' nod. Annah's grin widened. Finally, Emma thought, someone got her expressions. "I was never very fast with the running," she said. "But I play softball in the summer."

It was three more innings before Samuel noticed Emma in the stands. He gave a big wave as he swaggered up to bat. Two strikes later, he nailed one to the outfield for an easy double.

"Yeah!" Emma jumped up. Annah looked up at her, and Emma shrugged. "It was a good hit." She settled back down. "So, have you been thinking about college yet or is that too soon?"

"Oh I know what I want to do." Annah let out a long sigh. "But trying to get my mother to listen is like talking to a wall."

Emma stifled a laugh. Was she ever this melodramatic about her own mother? Probably. "So what do you want to do?"

"I want to be a writer." Annah watched her, waiting, it seemed, for Emma to pass judgment.

"And your mother?" Emma asked, sensing the source of Annah's sensitivity.

"She wants me to major in bio-engineering so I can join her company when I graduate."

Emma nodded. "Bio-engineering. That's a complicated field. Do you have the grades for it?"

"Yeah." Annah shrugged, looking back at the ball game. "I mean, I like the math and all, but where's the creativity?"

"Well, it comes when you apply the math or science to real-world problems." Annah glared at her. Emma held up her hands. "Hey, don't shoot the messenger. I'm a graduate math student, so this is my thing. I'm not saying I'm siding with your mother here."

A voice from behind interrupted them. "Oh, heaven forbid anyone side with her mother."

They turned in unison. Marina stood behind them, her hands on her hips, but a smile played on her face.

"Mom, you're early," Annah complained.

"Sorry. I wanted to see Samuel play. I didn't realize you had company," Marina replied as she sat next to them.

Emma watched the game with feigned interest. Marina reminded her of her father, and that still hurt too much. Annah glowered at her mother. Maybe Emma never had such an antagonistic relationship with her mother because that's all she had growing up.

She turned to Marina. "So, you have your own company?" she asked, breaking the tension that had settled on them all.

Marina shrugged. "Well, sort of. We founded Neo-Tech, but the reality is that the venture capitalists control the majority of the company by now. You said you're doing your graduate work in math? Have you chosen a thesis topic yet?"

"Riemann surfaces," Emma said, glad for the neutral topic.

"Really? That's a difficult subject."

Annah let out a loud sigh. "Do you have to geek out, Mother?"

"Sorry," Marina said. "It just happens to be a core technology for Neo-Tech." She smiled, mischievously. "Annah loves to hear about my work, don't you honey?"

That comment warranted a penetrating, burn you on the spot stare from Annah. Emma turned away so as not to be caught smirking herself. She sensed that mother and daughter thrived on taunting each other. The rest of Samuel's game was spent with neutral comments on his play and the relatively benign weather they were experiencing for a late spring evening. By the time the game was over and Samuel came trotting over, Emma was glad to be heading home. The event had turned out to be more of a chore than she'd expected with Marina there.

Emma arrived home feeling more confused than ever. Grudgingly, she accepted that Marina was an okay person, possibly even interesting. Emma got along well with Annah, to the point of agreeing to meet up with her for sprint training. Not that Emma ran sprints, at least not well. But Annah seemed thrilled by the notion, and if Emma were honest with herself, she was also warming up to the notion of having a sister.

The apartment was dark, but not empty when Emma unlocked the door. She steeled herself for another scene with Jasmine and Maya if they were in the living room. She flicked on the hallway light. It cast enough light to just make out Jasmine sitting in the kitchen, her head resting on her arms on the old pine table. Emma peered around the corner. No sign of Maya. So far so good. Jasmine didn't move, so Emma walked around to turn on the living room lamp. Guessing that Jasmine was hung over again, Emma asked quietly, "You need Motrin or something?"

Jasmine lifted her head. Her face and arms remained in shadows, but somehow the shadows were wrong. Emma had her hand on the switch for the kitchen light when Jasmine finally spoke.

"No lights, please."

Emma looked closer at Jasmine. Something was definitely off. "What's wrong?"

"Nothing. I just don't want the lights on."

Emma crossed over to Jasmine and pulled up the seat next to her at the kitchen table. Jasmine cradled her left arm, and the red patch on her cheek certainly wasn't makeup gone awry.

"What happened to you?" Emma asked, her voice thick with worry.

Jasmine looked away, covering her face in shadow. "Nothing. I fell."

Into someone's fist maybe, Emma thought. "Who did this to you?" Emma's fists clenched. "Did Maya do this?"

"No! No. We ran into, into some bad people. I'm okay. I'll be okay."

"You got jumped?"

"Sort of."

Emma rested her hand on Jasmine's shoulder, praying it was a bruise-free zone. Jasmine didn't flinch, so maybe she lucked out. "You want to talk about it?"

"No."

Emma slid out of her chair and went to the fridge. She cracked free some ice cubes and wrapped them in the red checkered kitchen towel.

"Try this on the arm," she said, holding out the ice pack.

"Thanks," Jasmine said, placing the pack on her left arm. She winced.

"Any chance it's broken?" Emma asked.

"No, just a bad bruise."

Silence engulfed them for a time as they sat in the dark kitchen. Emma had a feeling Jasmine's injuries were worse than she let on, but the awkwardness between them prevented her from pushing further. She wanted to know where the attack happened and did they call the police. And did Maya look as bad as Jasmine? Did Maya try to defend her?

Finally, Emma couldn't take the silence anymore. "Look," she began, "About the other day..."

Jasmine looked up. Emma could see the salty tracks of dried tears on her cheeks.

"I'm sorry for what I said," Emma continued.

Jasmine smirked. It seemed painful. "You mean about hating my guts?"

"Yeah, the whole hating thing. I didn't mean it."

Jasmine tried to shrug, but it jarred her arm. She winced instead. "It's okay. We kind of made a mess out of things with you and Nicole, eh?"

"I guess. I haven't heard from her in awhile."

"Sorry," Jasmine murmured, lowering her head.

"Hey, not your fault. If anything, Maya started it all."

"I know you two don't like each other."

There's an understatement, Emma thought. She chose not to address that topic for now. "Well, I probably should have told Nicole by now that I'm a lesbian."

"Think it would have mattered?" Jasmine asked.

"Who knows, probably not," Emma said. If Nicole were homophobic, then that about ended any hope they had of remaining friends. She'd get over Nicole, she told herself. Probably. Someday. "How's the arm?" she asked, wanting to change the subject. "Can I take a look at it?"

Jasmine lifted the ice pack. Emma strained to see in the dim light from the living room. A swollen area, just starting to color, spread from below the elbow and wrapped half way around Jasmine's narrow forearm.

"Can you move your fingers and wrist?" Emma asked.

Jasmine tried. Everything worked, but painfully. She shifted her arm out of the shadows, and Emma got a good look at it. Emma's eyes grew wide, not from the injury, but from the collection of tiny punctures in her roommate's arm, multiple injection sites.

"Jasmine."

Jasmine saw her expression and covered up her arm. "I'm going to bed," she announced, standing.

Emma tried to keep her there but Jasmine pulled away.

"I'm a big girl. I can take care of myself," Jasmine said.

Emma watched her roommate limp into the bedroom and collapse across the bed, curling into a ball. She quietly closed Jasmine's door. Something awful was going on, and she'd be damned if she was going to sit by and let it happen. She flicked on the kitchen light and started pacing.

ADAM TREATED NICOLE to an exquisite dinner in Harvard Square. At least it should have been if she could have kept her mind off unwelcome thoughts. She indulged in her second glass of red wine, trying to tune out those stray thoughts.

"You're in a state tonight," Adam said.

Nicole sipped her wine, enjoying its warm, woody taste. "Just relaxing and enjoying your company," she said.

"You want any dessert?" he asked.

Nicole perused the menu. Nothing seemed as good as the wine in her hand. Maybe she'd open another bottle when they got back to her apartment. She looked up at Adam. His blue eyes crinkled when he smiled. She watched him coyly. "No dessert tonight, love. Take me home."

Adam called over the waiter and settled the check. He led Nicole out of the restaurant into the wall of humid air waiting outside the air conditioned establishment. Harvard Square teemed with late evening activity, fed by the rich diversity of shops and the overflow of post-exam students. They entered the garage where Adam had parked his car. Nicole leaned on him as they walked up the stairs to the second level.

"Why do we always drive?" she asked. "Traffic around here is such a pig."

He gave her arm a pat, "Because I hate taking the train. It smells, especially on days like today, with all the heat and humidity." They paused at the BMW as he unlocked the doors. She banged her head on the way into the car. "You all right?" he asked.

"Yes, just a bit tipsy," she said, rubbing a growing lump on the top of her head.

Adam started the engine and flipped on the air conditioning. It took a block or two before cool air flowed over Nicole's chest and face. She had to admit, there were benefits to driving, even with the traffic mess of Cambridge. She felt restless, playing with the stereo as the streets rolled by.

"What's up? You're all fidgety," Adam said.

"Nothing, just too much excess energy." She looked at her future husband. His wavy blond hair curled around his ears. She brushed it back for him. "Will you come up to my apartment?" she asked softly.

Adam gave her a broad smile. "I wish. I have to head back to Neo-Tech after this."

She slumped in her seat. "I'm getting sick of that company." She doubted she was the only lonely start-up spouse. It used to bother her more, but the past week, she'd been glad for the solitude. She felt guilty for brooding over her feelings for Emma, but she couldn't stop thinking about her.

Adam patted her leg. "Sorry, we're preparing a presentation for the investors tomorrow. Paul wants to review the slides tonight."

Nicole curled away from him to stare out the window. She didn't want to hear about Paul today. It tugged at her heart to think of what Emma might be doing right now, how she might be feeling about her father and his family. Nicole wanted to call her, but something held her back. Her mind focused on Maya's face, knowing just what had kept her away from Emma for so long. She took her frustrations out on Adam. "Your company needs to remember you have a fiancée who's tired of being left alone at night."

Adam pulled to a stop in front of her building. "It's the way it is, Nicole. Neo-Tech has a long way to go before we can sit back and relax."

She got out of the car and stood alone in the warm night air. Adam blew her a kiss and sped off, his red taillights glowing like demon eyes as he drove out of sight. She stood there a moment, indecisive. She thought about visiting Emma. But no, she wouldn't. She couldn't bring herself to go back to that apartment and risk running into Maya and Jasmine. It was all too unsettling. But she missed Emma desperately. She hadn't heard from Emma for a week, and she worried that her friend didn't want to see her. And she wasn't sure what she would say to Emma. She was ashamed of the way she had run out of the apartment, and afraid she'd embarrassed Emma by her awkward behavior.

Nicole turned and trudged her way up to her apartment. She'd love a good long soak in the tub, but the humid weather made her shy away from a hot bath. Maybe she'd call her mum in England in the morning. Nicole smiled for the first time in days at the prospect of having someone to talk to. Maybe she could explain enough of her situation with Emma to her mother without letting on the true nature of her feelings.

Chapter
Eight

EMMA HEARD THE phone ring while she was in the shower,
but either Jasmine or the answering machine would pick it up. She
let the hot water beat down on her back, releasing some of the
tension of the past few days. She was glad that she'd met up with
Annah yesterday, but even that had turned into a stressful event.

The weather report promised sunny and warm, and Emma was
determined to get out and shake off her moody attitude. Seconds
after she shut off the water, she heard Jasmine knocking on the
bathroom door. She didn't think she'd been hogging the bathroom
that long.

"What?" she shouted.

"Hurry up, get dressed." Jasmine sounded excited.

She dried herself off and pulled on navy blue shorts and a
white Red Sox baseball shirt. She came out of the bathroom with a
spare towel.

"What's the emergency?" she asked, drying her hair on the
towel.

Jasmine did a silly dance and handed Emma a note. "Someone
wants to see you," she said in a sing-song voice.

Emma read the note, and her heart skipped a beat. Nicole had
called. Emma forced herself to calm down. As her initial excitement
faded, she crumpled the paper in her fist. She'd be glad to talk to
Nicole, but she was determined to get over her unwanted attraction
for a straight woman.

Jasmine's enthusiasm continued. "So, does this mean our date
is off for tomorrow?"

"No way." Emma stuffed the note in her pocket. "I'm sick of
being in this apartment. And I promised you I'd try to get along
with Maya. You can't ditch me that easily." And she wanted to
figure out a few things about Jasmine's girlfriend. She'd pushed
herself into getting an invitation to join them at a gay bar, and she
wasn't backing down now.

"Okay, but you are calling Nicole back, right?"

Emma's pulse quickened, despite her efforts to control herself. "Yes, I'll call her back. She's still a business client."

"Sure, sure. All business clients get you that red in the cheeks," Jasmine teased.

Emma turned away. She'd get over these feelings, damn it.

EMMA AGREED TO meet at Nicole's apartment at ten o'clock. That gave her enough time to keep her lunch date with her mother in Copley Square afterward. She stood once again before Nicole's apartment, willing her heart to settle and her mind to focus on business. She'd never had such a hard time getting over someone she hadn't actually dated. Not that she specialized in hopeless infatuations or anything. No, not her.

As Nicole opened the door, Emma couldn't help but notice the blue cotton pants and tight tank top that revealed the delicious contours of Nicole's body. Emma mentally slapped herself. Focus on the eyes, she told herself. Not the shirt, the eyes. Her gaze locked onto Nicole's. Nicole took a step closer to her. Emma felt a rush of heat through her body as she watched a flush creep over Nicole's face. She stood for a moment, unable to break the silent intensity between them. Nicole's breath came in short gasps, and it was then that Emma realized that what she felt for Nicole was not unrequited attraction. Her senses filled with an awareness of Nicole, and she knew her friend felt at least some of it as well.

"Hi," Emma said. Her voice came out steady. Bonus points for her. The single word broke the spell between them, and Nicole backed up a few steps into the apartment.

Nicole smiled shyly. "Come in, please. Would you like something to drink?" she offered as they walked to the living room. The open windows let in a warm breeze and the scent of flowers from somewhere outside.

"Water would be great, thanks. It's getting pretty hot outside." Emma schooled her wayward thoughts, deliberately not watching Nicole as she left to get the drinks. Emma walked over to the sofa and spread her wedding notes out on the cherry-wood coffee table. Nicole returned with a glass of ice water for each of them, complete with a slice of lemon balanced on the rim.

They sat in awkward silence for a moment or two, until Nicole finally spoke. "I'm sorry about last week."

"No need to apologize," Emma interrupted.

"No, I should. I behaved badly, and I'm sorry."

Emma just shrugged. She'd rather not be having this conversation. If Nicole asked, she would not deny her attraction. Just being in the same space with her excited Emma as no one else ever had.

"I just wanted you to know," Nicole continued, "I don't have a problem with you being, you know."

"A lesbian?" Come on. It wasn't a swear word, she thought.

"Yes, lesbian. I'm not homophobic or anything."

Uh-huh. Emma was regretting that she'd agreed to meet Nicole face to face. She hated being defensive with Nicole, but she refused to believe that there was anything wrong with her sexuality.

Nicole's fingers played with the droplets of condensation forming on her glass. "I'm not really handling this well, am I?" Her gaze held Emma's, as if searching for assurance.

Emma's stoic attitude melted. "Sorry," she said. "I'm not being very helpful. I probably should have told you before."

"No, not really. I mean it wasn't any of my business, was it? It's not like you should carry a card or something to announce who you are."

Emma smiled. "True."

"It's just, the way it all came out, with your roommate and her girlfriend. It was uncomfortable for me. I'm sorry."

Emma put down her glass. She wanted to take Nicole's hands in hers, to re-assure her. But the embarrassment of her outing by Maya remained between them. She picked her glass back up again to give her hands something to do, and to keep her from making any mistakes.

"Maybe we should just start over here," she suggested.

"Yes," Nicole agreed. She held out her hand. "Hello, I'm Nicole Davis."

Emma took the offered hand, warm in her own. "And I'm Emma, lesbian wedding planner. Glad to meet you."

The tension eased between them. Emma didn't dare let her hand linger in Nicole's, and she gently pulled it free. They spent the next hour going over the wedding details. They had less than three weeks left. When Emma left to meet her mother for lunch, she felt like they had salvaged something out of all this. What that something was still confused her, especially when Nicole walked with her down the stairs and out the front door. It was as if Nicole did not want their time together to end. In a rush of words, Nicole invited her to a game of racquetball later that day, and Emma gratefully accepted the excuse to see her again.

THE TRAINS WERE a mess, and Emma arrived a half-hour late for lunch with her mother. She found her standing outside the Indian restaurant where they'd agreed to meet, her arms crossed.

"Sorry," Emma said, running up. "The Red Line took forever."

Margaret frowned. "Where were you coming from?"

"I was visiting Nicole." Emma led the way into the restaurant. They served buffet style, so they were settled in no time and plowing through plates of chicken tikka masala and curried lamb. A dozen other patrons jammed the popular, tiny restaurant. Her mother regaled her with the latest family gossip as they ate. Emma listened half-heartedly, her thoughts active with the memory of her renewed friendship with Nicole. Lunch was nearly finished before Emma made a serious slip-up.

"Who's Annah?" her mother asked after Emma went on about the ball game the day before.

Emma studied her plate, pushing the few remaining grains of rice around with her fork. She could probably make up a story about meeting someone named Annah at a bar. Her mother wouldn't question that. She stared up into her mother's grey eyes. No, she wouldn't lie. She scooped up her last bits of rice and swallowed them. "Annah is my half-sister."

Margaret's eyes narrowed. "What are you talking about?"

"I met my dad a couple of weeks back. He has a wife and two kids."

"That man doesn't deserve the title of father," her mother said through clenched teeth.

"Look, I know you don't like him," Emma said, not entirely sure why she was defending her father.

"He's a disgusting bastard. Emma, how could you do this to me?"

"It wasn't my fault." Emma's face flushed with guilt. "I went to a friend's party, and he just showed up."

Her mother pushed away from the table. "And his kids just happened to show up at the ball game you went to? Don't lie to me, Emma LeVanteur. You never were very good at it."

"Don't take it out on me, just because you and Dad didn't get along," Emma said. A knot grew in her stomach. This was the argument she'd been trying to avoid. When she was younger, she'd blamed her mother for her father's disappearance. It was unfair, but she felt the same old bitterness resurface.

"Didn't get along? Is that what you think?"

Emma shrugged. "You never talk about it, so how would I know why you two divorced? I just know he left and never came back."

"That's right and don't forget it." Her mother leaned across the table to speak in a harsh whisper. "Just think about this, with your new extended family. How old is Annah, and how old were you when your father left us."

Emma sat back, confused. Her mother tossed twenty dollars on the table and stormed out of the restaurant. Flustered, Emma remained to pay the waiter and then ran outside. Her mother was nowhere in sight. She walked across Copley Square. Why did her mother bring up Annah's age? Had she known about her father's new family? What had Annah said, that she was about to turn sixteen?

Emma stopped short. Her mind whirled. Why hadn't she realized it sooner? If she were ten when her father left, then Annah was already at least three years old. Her father hadn't just left them, he'd cheated on her mother for three or four years before they split.

She walked past the courtyard of the old Trinity Church in a daze. Pigeons scattered in front of her as she paused before the effigy of some saint, looking up into its hollow eyes. Why did her father have to ruin everything? Now he even tainted her friendship with Annah, because he left Emma behind to raise his new daughter. She moved past the church, walking along the busy sidewalk shops that lined Boylston Street. She wanted to scream at something, but she wasn't even sure at what or whom she was mad. She wanted to wish he'd never come back into her life, but a part of her knew that wasn't true. She liked Annah and Samuel, even if she was jealous that they had her father all these years.

Emma wandered down into the Boylston Street Station. Cool air from the underground station pushed past her as she walked down the stairs. She needed to get away from all this, the tangled web of her father's messed up life. She looked at her watch. In two hours she would meet Nicole for racquetball. That gave her just enough time to get home and kick the wall for an hour before she had to leave again.

NICOLE RUSHED AROUND her bedroom, changing into workout clothes while Katie lingered around Nicole's apartment. Nicole had less than a half hour to get ready for racquetball, and her patience for Katie's idiosyncrasies hadn't returned after the incident with Paul. Nicole flipped through her wardrobe, choosing the lightest pair of track-suit pants she owned. She pulled on a sports bra and then a light tank top over it that left the black straps of the bra exposed. She studied herself in the mirror and decided against any makeup, but did restyle her hair. Happy with the overall result, she walked back to the living room to politely tell Katie that it was time to go.

"That's a good look for you, sporty and sexy," Katie admired from her perch on the sofa.

Nicole suppressed a smile. If she'd impressed Katie and her

impeccable taste, then it was a job well done. "Sorry to have to leave on you like this," she said half-heartedly as she grabbed a racquet and ball from her hall closet.

"Are you meeting Adam?" Katie asked.

"No, Emma." Nicole tried to hide the flush she felt at the mention of Emma, occupying herself by stuffing her equipment and a towel into the duffle bag on the floor of the closet.

"You know she's gay," Katie announced.

"What?" Nicole stood up too quickly and banged her elbow on the closet doorframe. She stepped into the living room, rubbing her bruised arm. "How did you know?"

Katie's face pulled into an unpleasant mask of smugness. "The way she looks at you? If she got any more obvious, she'd be wearing a sign."

This time, Nicole had nowhere to hide the deep color that rushed to her cheeks. Was Emma really attracted to her? The thought sent a rush of heat through her body. She turned back to the closet, realizing that Katie had already seen some of her reaction. She heard Katie approaching as she picked up her duffle bag.

"You're just encouraging her, dressing like this." Katie emphasized her words by snapping Nicole's exposed bra strap.

Nicole pulled away from her. "Don't be silly. She's planning my wedding. I think she knows I'm straight." The words felt hollow to her right now, but she wanted, needed, to move Katie off this conversation track.

"Straight or not, you need to put that girl back in her place."

Nicole stared into Katie's cold, blue eyes, wondering how she'd ever become best friends with this woman. "She has no place to be put back into. She's my friend, and if you'll excuse me, I need to leave now or I'll be late." She pushed past Katie and walked out the door. Katie followed sullenly behind her. Nicole breathed a sigh of relief when Katie walked off in the opposite direction without another word.

NICOLE ARRIVED AT the racquetball court at the same time as Emma. Emma's athletic form mesmerized her. She watched as Emma took off her watch and a pinky ring that she always wore.

"Is there a story behind the ring?" Nicole asked as she pulled out her racquet.

Emma fingered the ring before showing it to Nicole. "My dad gave it to me on my eighth birthday.

Nicole looked at the silver band. A small blue stone glimmered in the florescent light. "It's pretty. What's the stone?"

"Topaz, I think," Emma said as she put the ring away. "Are you ready for a workout?" she asked with a gleam in her eye.

"Yes, but I thought I'd beat you at a few easy rounds of racquetball first," Nicole jibed in return. For the next hour or so, she was determined to block out all thoughts of Katie and the wedding. The court was just emptying. Two sweaty figures walked out as Emma and Nicole took it over. Fenced-in lights embedded far up in the ceiling illuminated the enclosed court. Dark, rubber ball marks streaked the walls and floor. Nicole ignored the stench of sweat that lingered in the court as she stretched.

"You serve first," Emma offered.

Nicole bounced the small blue ball a couple of times, then fired off a hard hit. Emma returned the volley and an intense match ensued. For every hard hit that Nicole had, Emma had a strong return volley. Even shots off the opposing wall didn't stop Nicole's opponent.

After four games, they were even, two for two. Sweat dampened Nicole's top, and a sheen covered Emma's red face.

"Had enough, Professor?" Emma taunted.

Nicole bent over, breathing hard. Definitely an intense workout. "I'm willing to stop. Don't want to cause you serious injury or anything."

"So very kind of you," Emma said.

Nicole gave her a playful swat on the backside with her racquet.

"Hey."

"You love it," Nicole said with a smile. "We make a good match."

Emma wiped sweat off her forehead. "Yes, we do," she agreed as they gave up the court for the next pair of players. She sniffed at her shirt. "I need a shower in a bad way."

Nicole disagreed, but she kept her thoughts to herself. Emma's face glowed, and her damp bangs hung down across her dark eyebrows. All very beautiful and incredibly enticing. Nicole berated herself for wayward thoughts as she stretched her right arm out, rotating her shoulder in a circle.

"Did you pull a muscle?" Emma asked.

"Possibly. I have a knot right between my shoulder blades." Nicole reached back and struggled to push against the source of her pain.

"Let me help you with that," Emma offered as she positioned herself behind Nicole. She pressed against Nicole's tight back muscles until her fingers found the source of Nicole's pain. She massaged the area, rolling her palms into Nicole's back. "How's that?" she asked as she pressed down.

"Oh, that's good," Nicole moaned. Heat shot through her body, centering below her waist. She had to step away. The intensity of her reaction to Emma's touch embarrassed her. She couldn't deny the sexual tension she felt in Emma's presence. She prayed that it wasn't as obvious to her friend.

"Hope that helped some," Emma said.

"Yes, thanks." Nicole brushed her damp hair off her forehead.

"Next time you should wear shorts," Emma said. "Those sweats don't help you stay cool."

Nicole looked down. "We talked about that already, remember, scars?"

"So what? Who cares if you've got some scars? This isn't a fashion show."

Nicole shrugged. "Adam would rather I keep them covered in public."

"Well, he's wrong." Emma clenched her jaw.

Nicole smiled and reached for Emma's hand. A welcome warmth spread through her.

"How did it happen?" Emma asked. "The scars?"

"I had an accident on my tricycle when I was very young. Peddled around a hedge and ran into a lorry."

"Ouch."

"My tricycle was destroyed. I ended up needing a plate in my leg until the bone healed. So I actually have two scars, one for putting the plate in and another for cutting it out eleven years later when my bones grew around it."

"Still, you shouldn't feel like you have to hide it. New England summers are pretty hot for long pants."

"Maybe." Nicole grinned, letting go of Emma's hand so she could pack up her equipment. "So, what's up for you this week?"

"Not much. Going clubbing with Jasmine tomorrow."

"Oh." Nicole felt as if a bucket of icy water had just been dumped on her head. She should have realized a woman as attractive as Emma would have a girlfriend. Maybe more than one. The thought burned inside Nicole as they packed their gear in silence and left the building. Nicole paused outside. She wanted to know, she needed to know. "Um, I never asked, but do you have a girlfriend?"

Emma watched her closely. "No," she confessed. "Jasmine was the last and only girl I've ever fallen in love with."

Nicole stared at Emma as a wave of jealousy overwhelmed her. "You two were a couple?"

"Yes, during freshman year."

Nicole relaxed. At least it was long over. "Oh, that must be hard. I mean to still live together."

Emma shrugged. "We didn't become roommates until senior year. I've long since gotten over her."

"Well that's good," Nicole said, hoping she didn't sound too enthusiastic about the news. "I mean, for you," she added. Emma didn't mention any other girlfriend.

Emma walked Nicole to the Red Line train station on the next block. The light breeze dried the sweat on Nicole's arms and face as they walked. She wanted a good, long shower when she got home, but as they neared the station, she felt reluctant to part company with Emma. "When did you know you were gay?" she asked.

Emma thought a moment. "I don't know, by high school I guess. I mean, I realized I wasn't attracted to boys. Then I met Jasmine my freshman year at college. The rest is history."

Nicole masked her irrational envy of Jasmine with a laugh.

"So," Emma asked. "When did you know you were straight?"

Nicole looked away from Emma for a moment, unsure any longer just how straight she was. "I met Adam two years ago. He's been quite sweet to me." She turned back to see Emma staring at the ground.

"Well, I'm glad you found someone. I hope he's good enough for you." She gave Nicole an odd, unreadable look, but didn't say anything more on the subject.

Nicole enfolded Emma in her arms for a moment when they reached the station. "I'll see you tomorrow?" Nicole stuttered, unable to control the excitement that tingled through her body wherever it touched Emma's. She took a step back, letting Emma go.

"Yes, bye." Emma waited at the top of the train station entrance as Nicole walked down the steps. When Emma disappeared from view, Nicole ran down the damp station tunnel. She was confused, not so much by her reaction to Emma, but by her illogical jealousy at the thought that Emma might have a girlfriend. How foolish was that, given that she herself was getting married in a few short weeks? It all made no sense, and Nicole had no one she trusted enough to talk to about it all.

EMMA MET NICOLE at her campus office the next day. She was glad that classes were over. Toward the end of the semester, they'd gotten a few stares, since she and Nicole had left every lecture together for the last month, but Nicole didn't care. As an audit, Emma's grade had no bearing on her college record, and Nicole insisted there was no ethical issue with the two of them being friends. Still, they maintained a casual distance until class ended for the semester.

Nicole had just unlocked her office when Emma arrived. Nicole asked about the box that she carried, but Emma refused to tell her what was inside. When they entered the office, Emma placed the box on the spare chair and collapsed into the other seat as Nicole dropped her satchel on the floor and leaned on the desk, staring down at Emma.

"Yes?" Emma asked, trying to mask the smirk that threatened to reveal itself across her face.

Nicole folded her arms. "Are you going to show me what's in the mystery box you've got there, or do I have to torture you for the information?"

Emma got up from her chair and stood next to Nicole. "Torture, you say?" She tapped a finger on her temple as she feigned concentration. "Now, what kind of torture did you have in mind?"

Unfolding her arms, Nicole pushed off the desk and leaned into Emma. She pulled Emma's hand away from her temple and held it close to her own chest. "What torture are you most susceptible to, Ms. LeVanteur?"

A lump formed in Emma's throat, stealing her ability to speak for a moment. The closeness of Nicole's body sent her pulse racing. "Okay," she said. "I give up."

"Well, that was too easy," Nicole said as she let go of Emma's hand. Emma picked up the box and handed it to her. Nicole glanced from the box to Emma. "You mean I get to open it?"

Emma grinned at Nicole's childlike excitement. "Yes, it's for you."

Nicole placed the box on her desk and opened the lid. The sweet scent of lavender surrounded them as Nicole lifted a small arrangement of flowers. Emma glanced at the sample bouquet, white roses wrapped in lavender blooms, which the florist had made for Nicole.

Nicole sniffed the bouquet, closing her eyes as she inhaled. "It's beautiful," she whispered as she opened her eyes. She turned the bouquet around, touching and smelling each flower. Then, she put the flowers on her desk and closed the short distance between her and Emma. She ran her fingers through Emma's hair. "I don't know what to say, but thank you." She leaned in as Emma wrapped her arms around Nicole's waist.

Nicole pulled her closer, and Emma felt warm lips on her cheek. She could barely breathe as she stroked the tight muscles of Nicole's lower back. Nicole wrapped her arms around Emma's neck. Emma felt the heat of Nicole's body, and all self-restraint dissolved. Nicole's eyes drifted shut as Emma leaned in and pressed her lips to Nicole's. A burning heat shot through her body.

Nicole's lips explored Emma's and her hands stroked the back of Emma's neck. The kiss seemed to both last forever and be over in a heartbeat.

Breathless, they stood in each other's arms. Emma tried to formulate words, to ask what had just happened between them, when a hard knock on the door shocked them both, and they jumped apart.

The office door swung open, and Katie stepped inside, pausing when she glanced between Nicole and Emma. "Am I interrupting something?" she asked as she stepped into the office and shut the door behind her.

"No, not at all," Nicole said. "I was just thanking Emma for the flowers she gave me." The words seemed to tumble out of her mouth as she stepped behind her desk, distancing herself from Emma.

"They're a sample of the florist's work," Emma explained, hoping in vain that the flush in her cheeks wasn't as obvious as the deep crimson coloring Nicole's fair features.

"I see," Katie said. Her penetrating stare fell on Emma. "Well, it was kind of you to drop them off." She turned away then as if Emma were no longer in the room and spoke to Nicole. "We should get going. Mother's expecting us by four o'clock."

"Yes, of course," Nicole said. She addressed her words to Emma, but avoided eye contact. "Sorry we have to run. I'll...um... I'll call you tomorrow?"

"Okay." Emma watched as Nicole shoved papers into her satchel and then paused to touch the flowers one last time. Nicole glanced up at her for an instant, and a rush of jumbled emotions washed over Emma. She wanted to say something, but with Katie standing guard, she had no opportunity. She followed them out the door and could only wave mutely as Katie rushed Nicole away.

When they finally disappeared from view Emma leaned back against the sun-warmed brick wall of the Humanities Building and slumped to the ground. What had just happened between them? Whatever doubt she had about Nicole's attraction to her disappeared. She closed her eyes and felt the intensity of their kiss once again. She pushed herself up and blindly made her way across the campus, wondering where their mutual attraction would lead them.

THE WEAK AIR-CONDITIONING in the club couldn't compensate for the throng of warm bodies dancing inside. Emma leaned against the bar, waiting for her second beer. She glanced at the other women around her, but not long enough to establish eye contact. Getting picked up was not part of her plan for the night. She kept an eye on Jasmine and Maya as they gyrated around the dance floor. But she found it hard to concentrate on why she was here with them. Confusion and a bundle of mixed emotions had swirled through her mind since that afternoon. She'd called Nicole's apartment, but only got the answering machine. She didn't leave a message. What kind of message could she have left without sounding desperate?

So far, the night had been uneventful. But there was nothing about Maya that Emma liked. The woman pushed Jasmine around like she owned her, drank too much, and spent an inordinate amount of time eyeing the other women at the bar. Emma had no idea what Jasmine saw in her.

"That'll be three bucks," the bartender said. Emma paid for her drink and moved into the back of the room. Her black pants and navy t-shirt would help her blend into the shadows. She'd already turned down two offers for a dance and one proposition she felt embarrassed to even remember. Somehow the bar scene just didn't suit her, especially tonight. No one there could compete with the memory of Nicole in her arms.

Jasmine and Maya found her after their dance. So much for her dark camouflage. Jasmine's eyes were glazed over already. Drugs or alcohol. Emma wasn't sure which, but it bothered her. Jasmine had never been into drugs before dating Maya.

Maya seemed to be fine, if a bit tense. She kept eyeing the crowd as they chatted over the sound of the music. Emma watched as Maya focused on one woman in particular, their eye contact obvious. Why on earth did Jasmine not notice all this? Even if they didn't have a monogamous relationship, common courtesy meant that Maya should keep her outside flirting to times when she wasn't with Jasmine. Whenever that was.

The other woman headed toward the restrooms.

Maya pushed Jasmine off her arm. "I need to take a piss," she announced and walked off.

Pleasant, Emma thought as she watched Maya leave. Was she nasty enough to grab some bathroom sex while Jasmine waited on the dance floor? Time to find out.

"Can you hold this? I think I need to go as well," she said, handing her beer to Jasmine. Emma wove her way through the crowd in time to see Maya avoid the restrooms and slip down the dark hallway to the back door. Emma looked around and then followed quietly behind. She stopped before the hallway curved around to the back. She heard voices, one definitely Maya. It was all beginning to feel too cloak and dagger for her.

"How much you want?" Maya asked.

The other woman spoke too softly for Emma to hear. Emma looked around again to be sure no one was watching, and then peered around the bend. Maya stood very close to the woman she'd watched in the bar, leaning over her. Emma saw the woman pull out something from her pocket and exchange it for a small packet from Maya. Emma pulled her head back quickly when the woman looked in her direction.

She found her way back to the restroom and joined the small line inside. She'd seen enough to know Maya wasn't a cheap slut; she was something worse...a drug dealer. By the time she came back from the restroom, Maya and Jasmine were ready to dance again. Maya handed Emma her beer, and Emma found herself a seat. She sipped her beer as she contemplated what she should do next.

Emma felt strange by the end of the night. Not drunk, since she'd only had the two beers. But she felt nervous and jittery. When they finally left the bar, she felt sure she was being followed. Sweat beaded up on her forehead even though the evening was cool. She kept turning around as they walked to the train station.

Jasmine finally stopped. "What's your problem?"

Emma looked around to be sure no one could hear them. "Someone's following us," she said in a throaty whisper. She shook her head, trying to clear the fuzzy feeling that was growing inside her. Her eyes crossed and uncrossed as the streetlights pulsed around her to some hidden beat.

Jasmine looked around. "You're nuts."

Emma held her arm, "No, I'm serious. I can feel their eyes on me. They're crawling all over me." She scratched at her legs, trying to get through the blue jeans to her skin. Someone was coming for her, she could feel it.

A man walked by with his dog. Emma lunged for him, but Maya grabbed hold of her. Emma shouted at the shocked man, "Get away from me! I'll kill you, you dirty bastard!" The man backed into a storefront and then half ran down the block. Emma pulled away from Maya. "Don't touch me. Nobody touch me." She scratched at her arms where Maya had held her.

Jasmine's face swam in her double vision. Maya's evil grin superimposed itself on Jasmine, fading in and out with the beat of Emma's heart.

"Don't let them take me," Emma pleaded. She felt the lights breathing down on her as stinging sweat dripped into her eyes. "They have cameras there." She pointed up. "Keep them away from me!"

Jasmine pulled Maya out of Emma's vision. Emma's head throbbed to the beat of the spying lights. She heard Jasmine arguing. "Keep them away," Emma whimpered, hugging herself as she squatted on the sidewalk. Keep them all away. She could hear them whispering, threatening her. She rocked back and forth, afraid to stand, afraid to look up.

Jasmine came back, tugging at her.

"Let go!" Emma screamed. Jasmine backed off.

"It's okay, Emma," Jasmine said. "It'll wear off in a few hours."

Emma hid behind Jasmine, ducking from the pulsing lights. "Take me home," she begged. Jasmine wrapped an arm around her waist, but Emma pulled away. Maya seemed to have disappeared. She hoped the lights had gotten Maya as Jasmine led her to safety.

COOL OCEAN WATER lapped at Nicole's bare legs. She stood in the foamy surf as waves splashed against her and then retreated, in a slow, sensual rhythm. Warm sunlight bathed her face. She closed her eyes against the light. Someone approached her from behind, and she suppressed a smile. Cool, firm hands massaged her back, working taut muscles. Nicole felt the heat of her lover's body against her as familiar fingers pressed against her neck and shoulders. A shudder rolled through her as one hand wrapped around her bare waist while the other caressed her arm. Up and down, rhythmically, with the movement of the ocean. She leaned back, wanting to feel that body pressed against her. She tilted her head to the side, accepting the seductive kisses along her neck with a soft moan. The hand on her arm brushed down her wrist and intertwined with her fingers. Nicole couldn't wait any longer. She needed more. She wanted more. She turned around to face her lover. Lifting her hands, she ran her fingers through long, chestnut hair. Staring into intense pale brown eyes, she leaned in to feel warm lips pressed against hers.

Nicole awoke to her own throbbing need. A tangle of sheets wrapped around her in her dark bedroom. Not opening her eyes, she raked her fingernails across her erect nipples and then dipped her fingers into the dampness between her thighs as she struggled to recapture her dream. She remembered the maddening swell of desire as her lover's lips pressed against hers in the dream.

And then she remembered whose lips had kissed her. She knew those intense eyes, that long, brown hair. She knew the touch of those agile fingers, though not in such a teasing, exciting way. She draped an arm across her eyes as her fingers stroked her moist folds until her body trembled. The vision of that beautiful face swam before her as she climaxed.

Emma.

THE NEXT MORNING, Emma woke up sweaty and stinking of who knows what. Her head throbbed, and her eyes felt heavy as she squinted at the sunlight that burned through her open window. She sat up and shut the blinds. She didn't want anyone seeing in. She crawled back into bed, jittery and confused. Someone knocked on her door. She wouldn't get up. They couldn't come in if she didn't get up. The door swung open, and Emma ducked under the bed.

"Emma?" Jasmine's voice floated to her.

"Are you alone?" Emma called from behind the bed.

"Yes."

Emma peeked up. Her eyes focused on Jasmine in the doorway. "Close the door, quick," she ordered.

Jasmine shut the door. "Damn it, how much did Maya give you?"

Emma crawled up on the bed, clinging to her pillow. "What are you talking about? Is anyone else here?"

Jasmine tried to sit on the bed, but Emma jumped, so she backed away. "Look," Jasmine said with a frown. "I'm sorry. Maya slipped something in your beer last night. You're having a bad trip, okay?"

Emma realized that at least the lights weren't pulsing anymore. "Slipped me what?" She still didn't understand. "Are you sure we're alone?"

"Yes, just you and me here." Jasmine let out an exasperated sigh. "I don't know how much she gave you, but you're obviously still feeling it. Maybe you should take a shower?"

"No. I'm not going out there." Emma shrank back into her bed, making herself as small as possible. Her arms itched. She looked down at them. Red welts lined both her arms and legs. "What happened to me?" she asked, her voice cracking.

Jasmine stepped closer. Emma tried not to flinch. "You kept scratching yourself last night. You gave me this when I tried to stop you."

Emma peered over her bed sheet as Jasmine lifted her shirt above her waist to expose a deep blue bruise. "I don't remember," Emma mumbled. She wasn't really clear on what Maya had given her. An hallucinogen, maybe?

"Yeah, apology accepted," Jasmine said. "You want something for your scratches?"

"No," she squeaked. No medicine, no drugs. The phone rang, ending their conversation. Jasmine disappeared to answer it. Emma pulled herself out of bed just long enough to shut her door. The close confines of her own room settled her rattled nerves.

"It's for you," Jasmine called through the door.

"I'm not here," Emma answered.

"Not even for Nicole?"

Nicole. Oh God, please, Nicole can't see her like this, she thought. "No. Take a message." Jasmine came back a few minutes later carrying a glass of orange juice. Emma tried not to jump again when the door opened, but she failed. She managed not to duck behind the bed, though. Things were improving.

"You thirsty?" Jasmine held out the glass. Emma looked from the juice to Jasmine, licking her parched lips. "It's clean. I promise." Jasmine's face darkened in anger. At her? At Maya? Emma didn't know. She reached out and took the glass. She gave it a sniff.

"I said it's clean."

She took a small sip. Seemed okay. She drank more, in big gulps. She drank too fast. A moment later, she burped loudly, and her bladder woke up. Emma fought the urge to go to the bathroom. It meant she would have to leave her room, and she definitely wasn't ready for that excursion. Her bladder battled with her paranoia for control of her actions.

Her bladder won.

Emma stumbled out of her room to the bathroom. She rested her head on the cool porcelain sink beside the toilet as she sat. Her eyes drifted shut, but she forced them back open. She wanted to be back in the safety of her own room. She looked up to see Jasmine staring at her from the bathroom doorway. Obviously, she'd forgotten to kick the door shut.

"Look," Jasmine said, "I don't think you should be alone today. You want me to call someone? Your mother maybe?"

Emma stood up at the sink. Her reflection stared back at her from the mirror, bloodshot eyes surrounded by a tangled mane of hair. "No. I want to be alone." She turned on the tap and swirled some water around her mouth, spit it out, and then turned the tap off. She staggered back to her room. The doorbell rang. Emma bolted, and Jasmine cursed.

"Don't let them in!" Emma shouted from her room as she shut the door again. She crawled back under the covers, waiting for the wave of paranoia to subside.

Chapter
Nine

PAUL WAITED FOR the elevator to stop on the ninth floor. He walked to the open door three apartments down on the left. A small, dark haired woman stood there, dressed in a sharp light-blue blouse and slacks.

"So you're Emma's father," she said, studying him as he approached.

"Yes. And you are?"

"Jasmine. Her friend. Let's see some I.D. first." Jasmine waited at the door, tapping her foot. Paul pulled out his license, frustrated at being a stranger in his daughter's world.

"Hmm. Okay, you're legit," Jasmine said, handing him back his license. "Emma's pretty sick today. Does she know you're coming?"

"No, not really. But we met a week or so ago, and she has met my wife and children," he added.

"I thought she hated your guts."

Paul pushed back the pain from those words. "We've reconciled our differences," he lied. He knew if he could just talk to Emma, she'd understand why he'd been forced to leave her.

Jasmine shifted from foot to foot as she seemed to consider some internal decision. "All right," she said at last. "I need to get to work, so that means you have to stay with her or get someone else to watch her." Jasmine frowned. "She can't be left alone, you understand?"

Paul nodded. "Does she need any medication?"

Jasmine smirked, "She wouldn't touch another drug now to save her soul." She waved him inside. "That's her room there, the closed one. Remember, don't leave her alone."

She grabbed a tan briefcase and slammed the door behind her when she left. Paul stood in Emma's apartment, weighing the conflicting emotions inside him. The little girl he left so long ago was a virtual stranger to him now. He lucked out that her roommate let him in, but now what? Would she even want to see him after so long?

He wandered through the silent apartment. It seemed cramped compared to his own home, but then she was still in college, according to Annah and Marina. He scanned the small kitchen, with a pile of dishes in the sink and an open box of danishes on the counter. His gaze shifted to the open living room. A worn sofa and coffee table dominated the tiny space, with the walls lined with book cases. He couldn't tell what belonged to Emma and what belonged to her roommate, and that bothered him. She was an adult now, his little girl. Independent. She didn't need him in her life anymore, and maybe she wouldn't want to know him either.

He pushed down his fears and walked over to the bedroom door. He knocked twice.

Emma's voice shouted back, "Go to work, Jasmine!"

He cleared his throat. "Jasmine left. It's me, Emma, your father." He heard a shuffle of movement inside.

"What the hell are you doing here?" she said from somewhere inside her room.

He rested a hand against the door. "I just want to talk to you."

"Well, talk to the door, cuz the daughter don't want to hear it."

"Please, can we just talk? Your friend said you're sick. Is there anything I can get you?"

"Yeah, a Dad. A real one who won't desert me for his illegitimate brats."

That stung. "I'm sorry. It's not something that can be explained away. I made mistakes, I know that."

"Yeah, who were the mistakes, me or Annah and Samuel?"

The bedroom door opened, and Paul nearly fell inside. Emma leaned on the door, her ashen cheeks a harsh contrast to the black circles under her eyes. Worse than that, there were deep red scratches all along both arms.

"What happened to you?" Paul asked, frowning.

"What? Haven't you been listening? My dad dumped me for his new family. Try to keep up." She crawled back into her bed, covering herself with a wrinkled blue sheet.

"I didn't dump you. I fell in love with someone besides your mother."

Emma snorted. "Had a little sex, had a little kid, decided out with the old and in with the new."

"I wanted to see you, so many times, Emma."

She sneered at him. "Sure you did. But oops, one thing led to another, and you never got around to it."

Paul drew back. "No. I wanted to, but I couldn't. Legally."

Emma frowned. "What do you mean, legally?"

"Your mother got sole custody in the divorce. She had me

declared an unfit parent. When I tried to see you after school one time, she got a restraining order against me. If I did anything else, they'd have taken Annah away from me, too."

"Were you?" Emma asked, sitting up. "Unfit?"

Paul sighed. "No, I don't think so. Your mother was very bitter when she found out about Annah. She was three when I left you."

Emma watched him with a hard glare. "That was a nasty thing to do, cheat on my mom for years like that."

"Yes, I know. I still don't think it warranted having my eldest daughter taken from me." Paul's voice cracked as he spoke. "But that's all the past. Can we start anew?"

Emma didn't reply one way or the other.

"What happened to you?" he asked again, "You look, I don't know..."

Emma curled back into a ball. "Drugged? Would you be shocked if daddy's little girl was a drug addict?"

Her voice was still angry. Paul stared at her as he spoke. "It doesn't matter. You're still my daughter. I should have come to you when you turned eighteen, when the restraining order ran out."

"I'm not." She looked away. "An addict, that is. Someone did this to me. Someone who's going to get her ass kicked into the middle of next week when I get my hands on her."

Paul relaxed, wanting to believe her. He meant what he said, but still, it was easier to believe, or hope, his daughter wasn't into drugs. He was only just dealing with that fear, now, with Annah. "Your roommate was adamant that you shouldn't be left alone. So, any chance I can entice you onto the sofa for a bad video marathon?"

She looked him up and down. "Maybe."

Hours later, when Emma finally had the stamina to take a shower, Paul insisted on staying around until she finished, just in case. He spent the time wandering around the small two bedroom apartment. It felt good to be getting to know his daughter again. He scanned a bookcase that occupied the left hand side of the living room. The small particle-board shelves were overstuffed with books. He read titles like *Differential Equations*, *Numbers Theory*, *Fourier Analysis*. He remembered Emma's love of math, even as a child. The next set of shelves had an odd assortment of books. Paul frowned as he read some of the titles. When he got to *Best Lesbian Erotica*, he backed away from the bookcase in shock.

Emma emerged a half hour later, dressed in clean clothes and drying her hair. Paul stood by the bookcase, his arms folded across his chest.

"What's up?" she asked.

He pointed to the books. "Tell me these belong to your

roommate." His voice had an edge to it that he didn't much like. But something was wrong here, and he needed to find out what.

She folded her arms, a mirror image of his own. "They belong to both of us. Why?" Her gaze bored into him. He remembered her stubborn streak now.

"Are the two of you involved then?" he asked.

"No."

Paul felt himself relax. Maybe she wasn't...

"Not anymore," Emma added.

He felt the bile rise in his throat. "You mean you're..." He couldn't bring himself to say it.

"Lesbian. Yes, Daddy dearest, I am. You have a problem with that?" Her expression carried that mask of anger that he'd seen all too often on her mother. He clenched his jaw.

"I'm sorry," he said. "I should accept some responsibility that you turned to, well, to women. You didn't have a good male role model in your life." He didn't know how to take it when she laughed out loud. He should probably try to do something, help remedy the situation. "Look, my company has a good medical plan," he said, trying to think clearly in the strange situation he found himself in. "I could get us to a good therapist to help us figure all this out."

Emma stopped laughing. Her expression was cold, her eyes narrow. "Figure out what? That I'm a lesbian? News flash, I already know."

Paul held his temper in check. "There are places that can deal with homosexuality. You don't have to be this way."

"Get out."

He didn't move. "Let's just take this one step at a time."

She picked up a book from the coffee table and flung it at him. "Get out of my face, you homophobic bastard!"

He blocked the book as it sailed at him. "Fine. We'll talk about this after you've recovered."

"The hell we will."

Emma stood firm, glaring at him as he left her apartment. Paul's stomach felt queasy by the time he made it to the downstairs lobby. So much had gone wrong in Emma's life. His anger grew, anger at the way his daughter turned out, with drugs and lesbians. An anger that centered the blame on his ex-wife.

Paul arrived home in time to hear his wife and daughter at each other's throats, again. He never realized just how much teenage girls don't get along with their mothers. Of course, Marina didn't help matters. She knew how to push their daughter's buttons, and he swore sometimes she did so just for the thrill of it. He wished he'd asked Emma how things went with Margaret at that age. But there was still time for that, once they solved her other problems.

"I'm home," he announced, walking through the well-lit foyer. Samuel waved at him from the living room as he passed by. He was watching TV, as usual. At least his son wasn't of dating age, yet. That was one less worry in his life. By the time Paul made it through the dining room, Annah was accosting him.

"Would you talk to Mom, please? She's being unreasonable."

Paul wrapped an arm around Annah. She was nearly as tall as he was. "What's she being unreasonable about today?" He let her go and pulled out his chair at the dinner table to sit down.

"She's insisting I take AP chemistry next year, and I want to take creative writing."

Marina came in with the dishes just as her accuser finished. "That's not what I said, Annah. I said you should consider AP chemistry over the writing class. It holds a lot of weight on your college applications."

"See?" Annah gesticulated as she spoke. "She just wants me to follow in her narrow little footsteps. Well it's my decision, not yours. I get to decide who and what I want to be."

Paul rubbed his temples, trying to push back the start of a headache. "Calm down, Annah. We're not trying to dictate your future career here. As for college prep classes, we'll look at your schedule later. Maybe you can fit in both."

"Paul," Marina said, "You're giving in to her again."

He shrugged. "Well I didn't say creative writing was a good idea." He held up his hands before Annah raged at him. "But, if you've got room in your schedule after the serious classes, then maybe."

Marina rolled her eyes. "Care to make yourself useful in the kitchen?"

He followed his wife into the kitchen and rolled up his sleeves to prepare the vegetables. With luck, he could get through dinner without more melodrama.

But, luck wasn't on Paul's side. Half way through dinner, the topic of Emma came up.

Marina started the conversation. "So Annah had an idea about her sweet sixteen party."

Annah looked at her mother over her glass of milk. "You mean inviting Emma? Yes, I want her to come."

"And I said we'd have to discuss it with you," Marina said, looking at Paul.

"What's the big deal?" Annah frowned. "She's my half-sister, and I want to invite her."

"Yes. And she's also just found out she has a half brother and sister." Marina sighed. "I know you're anxious to get to know her, but did you ever think that maybe she needs time to adjust to all this?"

Paul cleared his throat. "I don't think it's a good idea, Annah."

His daughter turned on him. "What?"

"I'm glad you've taken an interest in Emma, but there are issues that she and I have to deal with first."

Annah scooped up her dishes, rammed them into the dishwasher, and stomped her way out the front door.

"That went well," Paul said around a mouthful of mashed potatoes. So much for the quiet evening.

"Pass the peas?" Samuel asked. He'd quietly sat through another of his sister's tirades.

Paul felt Marina staring at him. He swallowed a forkful of peas. "Yes?"

"So, care to share what issues there are? You left here this morning Mr. High Hopes and fatherly love. Now suddenly there are issues. What's up?"

He put down his fork. "I don't think we should discuss this in front of Samuel."

Samuel looked up from his plate. "I can go eat in front of Cartoon Network." Marina nodded, and Samuel scooped up his plate and left.

"Well?" she asked.

"Emma was recovering from some bad drug trip today."

"Really? Do you know what kind of drug?"

"No," Paul said. "She claims someone slipped it into her drink last night, but after what else I learned, I'm not sure I believe her."

Marina leaned back. "That doesn't sound good. But then she's what, twenty-two or something."

"Twenty-three," Paul corrected.

"Anyway, a lot of people experiment with different things at that age."

He thought a moment. "Yes, you're right. Maybe she's just going through a phase."

"What else did you learn about her that makes you think she's lying?"

He looked at Marina. "She claims she's a lesbian."

Marina sat there a moment. He couldn't read any reaction on her part to the news.

"And?" she said finally.

He sat back. "And? And well, that's it." He wasn't sure what else she was looking for. He certainly wasn't going to describe what was on Emma's bookshelf for anyone to see.

His wife folded her arms across her chest. That was never a

good sign. "So, she's a lesbian. And somehow that makes you think she's a liar?" she asked.

Paul recognized Marina's tone of voice. This conversation needed to end. "Look, I don't want to argue about liberal politics here. Emma's got problems, and I don't want Annah exposed to them."

"Problems?" Marina's voice rose as she continued, her dark face coloring. "Okay, maybe the drug issue is real, or maybe it's not. But don't tell me you think homosexuality is a problem, Paul LeVanteur."

He held his ground. "Well, it certainly isn't normal. I offered to take Emma to therapy for it, but she threw me out of the apartment. A woman with a woman? It's just not right."

Marina stood up and leaned over the table, forcing herself into Paul's face. "Funny thing. If you and I lived some fifty years ago, assholes like you would have said the same damn thing about us. Hell, some of them still do." She threw down her napkin and stood straight. "Now you can take your bigoted-ass self and clean up the dishes. And the only one going to be getting therapy around here is you. Tomorrow!" Marina shouted as she left the dining room. "Dang, no wonder she kicked you out. I'd have kicked you out, too."

Paul rested his head in his hands as the headache pounded in his skull. Definitely no hope of a quiet evening at home.

Samuel walked in from the living room. "You going to eat those mashed potatoes?"

NICOLE WANDERED DOWN Newbury Street. The high scale shops glistened in the early evening as sunlight broke through the gray, overcast sky for a few minutes before hiding behind darker clouds. She was supposed to be shopping for a Maid of Honor gift for Katie, but her thoughts lingered elsewhere. She'd called Emma in the morning, but had to leave a message with her roommate. She couldn't help but worry that Emma hadn't called her back yet, especially after the kiss they'd shared. Nicole's body reacted just to the memory of Emma's lips on hers. She wasn't even sure what she wanted to say, but after learning that Emma was going out to a lesbian bar the night before, Nicole couldn't hide her own jealous feelings. She tried to tell herself that it didn't matter if Emma had found a date, but the thought of some other woman hitting on Emma left a sick feeling in the pit of her stomach. She knew she had no right to feel proprietary. After all, she was getting married to Adam within the month. And yet she had kissed Emma, and it had both thrilled and frightened her that she felt more from Emma's one kiss than she had from all the romantic moments she'd shared with Adam.

Realizing how close the wedding was didn't help Nicole's confusion, and she instinctively found something else to concentrate on. She stepped into a small jeweler's shop to get out of the annoying drizzle that had started. The shopkeeper eyed her over a pair of wire frame glasses, seeming to size her up and discard her in a glance. Nicole fought back the urge to just walk back out into the rain and decided to examine every display case instead. She paused in front of a case of narrow band rings, smothering a smirk when the shopkeeper sighed heavily and hoisted himself off his corner perch.

"Can I help you?" he asked with a voice that droned out his annoyance.

"I'd like to see the ring with the blue topaz stone, there on the left."

The shopkeeper placed the silver band in her hand. Nicole turned it around to catch the light. The stone was bigger, but otherwise, it seemed a perfect match to Emma's ring. She slipped it on her finger. It slid on and off, significantly larger than her ring size.

"It's a man's ring," the shopkeeper said, as if Nicole couldn't have figured that out for herself.

"Can it be cut down?" she asked. "To something like a size six?"

"Yes, but you might prefer something in the ladies' section," he said.

Nicole gave him back the ring. "No thank you." Her face flushed, but she grinned sheepishly at the shopkeeper's frustration. She walked out of the shop, surprised at herself for taunting the man. But his attitude was appalling. Besides, she liked the ring. The style reminded her of Emma's ring.

As the evening wore on, Nicole gave up any hope of completing her shopping excursion and headed back to the train station. Before entering the station, she rang up Emma. Her heart pounded as she punched in the quick dial number on her cell phone. She listened to each ring with tense anticipation. After the fourth ring, the answering machine turned on. Nicole hung up without leaving a message. Emma wasn't home. Maybe Emma hadn't come home at all after her night out? Or maybe Emma was avoiding her after the surprising kiss they'd shared. A cold feeling settled inside her as she walked down the stone steps into the train station.

EMMA FORAGED IN the fridge. Her appetite returned, but there was nothing much to eat. She dug in the back and found a yogurt that hadn't expired, yet. She sat at the empty kitchen table spooning up the creamy yogurt. Her head still throbbed, but at least she didn't think she was as jumpy as she had been earlier. She gazed at the scribbled reminder note that Jasmine had left for her. Call Nicole, it said. How could she? Emma might be clean and returning to normal, but what would she say to Nicole after the kiss that they'd shared. For Emma, it ignited a passion to be with her, to feel Nicole in her arms. But what had it meant to Nicole? And was Emma prepared for whatever Nicole might say to her?

With no small measure of guilt, she prayed that Nicole would want her as well, even at the expense of leaving her fiancé. But then, Emma would be the infamous other woman and responsible for breaking up a relationship. Yet the other option hurt just to think about, that the kiss might have meant nothing to Nicole, and she would proceed with the wedding as if nothing had happened.

The doorbell rang. Emma jumped. Then she cursed and forced herself to get up and answer it.

"Hello," she said into the intercom.

"Emma? It's Annah."

Great, more of Paul's family. Emma paused, considering her options. Was she ready to deal with homophobe junior? She shook her head. This day was just too much. "Look," Emma said over the intercom, "Your dad just ticked me off enough for one day. Maybe now's not the best time."

"He's a jerk. I'd trade him in for a good used car if I could."

Emma laughed, then buzzed Annah in. "Ninth floor, and I'll look for you in the hallway."

She led Annah into the apartment a few minutes later. "Home sweet home," she announced. "Not much, but such is the life of a grad student."

Annah looked around, taking in the living room and kitchen in a heartbeat. "I'd give anything to have half the size of this place, just to get away from my annoying parents."

Emma stood by the sofa. "Okay, Annah. Before we get all buddy buddies, I threw your dad out because he's homophobic." And Emma needed to know just how far the apple fell from the tree.

"Your dad, too," Annah corrected. "And don't blame me if he's a backward so and so." Annah's eyes grew wide as she caught on. "Oh my gosh, you told him you're gay?"

Emma steeled herself. "Lesbian, yes."

Annah guffawed. "No wonder he was a total spaz tonight."

"Well," Emma continued, "do you have problems with my

sexuality, too?"

Annah planted herself on the sofa. "Who cares? My best friend Aly's brother is gay. He moved to San Francisco two years ago." She turned back to Emma, who was still standing. "So, do you live alone or do you have a girlfriend?"

"No, no girlfriend right now." Emma relaxed. "But I do have a roommate."

"Cool. Do you two have lots of parties?"

"No, not really." Emma marveled that a jerk like her father could have an okay daughter. Then she corrected herself, two okay daughters.

"So anyway," Annah continued, unabashed. "My mom's being a pain about college." Annah's quick acceptance of Emma eased the tension she'd been feeling all day. So what if her father was a jerk? Emma wouldn't take it out on her half-siblings. As Annah droned on about the latest problems with college and her family, Emma settled herself into the sofa for a long parental rant.

An hour and a half later, Emma insisted on taking the train ride back to Annah's house. It wasn't that late, but she still felt she should make sure Annah got home safely. When Emma finally managed to struggle back to her own apartment, she was exhausted. At least she managed to face the outside world without quivering like an idiot.

When she unlocked the apartment door, she found Jasmine on the sofa, alone for once.

"Feeling better?" Jasmine asked.

Emma nodded. "Mostly. Majorly tired, though."

"I'm sorry about what happened." Jasmine stood up. "If it helps any, I broke up with Maya today."

Emma walked over to the sofa and took Jasmine's hand in hers. "I know it wasn't your fault. That woman's into some bad business. Can't say I'm sad to hear you dumped her."

Jasmine smirked and sat back down. "I didn't think you would be."

Emma leaned against the sofa. "Any chance you brought home something to eat?"

"Leftover Chinese in the fridge." Jasmine pointed as her attention returned to the TV. "Help yourself." With a TV sitcom droning in the background, Emma devoured all the leftovers and an extra serving of ice-cream she found in the freezer. With a full belly and heavy eyelids, she crawled her way into her bedroom and collapsed on the bed for the night.

Chapter
Ten

EMMA WAITED OUTSIDE Nicole's office, where they'd agreed to meet. A couple of staff members passed her as she waited, but neither paid her any attention. She looked like any other student waiting for a teacher. That she wasn't Nicole's student anymore eased her conscience, a minor relief given that she had no idea what Nicole would say once they met.

Nicole's familiar figure walked down the corridor toward her. Emma's heart leaped into her throat, and any thoughts of taking the initiative and walking away from a relationship with Nicole dissolved. Nicole's pace slowed for an instant when she looked up and saw Emma at her door. A flush rose in her cheeks, and she looked away, digging in her pocket until she pulled out her office key.

Emma stepped to the side as Nicole approached, but Nicole still paused in front of her. Their eyes met, and Emma felt an electric connection to her. How could she walk away from Nicole, from how she made her feel? Nicole seemed uncertain, her gaze locked on Emma and her lips partially open. Emma wanted to close the gap between them, but realized it would be a bad idea.

"Sorry to keep you waiting," Nicole said as she stepped to the door and fumbled with the lock. A moment later, she held the door open and waited for Emma to enter. Emma walked passed her, breathing in the scent of lavender that permeated the small office. The bouquet sat on the desk, as it had when they'd left the office two days ago. Emma couldn't believe how much had happened since then. So much was spinning out of her control.

Nicole closed and locked the door behind her. She dropped her satchel and stood awkwardly in front of Emma. Silence lingered between them, until finally, they both spoke at once. Nicole laughed, "Sorry, you first."

"I'm not really sure what to say," Emma said. Everything that she considered saying disappeared as she stared into Nicole's sad eyes.

Nicole stepped closer to her. "Me either. I'm sorry I had to leave the other day. I mean, when Katie showed up."

"Did she say anything to you, about, you know?"

Nicole looked down, nodding. Emma reached out and lifted Nicole's face. She saw the start of tears in Nicole's eyes.

"What did she say to you?" Emma asked.

Nicole shrugged. "Nothing pleasant."

"I'm sorry." Emma put her hands on Nicole's waist and was amazed to feel Nicole lean into her. Nicole rested her head on Emma's shoulder and sighed. Emma stroked her hair, feeling its silky strands drift through her fingers as Nicole wrapped her arms around Emma and pulled her closer. The sensation of Nicole in her arms overwhelmed her, and she kissed the top of Nicole's head. Nicole shifted, and traced a string of kisses along Emma's neck. A fire burned inside Emma, but she couldn't go on, not without knowing what it all meant. "Nicole," she said.

Her voice seemed to shock Nicole, who pulled away from her.

"I'm sorry," Nicole said, stepping back further. "I shouldn't have done that."

"It's okay," Emma said. She wanted to reach out to Nicole again, but she needed answers more. "What's happening here?"

Nicole crossed her arms, avoiding eye contact. "I don't know," she said quietly. "I care about you a lot."

Emma felt as if she'd just fallen into a bucket of ice. She knew what was coming next, and didn't want to hear it. She'd give anything not to have to hear it, but running away wasn't an option.

Nicole stared at the floor. "I'm getting married," she said.

"I understand," Emma said. She wished her words were true, but she willed herself not to ask for an explanation. Nicole was getting married, and Emma just needed to back away from it all. "I need to go."

Nicole looked up, confusion in her eyes. "So soon?"

Emma felt herself being drawn to Nicole again, but she'd only make a fool of herself. Instead, she broke eye contact. "I'll talk to you soon," she promised as she stepped past Nicole and all but ran out the door. Graceful exit, she thought as she hurried out of the Humanities Building without looking back. Distance wouldn't stop the pain in her heart, but it would keep her from embarrassing herself further. And not making a further fool of herself was all she could hope for at the moment.

NICOLE STARED OUT at the back yard as Pam complained about the wedding. She'd rather be anywhere but here. Adam's mother had grown tiresome, nosing about every detail of the wedding. Nicole regretted ever agreeing to have it in her house. Pam viewed it as an open invitation to be opinionated about everything to do with the wedding.

"The wedding cake style just isn't big enough for the guest list," Pam said. "I don't see how this caterer can put another layer in this design without it looking a mess."

"I've spoken with her multiple times," Nicole replied. "She's added layers to her other designs without problems. And Emma's seen a similar cake expanded."

"Like I trust that girl's opinion," Pam snorted.

Nicole turned to face Pam, feeling the blood drain from her face. Had Katie told her about what happened with Emma? "Excuse me?"

"Nothing. We've only got a couple of weeks left. Shouldn't you be wrapping things up with that wedding planner by now?"

Nicole stared out the window, unsure of what Pam knew, but not willing to question her further. The harshness of Katie's words still stung, and she didn't dare risk repeating that with Pam. "Soon, I suppose, yes." But she dreaded finishing her business arrangement with Emma. She knew in her heart that Emma wouldn't drift away like other friends had. But how could she justify her time with Emma to Adam and her future in-laws? Katie already knew that she had more than one reason for wanting to spend time with Emma. But what did the others know?

"Maybe you can finish up with her tonight then," Pam said. "We're meeting at your place to examine her party gifts, yes?"

Nicole shook her head, "Yes, but I can't finish everything tonight. We have too many things left to work out." And she needed that excuse to keep her future family from questioning her and Emma. She would have to stop seeing Emma, eventually, but she couldn't do it just yet. She leaned against the counter, her mood turning sour. She wanted to be anywhere but here with Pam. She wanted to be home, to call Emma and ask her to come over early, before everyone else showed up. She'd spoken to Emma on the phone a few times, but still hadn't found an excuse to get together with her. Nicole wondered if Emma had found someone when she went out, but she didn't have the courage to ask. She wasn't sure how she'd react if Emma was dating another woman.

"You're unenthusiastic for a bride," Pam jibed.

As if being around her couldn't turn anyone or anything sour, Nicole thought. She forced a smile. "Just getting nervous. There's still so much to get done before then."

"Nonsense. Everything is coming together nicely. Did you try on the wedding gown yet?"

"Not yet, not since the last fitting."

"Well you should. And make sure someone's with you to verify the fit. You still have time to bring it back for an adjustment."

"Yes, of course." Nicole pushed off the counter. "When are Adam and Henry due back?"

"Not for another hour. Go take a walk or something and snap out of this mood."

Nicole took her up on the offer and stepped outside. The day was overcast, but dry as she walked past the well-kept lawns around Pam's neighborhood. The gardens didn't have the same abundance of flowers as her aunt's had in England, but still, they were pleasant. One house in particular, at the end of the road, had a lovely patch of wild flowers along the front. Nicole wondered if Emma enjoyed gardening. She'd never asked her.

She remembered the feel of Emma in her arms, the sensation of warm lips pressed on hers. Even the memory thrilled her, as the kiss had. Her body's reactions amazed her, the intensity, the longing. She'd never felt so drawn to anyone else like she was to Emma. How could she end that, walk away from that feeling forever? But she was about to get married. She couldn't let her feelings for Emma destroy the future she'd built for herself, could she?

By the time she got back to Pam's house, Adam was waiting. His blue car sat in the driveway. Nicole felt a twinge of guilt for what she'd been thinking about. She painted a smile on her face and prepared to greet Adam. With luck, she could convince him to take her home soon. She wanted to clean her apartment before everyone arrived later and fix up some finger food. Maybe she'd get some chips and salsa for Emma. She bounded into the house with a smile on her face at the thought of seeing Emma, again. Nothing would happen between them with everyone there, so at least she was safe from her own desires, she thought as she greeted Adam and Henry in the kitchen.

EMMA PACKED UP the fragile wedding favors, examining each one as she wrapped them in plastic sheeting. She had faith in the man who'd created them for her, but she knew Pam would be casting a critical eye on them. Not that Pam's opinion mattered. These were made for Nicole. Although she hadn't seen Nicole in a few days, she still wasn't eager to meet with her tonight. This was mostly because Pam and Adam would be there, and Emma felt uncomfortable around them. Emma knew she would be under Pam's caustic stare all evening. She was sure Pam recognized her feelings for Nicole and despised her for it.

But Emma also dreaded having to be around Nicole and not being able to touch her or hold her in her arms. Nicole had made it clear that she would marry Adam. That left a leaden feeling inside Emma, that the woman she loved and who cared for her in return would still marry someone else. A part of her screamed to run away from it all, but she knew it was too late for that. She didn't have the strength to walk away.

She stuffed extra packing in the box and taped it shut. She looked at the time, six o'clock. Enough time to shower and blow-dry her hair. She knew she was primping herself up to see Nicole, but she had given up the notion of forcing herself to get over her feelings. Time would take care of that. Time and a wedding, she thought with a lump in her throat.

EMMA'S TIMING WAS impeccable, if impeccable meant arriving at Nicole's just as Adam dropped Pam off at the curb and peeled off to find a parking spot. Small talk with the enemy, Emma thought. Perfect. "Hi," she said as she approached, carrying the box of wedding favors.

Pam's face crinkled as if she'd smelled something off. "Oh, hello. I suppose you want me to help with the doors." Mrs. Congeniality held open the outer door for Emma to enter the apartment building. Emma had to prop the box up against the wall in order to ring Nicole's doorbell. When they arrived upstairs together, Emma let Pam lead the way. Nicole waited for them at her apartment door. Nicole's eyes locked on hers, sending a rush of heat to her face. Nicole glanced at Pam as her cheeks flushed pink. Emma took in Nicole's attire. She couldn't keep her eyes off the short cropped t-shirt Nicole wore, or off the enticing flash of tight stomach muscles exposed by it.

Pam voiced her immediate dislike of Nicole's attire. "Really, you're having guests, Nicole. You should dress up a little better."

Nicole lowered her head, and Emma wanted to drop her box on Pam, preferably on her head. Nicole led them to the small dinette off the kitchen where Emma put down her box. The doorbell rang, likely Adam. Emma opened the box and unpacked a few samples of the favors for the others to see, while Nicole let Adam into the apartment. Emma knew that Pam would insist on seeing all the party favors, but Emma wasn't about to be generous and open them all right away.

Adam and Nicole pulled up chairs by the table. "I like them," Adam announced as he picked up one of the glass favors and held it to the light.

Each of the favors was a unique, hand-blown glass ornament

that reflected the light in soft rainbows around its contours. Emma watched as Nicole's expression grew soft.

"They're beautiful." Nicole's gaze locked with Emma's over the table. Emma grinned and blushed. She'd fretted over the favors for two weeks, harassing the glass-blower for daily progress reports. She didn't tell Nicole, but she'd designed them herself.

"We should examine all of them," Pam harped.

Emma gave Pam a cold smile and began unpacking the rest for the older woman's critical examination. She gritted her teeth as she watched Pam paw each ornament, leaving her fingerprints all over them. Emma would have to re-polish them all at this rate.

"Well," Pam announced. "They seem good enough. You'll have to pack them in something better than this, though," she added.

Emma ignored the jibe as she got up and helped herself to Nicole's glass cleaner. Somehow she knew it would aggravate Pam to know that she was familiar with Nicole's apartment, and that felt good. They discussed more details of the wedding as Emma cleaned each ornament and packed them back into the box. She congratulated herself for being able to stay in Nicole's presence and not let her feelings overwhelm her. As long as they weren't alone together, she thought. She hated seeing Adam with her, but if Emma ignored that part, she felt more confident that maybe she did have the strength to return to a more platonic relationship with Nicole.

Pam created a timetable for the wedding day, jotting down when the caterer would arrive at her home, who would be setting up tables and chairs, and when to expect the cake. Emma was still cleaning the last few ornaments by the time the planning session ended.

"What about the wedding dress?" Pam asked. "Why don't you try it on now, and I'll take a look."

Nicole's gaze darted to Emma and then back to Pam. "Thank you, but I've already asked Emma to help me with that later."

News to me, Emma thought. She held her expression blank, but inwardly she tap danced at the subtle slap in the face Nicole just gave her future mother-in-law. She tried to ignore the way her pulse increased, knowing she'd be alone with Nicole.

"I guess you'd better take me home now, Adam," Pam announced, her annoyance obvious. Adam shrugged, oblivious to the tension between the two women in his life. He got up and gave Nicole a peck on the cheek, then waited for Pam to collect her purse. Nicole and Emma remained silent until after the other two disappeared out the door. Then Nicole held her sides and let out a long laugh.

"I'm sorry," she said. "I didn't mean to put you on the spot like that, but Pam was being insufferable, really."

Emma grinned, "No problem. But this means you do have to try on the dress for me. I wouldn't want to be implicated in a lie."

Nicole blushed. "Are you sure you don't mind?"

"Hmm. Seeing an attractive woman in a beautiful dress? Let me think about that one," Emma teased.

"You know, if I didn't know better," Nicole said as she walked over to her bedroom. "I'd think you were flirting, Ms. LeVanteur."

Emma gave Nicole her best I'm-so-innocent look. Nicole shook her head and disappeared into the bedroom. Emma paced the small living room floor as she waited. Her mind had envisioned Nicole at the wedding, though always without a certain bridegroom being present. She worried about how she'd react, seeing it for real. Would she be overcome by the reality that Nicole was straight and getting married?

A few minutes later, Nicole peeked out from her room. Her hair curled over her ears, and just the slightest hint of an off-white gown appeared at her shoulders.

"Come on, don't be shy," Emma said, ignoring the hammering of her heart.

"Very funny. I'm glad you find all this amusing, but I need some help with the clips in the back."

Emma walked into Nicole's bedroom. She avoided looking directly at Nicole, scanning the room instead. A crystal lamp in the corner cast a soft yellow glow across the cream-colored quilt covering Nicole's queen sized bed. A light maple bureau occupied one wall, while a full length mirror took up the other wall.

Nicole turned her back to Emma. "Can you see them? A row of clips along the back there." She reached a hand around to point out the problem area.

"Yes, I see." Emma's hands shook as she worked the clips through their matching hooks along the open back of Nicole's antique white gown. The contours of Nicole's well-toned back and shoulders held her mesmerized.

"Did you get them all?" Nicole asked, straining to see the back of her own dress.

"Um, yes." Emma let her hands fall to her side as Nicole moved a step away and then slowly turned to face her. The beaded gown hugged Nicole's sensuous curves, gently clinging to her hips. The neckline came up high in the front, covering Nicole's chest to the neck, but it managed to lift and shape her round breasts in the most exquisite way. Emma's eyes locked on the vision before her. Nicole was beautiful.

"Well, what do you think?" Nicole swayed to the left and right, making the base of the gown swirl around her legs. When Emma didn't answer, Nicole took a step closer to her. "Hello? Is there something wrong?"

Emma lost herself in Nicole's soft brown eyes. "No," she said, her voice husky. Forgetting herself for a moment, she let her hand stroke Nicole's bare arm, stopping at her wrist. "You're beautiful," she whispered.

Nicole kept her gaze locked on Emma's. A pink flush rose over her neck and cheeks. Her hand enveloped Emma's as she stepped closer, their bodies just touching. Emma's body felt electrified. She slipped her free hand behind Nicole, stroking the bare skin exposed by the low backed dress.

Nicole leaned into her. "I'm glad you like the dress," she whispered in Emma's ear.

Emma felt the heat of Nicole's body where it pressed against her. Nicole's lips brushed against her cheek, and Emma trembled. After a pause, where Emma thought her willpower would give out and she'd carry Nicole to the bed and damn the cost, the spell was broken, and Nicole stepped back. Emma's pulse thudded in her ear as she lost herself in Nicole's intense gaze. She knew Nicole wanted her, but Emma couldn't act on it, not with an almost-married woman.

Nicole lowered her head as she played with smoothing the dress where it clung to her waist. "So," she said quietly, "It seems to fit well."

"Yes," Emma agreed. "The length is a little long. Will you be wearing heels?"

Nicole gave her a sly smile. "Yes, but you don't get to see them until the wedding. There has to be some surprise." Nicole stared at her. "You will come, won't you?"

Emma forced herself to ignore what the price of her attendance would be to herself. "If you want me to."

Nicole studied Emma. "Yes, very much."

"Then I'll be there." Emma smiled. "Meanwhile, do you need help with unhooking the back again?"

"Yes, please. It's getting rather warm in here."

Emma unhooked the dress slowly, letting her eyes linger on the smooth skin of Nicole's back. Reluctantly, she left the room while Nicole changed back into her casual clothes.

NICOLE SHUT THE door quietly behind Emma and leaned her head on the frame. Her heart still pounded and her body tingled with the memory of Emma's touch. Why did Emma have such an intense effect on her? She closed her eyes, unwilling to let go of the memory of Emma in her arms. She'd never felt such a burning need as she did right then. She wanted desperately to call Emma back into her bedroom.

She willed herself to push away from the door. She had to undress, to take off her wedding gown. As the dress came off, the weight of what it represented settled on Nicole. Where was she going with her life? To Adam? To the rigid controls that his overbearing family represented? She felt lost and alone. She couldn't talk to anyone about her confused feelings. Katie already knew too much and voiced her intense disapproval of Emma. Nicole's other friends were too casual. She couldn't confide something this important to them.

She brushed the start of a tear out of her eyes. Dressed again in jeans and a short-sleeve top, she pushed back her tangled thoughts and painted a smile on her face. Emma wouldn't see the mess she felt inside. She opened the door. Emma stood up from the sofa and came to her as if pulled by Nicole's need. They stood together, separated only by inches, and Nicole once again felt the pounding of her heart. She knew that if she reached out, Emma would come to her. She wanted to, more than anything. But fear held her back. Fear of what it would mean to turn away from her planned future.

"I should probably head home," Emma announced after a moment.

Nicole hoped she hid her disappointment as she answered, "All right. Thank you again for the wedding favors, they're lovely."

Silence surrounded them. Emma stood close to her, so close Nicole could have pulled her into her arms and wrapped herself around Emma's lithe body. Emma's lips parted as she stared. How Nicole would love to feel those soft lips on hers again, feel Emma pressed against her, touch her.

"Nicole?"

Nicole felt her face turn crimson. She stepped back. "Sorry, you should go." She turned away from Emma, hiding her flushed face. She'd come so close to giving in. She was terrified of her own reactions.

"Will you call me?" Emma asked. Nicole nodded, unable to trust her voice. Emma left the apartment, and Nicole collapsed onto the sofa, burying her face in the soft material as the tears she'd been holding back came out.

EMMA WALKED DOWN the hallway, not daring to turn around. She ran down the stairs, fighting back frustration. She knew how much Nicole wanted her, but still, the wedding hung between them, a wall that blocked any hope of a future together. The touch of Nicole's body against hers burned into her flesh, a memory that would never fade. She remembered the rush of heat from Nicole's touch, and the look in the other woman's eyes that pleaded with Emma to take control, to cut through the tension that separated them. But which way did Nicole want her to act? Did she want Emma to seduce her? Or did she want Emma to be the strong one, the one willing to walk away from it all and leave Nicole to her married future?

Emma nearly knocked over an older woman as she barreled out the front door of Nicole's building. "Sorry," she mumbled as she rushed past and down the sidewalk.

She broke into a quick jog on her way to the train station. The night remained warm, and she started to sweat before she made it to the station entrance a few blocks away. She pushed past the turnstile and stood on the near-empty platform, staring blankly at the billboards posted across the tracks from her. How could she go to Nicole's wedding? Could she stand watching the woman she loved accept the vows of her proposed husband? Worse yet, watch as Nicole declared her love for him and let him kiss her? She took a frustrated wipe at her eyes as the train pulled into the station. She got on, but stayed by the doors as they closed behind her. She felt too jittery to take one of the open seats as the train pulled out of the station.

At the end of her ride, Emma got off the train in the same state that she'd gotten on it. She trotted along the dark, deserted sidewalks to her apartment building. It was midnight by the time she fought with her key at her apartment door. She paused as she opened it, hearing voices inside. If Jasmine had found a new girlfriend already, it would be some sort of record, even for her. She shut the door quietly behind her and walked down the hallway. Emma froze as she saw Jasmine pulling Maya into the bedroom. Jasmine wouldn't look at her, but Maya made a point of pausing at Jasmine's door to smirk at Emma before she let herself be pulled inside and shut the door.

Emma's shock turned ugly. She fought with the urge to burst into Jasmine's room and pound her fist into Maya's smirking face. She didn't think she had ever hated someone as much as she hated Maya. Emma didn't know how long she stood there, but when the unmistakable sounds of sex emerged from Jasmine's room, she knew she couldn't stay in the apartment in her current mood. Not if she wanted to keep her fragile grasp of self control and not pound Maya into oblivion. She turned and went back out the front door.

Chapter
Eleven

NICOLE WANDERED AROUND her apartment, cleaning up after her departed guests. She set the dirty glasses in the sink and packed the wedding to-do lists into her organizer on the kitchen counter. It was late by the time she finished, but she didn't want to go to bed. Kneeling on the chair by the table, she re-opened the box of wedding favors. She unwrapped the topmost one, being careful not to get any prints on it after Emma's diligent work to clean them. The fragile ornament captured a rainbow on its surface. Nicole traced a finger lightly along the smooth glass. The elegant uniqueness of the ornament captured her heart. It reminded her of Emma.

Warmth flooded her as she thought about Emma. There was something special and precious about her that Nicole cherished. She hugged herself as she thought of Emma, of how much she loved the time they spent together. What should she do? What could she do? Events conspired to pull her along a track she was no longer sure she wanted. And yet, just months ago, she'd been happy, she thought. Content in her future.

And now? What did she really feel, now? Could she turn her back on the man she claimed to love, whom she would marry soon? Or should she still go through with the wedding and never feel the heat of Emma's body pressed against her again, never feel those lips on hers again? Either option terrified her.

Unable to face her own frightened emotions, Nicole re-wrapped the ornament and closed up the box. She wandered back into her bedroom and flicked on the light. She needed to put the wedding dress away before she could collapse in bed and hope that sleep would quiet her spinning thoughts.

EMMA FOUND HERSELF outside Nicole's apartment building. She moved across the street and scanned the building, counting windows to where she thought Nicole's apartment was.

Soft light filtered through the closed blinds. Nicole was still awake. Emma watched, enthralled, as a shadow walked past the covered window. She could imagine Nicole getting a late snack or something. What if she wasn't alone? Emma wasn't sure she could handle it if she saw Adam's bulky shadow pass by that same window.

Part of her felt she should go home. She shouldn't be staring up at a window she thought was Nicole's, but she couldn't pull herself away just yet. Even the faint shadow of Nicole's presence soothed her tumultuous thoughts. She leaned against a tree as she watched the shadow sit down. As Emma's mind settled, she stifled the irrational urge to laugh. What would happen if the shadow opened the blinds, and it was some old man with insomnia? The shadow figure moved to another room. After a time, the window grew dark. Emma lowered her gaze. This was foolish. She needed to get back home.

After the ride back, Emma walked into her dark apartment and tossed her keys on the coffee table as she sank into the sofa. She managed to control herself for the train ride home, but now tears flowed freely down her cheeks. She loved Nicole. She loved the way Nicole's hair fell into her eyes. She loved to hear her accent, hear her stories of England and teaching. And she loved the feel of Nicole's warm hand in hers, the soft touch of Nicole's long fingers.

Emma's thoughts were interrupted by someone staggering out of the bedroom. The harsh bathroom light flicked on, and Jasmine stood swaying in the light. She looked at Emma, whose face was streaked with tears. Emma waited for something, some acknowledgment from Jasmine, but her best friend was too far gone. Jasmine's glazed eyes washed over her for a moment, then she stumbled into the bathroom and shut the door. Emma locked herself in her own room and fumbled for a tissue. She needed to be alone to nurse her pain.

EMMA WOKE UP late the next morning. The gray day did little to entice her to leave her bed, but hunger pangs motivated her to move. When she emerged from her bedroom, she discovered the rest of the apartment was deserted. She poured herself some breakfast cereal and devoured it at the kitchen counter. After cleaning up her dishes, she made herself some strong coffee. As she waited for it to brew, Emma noticed a light flashing on her answering machine. Probably for Jasmine, she thought as she triggered the machine to replay the message.

Nicole's warm voice filtered in through Emma's sleepy brain. Emma closed her eyes as she listened. Nicole wanted her to call back. Emma's hand was on the phone, ready to dial, but she couldn't bring herself to do it right away. She'd spent most of the night trying to convince herself that she needed to do the right thing, that she needed to leave Nicole to her chosen future. Talking to Nicole would only pull Emma back into her confused despair of the night before. She didn't erase the message, but walked away from the phone and sat on the edge of the sofa. She couldn't call Nicole, not yet. If she did, her resolve would crack. When the coffee finished brewing, she got up to pour herself a cup.

The phone rang. She let it ring three times before forcing herself to pick it up. She couldn't avoid Nicole. "Hello?"

An overly energetic voice answered her. "Hey! It's Annah. What's up?"

"Nothing much, just crawled out of bed."

"At eleven? My mom would have burned the mattress from under me if I ever slept that late."

Emma laughed. "Well, one of the perks of being on my own, I guess. What's up with you?"

"Nothing, bored. You want to meet up for sprints again?"

"I don't think I have that much energy today." Emma's voice echoed her lack of motivation.

Annah's enthusiasm remained. "Okay, well what about just hanging at a coffee house?"

"Your mother lets you drink coffee?" Emma asked as she eyed her own steaming mug.

"Please, as if she could stop me. Besides, they sell coffee at school. It's a staple of every teenager's diet."

Emma caved in. At least it would keep her from calling Nicole right away. "Okay, how about we meet in the Public Garden by the Boylston Street station?"

"Sounds great, see you there at like noon?"

"Make it one o'clock. I still have to shower."

Emma hung up and gulped down her coffee, burning her tongue in the process. She took a long shower, letting the hot water loosen the muscles down her back and shoulders. When the guilt of wasted water weighed on her mind, she turned off the shower and returned to her room, wrapped in a terrycloth towel. She felt the cool air blowing in from her open window as she contemplated what to wear. It was cool and cloudy outside. Jeans and a t-shirt should do it.

Emma made her way out the door and managed to arrive at the Public Garden about twenty minutes early. The bustle of shoppers and tourists spilled past the cast-iron gating that surrounded the Public Garden. Newly planted annuals lined the fence on the inside, adding their sweet scent to that of the freshly cut grass.

"Hey," Annah said as she approached from Emma's right.

"You're early," Emma said.

"So are you." Annah stuffed her hands in the pockets of her loose-fitting jeans. Her curled hair was pulled into one frizzy ponytail, from which a lock had managed to escape. Or maybe it was left out deliberately, as Emma watched Annah twirl the strand in her fingers while they walked.

"I'm already wired on coffee," Emma confessed. "How about I treat you to a slush, and we can wander around the Garden?"

"Sure," Annah agreed.

Emma led the way to a slush vendor operating outside the iron fence. She bought traditional icy lemon slush for herself and what she considered sickly-sweet cherry slush for Annah.

They remained quiet as they walked past the wooden benches along the Garden's central path that led to the Common on the other side. Emma's thoughts kept drifting to Nicole.

"What's up with you?" Annah asked as she slurped the end of her slush and discarded the paper cup in the nearest trash can.

"Nothing much," Emma said. "Just having a hard time of things right now."

Annah gave her hand a little squeeze. "So tell me all about it."

"It's a bit much to dump on you," Emma said, ignoring her half-eaten slush.

"No way. I whine like forever about my problems. Now's your turn." Annah sat down under a large oak tree. Emma searched around for a place to dump the rest of her slush. After tossing her cup in the nearest trash can, she rejoined Annah by the oak tree.

"The best thing about the Garden," Annah said, "is that even with the tourists running around snapping pictures, you can still find a private corner to sit and talk."

Sitting cross-legged beside her, Emma delayed giving in to her half-sister's persistence.

So," Annah prompted.

Emma toyed with a blade of grass. "It's just the doldrums of a pathetic love life."

"Tell me about it," Annah interrupted. "My boyfriend dumped me a month ago, and I still haven't found a new one. Though my friend Jennifer's brother Michael, he's kind of a cutie."

Emma let Annah finish her ramblings. Teenage love hadn't been such a casual thing for her in high school. In fact it had been non-existent. She never liked boys and was far too closeted to ask any of her female crushes out on a date. That changed when she met Jasmine at college, but that was due to Jasmine's blatant advances. And now, maybe she was finally over Jasmine. But did she have the courage to start another relationship? And could she, with a nearly married woman? She'd hung back so many times before, afraid of repeating the pain that breaking up with Jasmine had caused her. Anything with Nicole would just guarantee further pain.

"Sorry," Annah said. "We were supposed to be talking about your love life, not mine."

"My lack of a love life," Emma corrected.

"Well, where do you go, I mean, to meet women?"

"I wish I knew. Clubs I guess, but it all feels like a meat market in there. How do you decide you want to date someone based on how they look in a poorly lit dance bar somewhere?"

"I wouldn't know. You think my mom let's me go out dancing at any twenties and under club? What about at school or work? Do you ever meet anyone interesting?"

Emma felt a rush of heat at the thought of Nicole, though she had been trying to avoid those feelings all day. Her face must have shown her reaction.

"So," Annah teased. "Someone must be interesting to you. Who are you thinking about with that sad, kicked puppy look on your face?"

Emma smiled despite her problems. "You wouldn't believe me if I told you."

"Try me."

She looked at Annah. Maybe it was time she opened up to someone. It had been ages since she could talk to Jasmine like this. "You remember that party where we met?"

"Mom and Dad's work party? Yeah."

"Remember that brown haired woman you helped me toss in the water?" Emma remembered Nicole standing outside the pool, her wet clothes clinging to her. The thought was maddening. Nicole was enticingly close and yet a world apart from Emma.

Annah's eyes grew wide. "No way. What's her name? She's a babe."

Emma had to laugh. "Nicole."

"You've got good taste," Annah said as she repositioned herself against the tree trunk. "So, are you dating?"

Emma lowered her head. "It's not as easy as that."

"She's not interested?" Annah asked, her expression showing sympathy for Emma's situation.

"Try she's getting married in less than two weeks." Emma felt the cold, familiar ache in the pit of her stomach as she related her feelings to Annah.

"Oh. That sounds like trouble."

"No doubt." Emma crumpled the blade of grass she'd been playing with and tossed it aside.

"Still," Annah continued, undaunted. "Has she given you any, you know, vibes that she's interested?"

Emma stared at Annah. "Vibes?"

"Yeah, you know. Do you catch her watching you? Or does she make excuses to, you know, stand a little too close or something?"

"You amaze me," Emma said, laughing.

"Yadda yadda. So? Vibes?"

Emma frowned. "Yes, a lot more than vibes. But then, she's about to be married."

"Well, maybe she's just realizing she's gay." Annah gave her a nudge. "Maybe you've opened her eyes to a whole new world."

Emma laughed out loud. "Don't I wish?"

"Maybe she'll dump that wanna-be husband and come sweep you off your feet."

"You're an insufferable optimist, aren't you?"

Annah shrugged. "Could happen."

"Yeah. Could more likely happen that she is straight, I'm just an idle curiosity, and she goes off on her honeymoon at the end of June."

"Pessimist."

"Optimist." Annah's enthusiasm lifted Emma's spirits, despite the topic of conversation. It was good to have someone to talk to.

Annah looked at her watch. "Crap. I have to get going. My Mom's dragging my dad off to a therapist later, and I have babysitting duties, again."

Emma stiffened at the mention of her father, their father. "What does he need a therapist for?"

Annah laughed. "Because he's being lame about you being gay, and mom's having a fit over it. She told him he had to see a therapist, or she'd kick him out of the house."

"Really?"

"Well, maybe not kick him out. But she was pretty mad about the whole thing."

"So was I," Emma said, trying to keep the bitterness out of her voice.

Annah gave her a quick hug before standing up. "Well, if he wants to be a jerk, that's his problem. At least we got to meet and stuff."

"Yes, we did." Emma stood up and brushed the dirt off her backside. Annah gave her a wave as she trotted off to the train station. Emma's mood lifted. She was glad to have Annah around. And thumbs up for Marina beating her father into reality.

She thought about their conversation, about confessing her feelings for Nicole, and admitting that Nicole shared at least some of those feelings. But, did Nicole care about her enough to question her own wedding? Would Emma want to be responsible for breaking that up? Emma wasn't sure she'd have the courage to push forward and find out, risking the pain and heartache if Nicole walked away from her like Jasmine had.

Afternoon thunderclouds formed in the distance as Emma wandered through shops along Newbury Street before making her way back to the train station. She didn't buy anything, but the stroll kept her mind off other, sadder thoughts. She didn't get back home until after four o'clock, but she was determined to call Nicole and find out exactly what Nicole's feelings for her were. She was mentally preparing for what she'd say to Nicole as she rode the elevator up to her floor.

Emma hustled through her apartment door as the phone was ringing. She picked it up before it switched to the answering machine. Her heart pounded, thinking it was Nicole.

"Hello, is this Emma?"

"Yes." Emma didn't recognize the female voice on the other end of the line.

"Thank God. This is Marina. Have you seen Annah?"

"Yes, she was heading back home about two hours ago, why?"

"Well, she's not here yet, and she was supposed to stay with Samuel for me."

Emma looked at her watch. "She should have been there at least an hour ago."

"I haven't heard from her, and it's not like her to not call if she's late."

Emma paused to consider her options. "I can backtrack on the trains, try to find her if you want."

"That would be wonderful. Paul's gone off to his appointment, but I'd like to stay by the phone in case she calls."

Emma tried not to think the worst. Maybe Annah bumped into a friend and just lost track of time. Then again, she was an open and friendly girl from the suburbs. Maybe she didn't have the street-sense necessary in downtown Boston. Scanning the train route to Annah's house was likely a waste of time, but it gave Emma something to hold on to instead of the irrational thoughts running through her mind.

It took her a half hour to get back to Boylston station and then start following the route Annah would have taken back to Cambridge. She got off every few stops to look around, but the effort was futile. When Emma didn't find any sign of Annah, she walked the four blocks to Annah's house directly, rather than call Marina. She remembered the route from when she'd accompanied Annah back home the last time. She kicked herself for not taking Annah back home this time, too.

Emma rang the doorbell on the two-story colonial that occupied a prime corner lot. They didn't lack for money. The house boasted dark cranberry paint with black shutters beside each window. Two pine trees dominated the front yard. There were no cars in the driveway. She rang the bell again, but no one answered. Somehow, this bothered her even more, and she debated whether she should stay and wait, or go back home.

Her thoughts were interrupted when a black two-door convertible pulled into the drive. The car door opened, and Paul stood up. They stared at each other for an uncomfortable moment before he spoke. "Good to see you again, Emma. I didn't know you knew where I lived."

She held her expression neutral. "Your wife called me. She hadn't heard from Annah and was worried."

Paul frowned. "Annah hasn't come home yet?"

"I don't know." Emma gestured at the door. "No one's home."

Paul walked past her, pulling out his keys. "This doesn't sound good." He unlocked the door, waved Emma inside, and walked to the front room.

A note was taped to the phone.

"It's from Marina," Paul said. "Annah's been taken to Cambridge Medical Center."

"Does it say what happened?" Emma's voice echoed her worry.

"No." Paul turned to her. "I'll give you a ride if you want to come along."

"Yes, thanks." The two of them climbed into Paul's car and drove in silence to the hospital. Emma imagined a dozen or more horrific excuses for why Annah was in the hospital, all of which she blamed on herself for not accompanying the younger girl back home. When they arrived at the hospital, it took them a long, frustrating time to find where the rest of the family was. The emergency room had four other clusters of people waiting to be seen. Emma stood to the side while Paul questioned the harried check-in desk clerk. Eventually, they were directed to the third floor recovery ward.

Paul and Emma popped out of the elevator together as soon as the doors slid open. The desk nurse asked Paul for identification before she would release Annah's room number, and then the nurse turned to Emma. "Are you family as well?"

"Yes, she is." Paul answered before Emma had a chance to reply. He led the way to Annah's room, and Emma followed. Marina sat by the bed, while Samuel sat in the side chair, staring out the window, bored already. Annah rested in the bed. Blood oozed through a bandage on her forehead, and her leg was wrapped in a cast from her foot to just below her knee.

"Hey," Annah said, unusually sedate.

Paul pulled up another chair and held Annah's hand. "What happened?"

"Sorry, Dad. I wasn't paying attention and got hit by a car."

"A pickup truck," Marina corrected. "But she'll be okay. She has a fractured ankle and some major bruises."

Marina turned to Emma for the first time. "Thank you for searching for her. We got a call from the hospital about twenty minutes after I talked to you."

Emma nodded, relaxing now that she knew Annah would be fine. "Nice cast," she said to Annah.

"Yeah. I'll probably hate it once the pain killers wear off." Annah gave her a weak smile.

"Looks like a walker cast, that's good." Emma said.

Paul interrupted them. "When can we take her home?"

"I haven't heard yet," Marina said. "Can you go ask the on-duty nurse?"

Paul left the room, taking Samuel with him for a walk. He seemed glad for the excuse to get out of the room.

"Sorry I didn't ride all the way home with you," Emma said.

"Hey, I'm a big girl. I can take care of myself."

"Sure," said Emma and Marina together. Annah made a face at them both.

"At least I don't have to do chores for the next couple of months," Annah said.

"We'll see," Marina said.

A FEW HOURS later, Paul offered to give Emma a ride home. Annah would spend the night in the hospital for observation, and though Marina fought to stay with her, Annah finally convinced her mother she would be fine by herself. When Emma got home, it was past ten o'clock and long past the time she was supposed to call her mother. She grabbed the phone and settled on the sofa.

"Hi, Ma."

"Emma? You're late." Her mother sounded tired. Emma should have called from the hospital.

"Sorry, I had an emergency."

"Really? Is everyone all right?"

"Yes. Annah got hit by a car, but she'll be okay. She'll be on crutches for a few weeks."

Her mother was silent. Emma really didn't want to have a fight about this. "Ma?"

"Well, sorry to bother you. Obviously, your new family has

priority these days."

"Don't be like that."

"Anyway, it's late. I'm going to bed. Talk to you later." With that, her mother hung up. Emma cradled the phone for a moment, debating whether she should call back. It was late. She'd call her mother tomorrow or maybe drop by for a visit. Right now she just wanted a long, quiet night's sleep. As she stumbled into her bedroom, she remembered her earlier determination to call Nicole, but it was too late for that as well.

Chapter
Twelve

THE LAST WEEK of June was baptized by a rolling set of thunderstorms. Rain pelted down on Emma's bedroom window as she finished her apartment-wide cleaning fit. She had a fan blowing in each room, with the hallway door open as the only escape for her cleaning fumes on the hot, rainy day. Jasmine remained scarce, which was much to Emma's liking, given Jasmine's renewed involvement with Maya. She'd been so angry with Jasmine that she'd considered moving out, but somehow, she couldn't really conceive of leaving her best friend, at least not yet. Besides, she was beginning to enjoy having the apartment to herself.

A knock on the open door startled Emma. She peered down the hallway.

"Nicole? What time is it? You're early," Emma said as she tossed her cleaning rag in the sink and dried her hands on a kitchen towel. She berated herself for not keeping better track of the time. She'd asked Nicole over with the determination to talk out what was going on between them, but now that the woman stood before her, Emma felt her resolve waiver. Was she ready for rejection?

"It's three o'clock, and I'm right on time," Nicole said as she entered. "Someone let me in downstairs." She looked around the clean apartment. "You've been busy."

"Sorry, I must have lost track of time." Emma hustled to shut the front door as Nicole took a seat in the living room. Emma looked down at her own clothes. She wore old nylon running shorts and a loose tank-top. And nothing underneath, she thought to herself, wishing she'd had a few minutes' notice before Nicole popped in her front door.

"I should probably change," she said, walking back to the sofa.

She watched Nicole examine her and fought back the rising heat inside.

"I think you look great," Nicole said.

The compliment took Emma by surprise and she felt a telltale flush rising in her cheeks. But she decided not to fight with Nicole's pronouncement and took a seat on the sofa. "So, is everything ready for next Saturday?" she asked, keeping her voice light while her thoughts scrambled for a way to start the conversation she wanted to have.

Nicole kept her gaze locked on Emma. "Yes, I think so. Pam's finally given up arguing over things."

"That's a relief," Emma said. Nicole's voice sounded hollow. Emma wondered if something had happened between Nicole and her future in-laws.

"You are still coming, aren't you?" Nicole asked.

"I said I would." Emma refused to think about the following Saturday, and what it would mean to her when Nicole got married.

"Great. My parents will be flying in on Thursday, so you'll get to meet them as well."

"Oh," Emma said, jumping up. "Just a minute." She ran into her bedroom and came back out with a small wrapped package. You're just delaying things, she thought as she handed the gift to Nicole. "For you," she said.

"But the wedding's not for another week."

Emma shrugged, trying not to blush. "Consider it a very late engagement gift, then. Go on, open it."

Nicole blessed her with a childish grin as she tugged at the ends of the ribbon on her present. She took her time unwrapping the box, and Emma squirmed in her seat, anxious to see Nicole's reaction. Nicole opened the black velvet box, discarding the wrapping paper. Her eyes grew wide as she pulled out a gold necklace from which hung a cluster of ceramic lavender flowers. "It's beautiful," she said.

Emma grinned from ear to ear, proud of herself for finding it. Not that she hadn't spent hours in the jewelers building in downtown Boston searching for just the right gift. "Glad you like it."

"Help me with the clasp," Nicole said, shifting her back to Emma.

Emma slipped the necklace around Nicole's neck, her fingers just brushing Nicole's skin as she clasped the necklace in place. "There you go."

Nicole turned around, her face glowing with excitement. "I love it," she said.

Then Nicole pulled Emma close and wrapped her arms around her. "It's wonderful, thank you," Nicole whispered in Emma's ear, so close that Emma felt Nicole's lips brush her cheek. The heat that shot through her body and centered between her thighs overwhelmed her as she held Nicole, trying not to shake. Her eyes drifted shut, and she inhaled the sweet scent of Nicole's hair.

A noise at the front door startled them both, and they separated. Emma heard keys in the lock. "Jasmine," she said.

"Oh," Nicole's face paled. "I don't relish seeing her, again. Not if she's back with that insane woman."

And Emma couldn't have the talk she needed to have with Nicole if Jasmine and Maya were around. She stood up, holding out her hand. "Come on, let's go into my room." Nicole's lips curved in a shy smile as she took Emma's hand. They slipped into Emma's bedroom and shut the door before Jasmine and Maya made it down the hallway. Emma leaned against the door. She could hear Maya's voice approaching. Nicole joined her, and they listened while Maya and Jasmine chatted.

Then the talking stopped. The sounds of kisses and soft moaning filtered into Emma's room. She and Nicole covered their mouths to stop from laughing. Movement beyond the door and the sound of another door closing suggested the other two had made their way into Jasmine's bedroom. Nicole tiptoed over to Emma's bed and buried herself and her laughter into Emma's pillow.

Emma joined her on the bed. "So, you find it hysterical to eavesdrop on girls making out?" she asked, teasing. She leaned back on the bed as Nicole calmed herself. Then Nicole turned on her, a mischievous look in her eye.

"What's the matter, don't you have any sense of humor?" Nicole asked. She gave Emma a poke in the ribs, followed by another. When Emma didn't laugh, Nicole started in earnest, tickling Emma until she squirmed on the bed, stifling her own giggles.

"Stop it," Emma said with a grin.

"Make me." Nicole's infectious mood was irresistible.

"You asked for it." Emma threw herself across Nicole, searching for her ticklish spots. They both thrashed, blocking and tickling until they were laughing and in tears. They'd given up being quiet until Nicole called a truce. Their arms and legs intertwined. They were both out of breath, but neither moved. From the other room came the unmistakable sounds of lovemaking. For a moment, Emma panicked, thinking Nicole would be upset by it. She looked at Nicole and saw that she was about to break down into giggles again. "Shh," Emma said.

That proved too much for Nicole, who buried her face in Emma's chest to hide her laughter. Emma was poignantly aware of Nicole in her arms. She felt her bare legs entwined around Nicole's strong thighs and Nicole's flushed face pressed against her breasts. Nicole's laughter stopped. She felt Nicole's cheek brush against her erect nipple as Nicole lifted her face to Emma. Emma stifled a moan.

She looked into Nicole's brown eyes. They were dilated, and her cheeks were a deep, warm red. Emma was too overwhelmed by the heat of her own desire to move. But Nicole moved. She lifted her hand to brush back the long strands of hair from Emma's face. Emma let her eyes drift shut as she felt Nicole's fingers caress her cheek. Her heart hammered in her chest.

She ran her hand along the small of Nicole's back. A soft moan from Nicole made her open her eyes. Nicole stared at her, aroused, vulnerable. Emma fought the urge to kiss the full red lips just inches from her own. When Nicole ran her tongue across those lips, Emma could no longer resist. She slipped her hand along Nicole's back until she cradled her head. She let Nicole's soft brown hair filter through her fingers.

Emma watched Nicole's face as she pulled her closer. Nicole's eyes drifted to Emma's lips, and then shut. Emma closed her own eyes. She felt Nicole's moist lips press against hers. Emma's resistance dissolved. She kissed Nicole harder, nibbling, then licking Nicole's lips until they opened, and she felt Nicole's tongue dance with hers.

Nicole moaned softly, and rolled on top of her. She felt Nicole's breasts pressed against her, felt hardened nipples pressing into her, and the growing sweat between their bodies. She kissed and sucked at Nicole's lips, her hands slipping under Nicole's shirt to feel the hot skin underneath.

Nicole rocked against her, pushing her thigh between Emma's legs. Emma felt herself grow moist, dampening the thin shorts that were the only barrier between her throbbing need and Nicole's thigh. Her hands slid down Nicole's back. She pulled Nicole's body further onto her, her own need intensifying. Nicole traced wet kisses along Emma's neck, rocking her thigh against Emma. She felt the intense heat between Nicole's thighs as they wrapped around her own bare leg, thrilling her and driving her passion further.

Emma's arousal reached a sudden climax, crashing around her as she moaned in response. Excitement ripped through her body. Nicole's breath came in short gasps. She rocked in time to match Emma's thrusts. Tossing her head back, Nicole went rigid as the orgasm rolled through her.

They lay in each other's arms, pulses beating frantically. Emma's breathing steadied. She opened her eyes as Nicole shifted in her arms. Nicole watched her for a moment, flustered, barely breathing. Then a frightened expression covered Nicole's face, and Emma's heartbeat thundered in her ears. Nicole pulled back, slipping off the bed. She covered her hot cheeks with her hands, tears filling her eyes.

Emma's world crumbled around her.

"Nicole," she whispered. But Nicole wouldn't answer. She only shook her head, standing up. Emma pushed herself off the bed as well.

"Oh, God," Nicole said, still shaking. "Oh, God." She pulled away when Emma tried to reach for her.

Emma stood by her bed, her arms hanging by her side. "I'm sorry," she said. Nicole didn't respond. She backed out of the room as tears spilled down her cheeks. Emma watched, helpless, as Nicole ran down the hallway and out the door, swinging it shut behind her.

Emma fell back onto the bed. She curled into a ball and rocked herself as tears flowed into her pillow. She'd gotten her answer after all, about Nicole's feelings for her, but it was a bittersweet pill. The look of anguish on Nicole's face as she fled told Emma everything she needed to know. Nicole wouldn't come back to her.

Chapter
Thirteen

EMMA SPENT A long night alternating between cradling her pillow to dry her tears and falling into fits of exhausted sleep. Her dreams were filled with the feeling of Nicole's body pressed against her. Upon waking, her thoughts lingered on the sensations of Nicole's lips on hers, Nicole's tongue teasing her lips and neck. And then she felt the crash of Nicole leaving all over again, the expression of shock and disgust she saw on that beautiful face.

By morning, she felt more drained than rested. Her mouth was parched. Brilliant blue sky peeked through the cracks in her bedroom blinds, a harsh contrast to her gray, depressed state of mind. She shut her eyes against the day.

Emma heard shuffling outside her room. She listened, hearing what she hoped was only one person out there. The sounds of pathetic crying filtered into her room, sounding at least as bad as she felt. She wiped a tissue across her face and dragged herself out of bed to see what was going on. Maybe it would get her mind away from her own tortured thoughts. She padded out of her bedroom to see Jasmine lying curled up on the sofa, trying in vain to control the hiccups that followed her crying fit.

"I didn't know you were here," Jasmine said between hiccups.

Emma sat down on the edge of the sofa. "Hasn't been a good night."

"No," Jasmine agreed. She looked up at Emma. "You look worse than me."

"Thanks, but maybe you should check a mirror before you say that."

Jasmine looked away. Her hand drifted to her cheek and she touched it gingerly, wincing. "Can you see it already?"

"See what?" Emma sat down closer. She saw the purple bruise spreading across Jasmine's cheek. "Did you get jumped again?"

"I never got jumped." Jasmine's shoulders slumped.

Emma sat silent for a minute as that statement sank in. "You mean Maya did this to you?"

Jasmine nodded, her head dipping lower.

"Why on earth did you let her do this?" Emma's fists clenched. "Why'd you go back to her?"

Jasmine looked at Emma, her eyes pleading for understanding. "She came to see me, begged me not to leave, swore that she'd change. And then, I don't know. Things just started happening."

Emma's anger at the world coalesced into a burning fury, focused on Maya. She tried to steady her voice and keep herself rational against the storm of her emotions. "Well, stop these things from happening," she said in frustration. "The woman's a bitch, a drug dealer, and now she's abusive."

"But she's not always like this. Sometimes she can be great."

"You're making excuses for her now."

"Maybe." Jasmine wrapped her arms around herself and turned toward the dark TV screen.

"Jasmine, look at me." Emma put a hand on her friend's arm. "Do you really think you deserve this kind of treatment?"

Jasmine wouldn't look at her. "I don't know. I don't have the greatest track record for keeping girlfriends."

"So? You're twenty-two." Emma let out an exasperated sigh. "You just got your first real job. Life's just starting out."

Jasmine turned to her. "Maybe." She brushed back a strand of Emma's long hair. "Maybe I should never have let you go, eh?"

Emma gently pushed her hand away. "Let's just not go there today, okay?" Jasmine wasn't the woman she wanted. Not anymore. She ached to feel Nicole in her arms, to feel her touch.

Jasmine gave her a half smile. "Okay. But you haven't told me yet what your bad night was all about."

It was Emma's turn to curl up, wrapping her arms around her up-drawn legs. "Nicole was here yesterday."

"And?" Jasmine perked up.

"And things got a bit out of hand."

"Woohoo!"

"Not really," Emma said. "When it was over, she pulled away from me like I had the plague."

"Oh, not so good," Jasmine said.

"She's disgusted with me."

"Well, if things got out of hand, and by the way, I do want details someday, anyway, seems like your Nicole has some issues she needs to deal with before this so-called wedding. When is the wedding?"

"In six days."

"Ouch. Maybe she'll come around," Jasmine added.

"Maybe." Emma tried in vain to feel the optimism that Jasmine projected for her. But she'd seen the look on Nicole's face. She prayed that Nicole would come around, but she didn't expect it. She'd let herself go out on that limb again, searching for love. And again, the limb had snapped underneath her.

NICOLE DIDN'T COME around. Not that day or the next. On Tuesday, Emma got a call from Pam, asking her for the final invoice on the wedding charges. Pam would mail her a check so that her business with Nicole was finished. Emma sank into her chair, clutching the phone after Pam hung up. Whatever glimmer of hope she'd been holding onto for Nicole faded. It was over. All the sweet and passionate sensations of Nicole in her life ended with that one phone call.

When the phone rang again, she picked it up, her body and mind working in some sort of automatic mode. It was Marina this time, asking if she'd like to meet up at Neo-tech for lunch the next day with her and Paul. Emma's numb mind agreed and she hung up. Her body felt strangely calm. She thought she should be crying, but she didn't. Perhaps she'd cried enough about Nicole already. Or perhaps tears were only a part of her wishful thinking that somehow this would all turn around, that somehow Annah's glowing fairytale would come true in the end.

By noon the next day, Emma's heart and mind had hardened. Her view of the world was tinged with bitter disappointment as she made her way to the outskirts of Cambridge by bus. The company was housed in one of the old Wang Computer buildings in an industrial park along Route 2A. As she stood before the tinted glass doors bearing Neo-Tech's dark emerald logo, Emma prayed she would not run into Adam while she was here. Even in her cold, detached state, that would be too much for her.

The lobby contained the usual abstract artwork that was endemic to most technology buildings. A series of awards lined the front desk, Best New Product of the Year, Best Innovation. *Rising Entrepreneur Magazine* must be prestigious, as the announcement of its "Innovator of the Year" award warranted a large blowup billboard behind the receptionist.

"Hello, I'm supposed to meet Marina LeVanteur for lunch," Emma announced as she approached the counter.

"Do you mean Marina Williams, the CTO?" the receptionist asked. She was an older woman with badly dyed black hair.

Emma raised her eyebrows. Marina hadn't taken Paul's name at work? "Yes, sorry."

"I'll call her and tell her you're here. May I have your name please?"

"Emma LeVanteur."

That elicited a barely suppressed stare from the receptionist as she dialed Marina's number. Emma walked away to look at the artwork on the walls. She would have read the awards but she'd never inquired what it was that Neo-tech built. She had enough time to register the blandness of the artwork before Marina's dark head popped out from a side doorway.

"Emma, glad you could make it." Marina held open a door off to the right of the lobby. "Thank you, Jocelyn," she said, waving at the receptionist as she directed Emma into the hallway. "Welcome to Neo-Tech." Marina wore a sharp black pantsuit offset by a cream silk blouse.

Emma murmured her thanks as she took in the crisp business surroundings that Marina led her past. Tan cubicle walls formed a maze of corridors, littered here and there by bookcases and discarded boxes. "What is it you do here?" Emma asked as she took a seat in Marina's plush corner office. The view from the window looked out onto a vibrant green lawn that surrounded a still, dark pond.

"You mean me personally or Neo-Tech?"

Emma looked back at Marina. "I can guess what you do, but what does Neo-Tech do?"

"You've heard of biotechnology?"

"Yes."

"Well, we are commercializing some of the more interesting aspects of that."

Emma felt interest perk up, despite her dour mood, as Marina went on to explain the products her company was creating. She asked detailed questions about the processes involved in what Neo-Tech was attempting to do. By the end of the brief conversation, Emma was impressed with both Marina and her company.

"Well, much as I've enjoyed this, we do have a date with your father," Marina said.

"Yes, I suppose we do." Emma's expression clouded over.

"Now, now," Marina stepped around her desk. "He's not that bad."

At Emma's doubtful look, Marina added, "Okay, maybe he is. But he's working on it. Come on. There's a cafeteria at the company next door, and they let us mooch off them."

Marina led the way through the maze of cubicles and out a back door. They entered the neighboring building by a side entrance that opened into a large sparkling clean cafeteria. "It's new," Marina said. "They have a chef service that caters to multiple cuisines. Chinese, Italian, grilled food. Even a vegetarian selection of the day. And, of course, pizza."

Emma took in the food options served from small stations

behind the registers. Lines of people huddled around the Italian and grilled food sections. "I'll go for vegetarian," she said.

"Good. Meet me by the counter, it's my treat."

Emma selected a vegetarian calzone and covered it with spicy red sauce and a sprinkle of Parmesan cheese. She grabbed a diet Sprite and waited for Marina. After Marina paid for their meals, they settled at a table with their lunches. Paul joined them ten minutes later, carrying a tray with a cheese-steak and a large cup of steaming coffee.

"Mind if I join you?" he asked as he sat opposite Emma.

Her stomach tightened as an uncomfortable silence settled on the table. She found Marina not just interesting, but technically very savvy. As for Paul, she could only remember his bitter words and no opening conversation escaped her tight lips.

"Well, you two. Let's make an effort here," Marina said when the silence had stretched on. She cajoled them into making at least polite conversation. Paul kept to neutral topics, focusing on Neo-Tech's position in the market and their main competitors.

"How about you, Emma?" he asked at last. "What's your thesis going to be on?"

She put down her fork and began her standard glossy coverage of her mathematical thesis work. She was surprised when both Paul and Marina asked probing questions, some of which furthered her own thinking on what she would write during her last year at Harvard. By the end of lunch, while she and Paul could hardly be called close, they were at least beginning to be civil to each other. So long as her sexuality was left out of the discussion, things rolled along nicely.

"Well," Marina said after they'd finished eating. "I think Paul and I have a two o'clock meeting to prepare for."

"Yes," Paul stood and held out his hand. "Thanks for coming."

Emma shook his hand, glad that the lunch went better than she thought it would. At least they hadn't argued. Marina enveloped Emma's hand in hers as they said goodbye, and Emma was surprised at how much she liked the older woman.

Emma arrived home in less than an hour. Jasmine would still be at work for another few hours, so Emma had the apartment to herself. The discussion of her thesis with Marina and Paul had given her something to focus on. Determined to push all other thoughts aside, she sat at the table and pulled out her notebook.

A couple of hours into her renewed studies, the phone rang.

It was her mother this time. "What are you up to, dear?" she asked.

"Working on my thesis." Emma tapped a pencil on her notebook.

"Don't you have the summer off?"

"Yes, but I just had lunch with Dad and Marina. They gave me some topics to review for my work."

"Oh." Her mother's tone changed.

"Ma, don't be like this."

"Well it's not me who's cutting loose her old family for her new one."

"That's not true and you know it. Just because I want to know my dad doesn't mean I'm cutting you out."

"It certainly feels that way to me." Her mother's voice cracked as if she were crying.

"Well, maybe if you just accepted that I do have a father and a right to get to know him, you wouldn't feel so threatened by him."

"I don't have to listen to you blather on about him, do I?"

"No, I suppose not." Emma struggled to control her temper. "Just one last question though, and I'll shut up about him."

"What?"

"Did you know he was homophobic?"

Her mother laughed. "Paul?"

"Yeah. He flipped over it when he found out I like girls. He wanted to drag me to therapy." Emma waited for her mother to finish laughing.

"Sorry," she said between breaths when she stopped laughing. "It's just your father, when he was younger, well he tried just about anything and everything you could imagine."

"Really?"

"Yes, including one fling with another guy. I never thought Paul would turn out to be a bigot. At least not like that."

"Well, just my luck, but he is."

Her mother's voice grew angry. "Well, you stand up to him. Of all the nerve, and this coming from an adulterer and virtual bigamist."

"Yes, I know," Emma agreed. "We don't have to talk about it anymore."

"Fine, but don't you let him make you feel bad about yourself. You are who you are, and you're a far better person than he can ever hope to be."

"Thanks, Ma." Emma didn't actually feel any better about the situation, but at least she and her mother were talking again. She hung up the phone and sat on the sofa. Her mind went immediately to Nicole. What would she be doing now? Emma stood up. She needed something to distract her from the ache in her heart. She turned on the television and hoped she could numb her mind and heart for a while.

Chapter
Fourteen

NICOLE SAT IN the corner of her overstuffed sofa, surrounded by pillows. She held a cold cup of tea in her hands as she stared absently at the rain pattering down on her kitchen window. The days were going by in a blur of last minute activity, including the arrival of wedding presents that were trickling in from her family and friends in England. Pam pushed her to open the presents early to get a head start on thank-you notes, but Nicole refused. The wedding and all it stood for loomed over her like an impenetrable dark shadow that both held her complete attention and triggered her abject fear. She couldn't face the inevitability of it by opening presents.

She glanced at the clock. Her parents should have landed at Logan Airport by now and be on their way to the hotel. She should get some finger foods ready for when they came by later, but she felt lethargic, unwilling to move just yet. With only two days left until the wedding, at least she wouldn't have to face Adam again until Saturday. Somehow she felt both relieved and guilty. It had been awkward between them for the last few days, with her being quiet and withdrawn. It was only a matter of time before he would ask her why she was treating him so distantly. She knew why, but the momentum of the wedding carried her like a leaf in the wind, leaving her little time to wrestle with what it meant to her, what Emma meant to her. And after she'd run from the apartment, would Emma even want to see her, again? Could she see Emma without wanting to touch her, to love her? Everything in Nicole's life lay in shambles around her, and she didn't know how to pick up the shattered pieces.

When the doorbell rang an hour later, Nicole still hadn't moved. She got off the sofa and called down to the lobby on the intercom. "Mum?"

"Yes, it's Mum and Dad, Love."

"Come on up to the third floor." She dumped her untouched tea down the drain and put the cup and saucer in the sink. She poked into the cupboard and took out some biscuits for her parents. It was all she had. She'd been too out of sorts to go grocery shopping. A soft knock brought Nicole to the door.

"Hiya," her dad said, wrapping his arms around her.

"Don, let her breathe. You'll crush the girl," Nicole's mother said.

"Now, Etta. Just ask if you want a turn," he said, letting Nicole go.

Nicole stooped to give her petite mother a gentle squeeze. "I'm so glad you're both here."

Etta squeezed Nicole before letting her go. "Sorry we couldn't come sooner, Love. Your father's business just wouldn't let him go."

"It's all right. You're here now." Nicole's spirits lifted as they all settled around the small kitchen table. Emma's box of party favors still sat on the side of the table. Nicole's gaze lingered on it for a moment, before her mother's quiet cough caught her attention. "Would you like some tea?" she offered.

"Oh yes. Do you get Typhoo Decaf here?" Etta asked.

"Not locally," Nicole said. "But there's a British Imports shop in Boston that stocks it. I still have some here somewhere." Nicole put the kettle on and searched her cupboard for her mother's favorite tea.

Her father watched her while she puttered around the small kitchen. "You look tired," he said.

Nicole kept her face averted. "It's been a long week."

Etta stepped into the kitchen. "Well, have a rest, then. We can take care of ourselves. Come along, Don, find the milk, and I'll get the tea pot warmed."

Nicole let her parents shoo her off to the sofa while they took control in the kitchen. She felt sleepy and calmer than she had in days.

BY THURSDAY, EMMA'S exhaustion took over. She'd been immersing herself in her thesis work. She hadn't heard from Nicole, and she didn't expect to, but as the wedding day grew nearer, she found it difficult to concentrate even on her school work. The thesis work had kept her from slipping further into depression, but it couldn't prevent the dreams she had each night. Nicole came to her in her dreams, pulling her along on a passionate sexual exploration. Lips, tongues, and fingers exploring all parts of each other. Whenever Emma woke up, it was Nicole's face she remembered and the sensation of Nicole's body on hers as she realized her hand was under her own panties, feeding her own throbbing need. When she came fully awake, she'd roll over, tucking her straying hand under her pillow. She wouldn't relieve herself, not that way, not when the last time it had been Nicole's body that had sent her cascading over the edge.

She had no ability to concentrate. She flipped through the channels on the TV, finding little worth watching, but at least it numbed her thoughts. She even fell asleep for a time. The ruckus of Jasmine coming home early woke Emma from her latest dream. She scrambled to sit up.

"You've been watching TV all day?" Jasmine asked.

"Not all day. Why are you home so soon?" Emma didn't know what time it was, but it certainly wasn't much past lunch time.

Jasmine sat alone at the kitchen table. "I met Maya for lunch today."

"What?" Emma leaned over the back of the sofa to see Jasmine more clearly.

"I broke up with her, for real this time. She was pretty pissed about it."

Emma was standing instantly. "Did she hurt you?"

"No. Just a lot of shouting."

"What did you do?"

"Nothing, went back to work."

Emma studied her roommate. "But you're home now."

Jasmine looked up into Emma's eyes. "Yes. I couldn't concentrate." She lowered her eyes. "So I said I was sick and came home."

"Probably a good idea." Emma pulled up a chair next to Jasmine at the table and draped an arm around her shoulder. She pulled Jasmine into a hug.

"What's that all about?" Jasmine asked as she let go.

"Just because I've missed you." Emma looked away. She wasn't going to get all sappy over it. At least not so that anyone could see.

"Ah, shucks." Jasmine teased.

"Brat."

"Sentimentalist."

"Is that even a word?" Emma asked as she let go of her best friend.

"COME HAVE A seat here," Etta pushed out a chair next to her at the table. "You've been so quiet."

Nicole left the sofa to sit with her mother at the kitchen table. "Sorry," she said. "It really has been a hard week." She felt her mother's intense scrutiny as she sat down.

"Well, what's left to do then?" Etta asked, still watching her closely.

"Not much I suppose." Nicole rolled a ceramic napkin ring between her fingers as she talked. "Adam's mother took over most of the wedding details on Tuesday. She's verified the caterer, florist and baker."

"What about your dress?" Etta asked.

Nicole felt herself blush as she remembered trying on the dress in front of Emma. "It's all set as well."

"Hmm. The rest of the wedding party?"

"All on Adam's side," she said. "His sister Katie is my maid of honor, and his college chum is the best man." Katie wasn't her closest friend anymore. Emma filled that role. At least, she had until Nicole had pushed her away. Now, Nicole felt hollow inside.

"Well, I don't want to sound opinionated, love," Etta said, leaning back in her chair. "But this is all sounding very one-sided. Isn't this your wedding, too?"

Nicole nodded. "I tried to keep the wedding party as small as possible."

Etta patted her hand. "You always wanted a house wedding. Are any of your friends going to be at the wedding, then?"

"Some, yes." But not the one person she wanted to be there. Not anymore. Nicole felt her eyes sting. She looked away.

Her mother must have sensed her discomfort and changed the subject. "So what's in this big box you've got hogging half your table?" Etta asked.

Nicole looked back at Emma's box. "They're the wedding favors," she said, her heartbeat thudding in her ears.

"May I?"

Nicole dragged the box over and pulled out a wrapped favor and handed it to her mother.

Etta unwrapped the ornament and held it up to the light. Rainbows once again danced across the glossy surface. "They're lovely," said Etta.

Nicole's voice caught in her throat. "Yes, they are," she said in a whisper.

"And such a novelty. Wherever did you find them?"

Nicole felt her tears well up as she watched her mother turning the ornament. She clasped the golden necklace that hung beneath her blouse, where it had been since Emma put it on her. The lavender flowers rested against the curve of her chest, elegant like the ornaments, a reminder of the special care Emma had shown her. "Emma had them made for me," she said in a shaking voice.

"Nicole?" Her mother put down the ornament and studied Nicole's face.

Tears flowed down Nicole's cheek. "Mum, I don't know what

to do."

"There, there." Etta wrapped her small arms around her. Nicole let go of her pent-up pain, sobbing into her mother's shoulder.

She felt her father's hand stroke her head as she shook from crying. "Let it out, Love. Then tell Mum all about it."

"COME ON, EMMA. Get up."

Emma tossed a pillow at the nuisance who shook her. "Don't you have to get to work or something?"

"I took the day off. Doctor's orders," Jasmine said, giving Emma a good shake again.

"Liar."

"Not a new one though. I told them I was getting sick yesterday. So I'm just extending the lie for another day."

Emma rolled away, ducking under her one remaining pillow.

"Besides," Jasmine said, emphasizing her words with a concerted effort to pull off Emma's covers. "You need to get out of the apartment today. You're beginning to smell like a hermit."

Emma rolled back to face her evil roommate. "And what does a hermit smell like?"

"You. Now get up."

"No."

"Yes. Brat. Annah's coming over in an hour."

"Who says?" Emma sat up.

"I says. She's been calling all week. We're going to Nahant for the day."

Emma pushed off her covers. "I smell a conspiracy."

"You smell your stinky self." Jasmine tossed her pillow back at her. "Go take a shower."

Emma knew what they were up to, but she didn't fight it. Maybe a quiet day on the beach would help. Still, she made loud groans of protest as she trudged off to the shower. "There'd better be coffee ready when I get out," she shouted from the bathroom before turning the water on. The hot water cascaded down her back and shoulders. But instead of clearing her thoughts, it only reminded her of erotic dreams she'd had of Nicole. She leaned against the cool tiles, wishing she could somehow just make the next few days disappear. If it were Monday, it would all be done with, she thought.

A steaming mug sat on the counter for her when she came out. She was clean but already regretting she hadn't fought harder to avoid the outing. The wedding was tomorrow and not even warm, sandy beaches would clear her troubled mind. She'd rather wallow in self-pity in the quiet comforts of her own room. She sipped at her coffee as she searched for a way out of the excursion. Annah arrived soon after she finished the mug of coffee.

"You're getting around well with that thing," Jasmine said as she let Annah in.

"Walker casts are the best. I mean if you've got to be lamed up and all," Annah said.

Emma leaned against the counter, her mind calculating the time remaining until Nicole would be legally wed.

"Hey, wake up," Annah teased. "Don't make me poke you with my cane." She held up a fluorescent green cane to prove her point.

"Hey," Emma said. "I don't want to disappoint, but maybe it's better if I just stay home."

"Nope," Annah said. "Not an option."

Emma pushed herself off the counter. "Seriously. I'm not feeling up to it."

Jasmine shrugged. "Okay, if you insist. Looks like we spend the day playing monopoly."

"Dibs on being the banker," Annah said.

Emma looked from one over-eager face to the other. "Maybe the beach would be better." At least she could take a long, quiet walk by herself.

EMMA WAS NEVER by herself. Wherever she went, one or the other of the conspiracy twins followed her. When she stood in the surf, Jasmine stood with her, the waves lapping at their bare feet. When she tried to go for a walk, Annah attempted to hobble beside her. Emma gave up the walk, for Annah's sake. But when they went so far as to have Jasmine trot alongside her on the way to the restrooms, Emma revolted.

"Look," she said. "This is over the top. Can't I take a pee by myself?"

"Nope," Jasmine said.

"Give me a break," she said. She could only take so much coddling.

Jasmine turned Emma toward her. "This isn't just about you, Emma. It's about me, too."

"What do you mean?" Emma felt a flush of embarrassment. She'd spent most of the day dwelling on her pathetic state and hadn't considered what her two companions might be feeling.

"I haven't had the best few weeks, either," Jasmine said, standing in front of Emma in the sand, her hands on her hips. "But somehow, you've been there for me when I needed you." Jasmine held her hand. "Don't block me out now. I need to be here for you, to help you like you've helped me."

Emma's resistance ebbed. "Sorry."

"'S okay," Jasmine said, resuming her walk. "Just don't let it happen again, or I'll have to let the kid give you a good swift kick in the butt with her mega-boot."

"Nice."

"Thanks. I try."

The warm sun beat down on them all afternoon. Annah was stuck on the beach because of her cast, but Jasmine dragged Emma into the ocean to swim and cool off. The waves off Nahant Beach were non-existent and they floated in silence on the salty water. Between the two of them, they managed to cool Annah off when they got out of the water by shaking all their excess droplets over the less than amused teenager.

"What's for dinner?" Annah asked.

Emma sank to the sand. Dinnertime. That meant less than twenty-four hours, and Nicole would be on her way to the Bahamas with Adam. Dark clouds settled over her spirit, separating her from the discussion over where they would go to eat. She felt a knot form in her stomach. She needed to be alone. "I'm going for a walk," she announced as she stood up and brushed the clinging sand off her still damp shorts.

"Okay, fun bus on the move," Jasmine announced.

Emma turned to her. "Not this time. I need time alone. Just let me go for a walk on my own." Something in her expression must have registered with them. Jasmine nodded in silence. Emma left the two of them and walked along the wet shoreline with the warm sun at her back. Somehow, she would have to get through the next twenty-four hours, and then maybe things would get better. Then she could give up any lingering fantasy that Nicole would come back to her. And then what?

The bitterness of her thoughts startled her. Thinking about the risk she'd taken with Nicole, she realized that she'd do it all over again, given the chance. Even knowing how it would all end. She took a chance and it failed, but that chance made her feel more alive than she had in years.

When Emma returned, she felt no better than when she'd left. Long solitary walks only worked in the movies. Jasmine and Annah were in the midst of a discussion about the incomprehensible nature of parents.

"How's your mother been?" Emma asked as she settled on her green and blue beach blanket. "Still dead set against the whole writer thing?"

Annah brushed sand off her cast. "She's been quiet about it the last week or so."

"Well," Jasmine said. "People have sympathy for the lame. She'll get back to it once the cast is off."

Annah laughed. "Yeah, maybe." She turned to Emma. "Meanwhile, we made dinner plans while you were walking off your doom and gloom."

"And the penultimate plan would be?" Emma asked.

"Pizza," they said in chorus.

"Again?" she grumbled.

Jasmine stood up and shook off the sand. "Nothing wrong with pizza. It has all the major food groups." She held out her hand to pull Annah up off the ground.

"Sand in a cast is not a good thing," Annah mumbled as she hobbled toward the parking lot.

"Next time wrap it in plastic," Jasmine offered.

Annah turned to give her a dirty look. "Fashionable, very fashionable."

Chapter
Fifteen

SUNLIGHT CASCADED OVER Emma's closed eyelids. She ducked under the thin cotton sheet, trying to regain the comforting state of her dreamless sleep. She turned away from the window and buried her head under the pillow. It was no use. Her mind and body were awake. She couldn't avoid worrying about what time it was. She gave up and lifted her head, pushing her unkempt hair out of her eyes as she searched for her clock radio.

It flashed 10:00 a.m.

Three hours until the wedding. Emma rolled back and pulled the sheet up over her head, willing herself not to cry. Tears would get her nothing but another dull headache. She told herself today would be the worst, and then it would be over. She could move on. Somehow, even being cut off from Nicole for the last few days wasn't final enough for Emma. When Nicole made her commitment to Adam, then it would be final. Then, Emma told herself, she could move on and struggle through this horrible summer.

Knowing Nicole's schedule for the day didn't help her. She pulled herself out of bed and made her way into the bathroom for a shower. Nicole would be doing just about the same thing. Emma looked at herself in the mirror. The brightness of the brown eyes that stared back at her belied the tired, drawn soul beneath. At least her bed hair accurately represented how she felt. A tangled mess of chestnut knots hung over her bare shoulders. She stepped into the shower, letting the steaming hot water beat down on her head and shoulders.

Nicole would have her parents with her by now, maybe even the maid of honor, Katie. Nicole hadn't thought a hairdressing appointment was necessary for the morning. She'd be drying her hair and possibly styling it by now, on her own. Emma hoped she wouldn't curl it. Nicole's hair fell naturally above her collar, perfectly framing her high cheekbones.

Emma poured shampoo into the palm of her hand and worked

it into her tangled hair. The scent of lavender filled the tiny bathtub shower, causing Emma to lean against the cool tile walls. She bought this shampoo after Nicole told her about the lavender bushes at her aunt's house. Emma choked back the tears as she rinsed it out, watching the foaming bubbles work their way down the drain at her feet.

She worked her fingers through her hair while the water tried to beat away her thoughts of Nicole. She managed to rinse off and dry herself before she wondered when Nicole would slip into that beautiful, beaded gown. Emma stepped out of the shower and sat on the toilet lid, her head in her hands. She had to stop doing this to herself. If she reminded herself, step by step, of every detail of Nicole's wedding day, she'd never make it to one o'clock.

Someone banged on the bathroom door. "You coming out anytime soon?" Jasmine shouted.

"Yes, just a minute." Emma wrapped a towel around herself and scooped up the shorts and t-shirt she'd slept in. When she emerged, she saw Jasmine standing outside the bathroom, looking her up and down.

"Nice packaging," Jasmine said with a wink.

Emma didn't bother to smile. She shuffled into her bedroom to get dressed. The glowing alarm clock said it was ten minutes to eleven. She had taken a long shower. She ignored her running shorts in favor of knee-length blue shorts and a white tank top. The warm air already blowing in through her open bedroom window told her it would be a hot, sunny day.

Jasmine knocked on her door. "You want any breakfast? I bought muffins."

"No," she said. Her stomach felt better empty today. Maybe she'd be up for food after one o'clock. She remembered the Beef Wellington with Yorkshire pudding entrée that Nicole had selected for the reception. Maybe Emma wouldn't be eating today at all. She sat on her bed, towel drying her hair. She could get a blow dryer for it, but there was no sense in rushing. She picked up her comb and worked out the worst of the tangles first, then applied her brush.

She began counting each brush stroke. She'd read somewhere that women used to do that for hours, probably back before the discovery of conditioners. Emma lost track after about twenty-five. She watched the hint of blue sky visible between her window and the top of the mechanic's garage that operated behind her apartment building. Emma brushed her hair until she was sure it was a frizzy mess. She felt along the length of it. No, it didn't seem too bad, for all the excess brushing it got this morning. She heard the doorbell ring. Maybe Jasmine would be going out, and she'd have the apartment to herself today for private moping. She looked at the clock. Less than an hour to go. She willed the numbers to change more quickly, but it didn't help.

She was startled out of her reverie by a soft knock on her bedroom door. "I'm still not hungry," she shouted.

Jasmine's voice came back from what seemed a long distance. "You've got company, Emma!"

Emma frowned and turned as her bedroom door creaked open. She froze a moment as the person in front of her walked in and leaned against the door until it quietly clicked shut.

"Nicole?" Emma drank in the sight of Nicole leaning against her bedroom door. Nicole was dressed in navy pants and light yellow v-neck top. Her hair wasn't curled, and for that Emma was grateful, but she did wear the slightest hint of makeup perhaps, with her lips deep red and her cheeks pink. She stood there watching Emma, not saying anything. Emma shifted to the edge of the bed, not sure if she should stand or sit. She wanted to verify the time. Maybe it was earlier, and Nicole just stopped by to say good-bye before the wedding? But Emma couldn't take her eyes off the beautiful, silent woman before her.

She noticed the dark circles under Nicole's soft brown eyes, a mirror to the marks under her own eyes. "Are you all right?" she asked. "Did something go wrong?"

Nicole pushed herself off the door and stood in the middle of the room, her hands working nervously on the edges of her top. "Emma. I, I don't know what to say."

Emma felt herself melt under the intense gaze of those brown eyes. She forced herself to look away. "I'm sorry," she choked out, "if that's what you are looking for."

"Sorry?" Nicole asked.

Emma nodded. "Last Saturday. Sorry for what happened between us."

"Are you sorry that it happened?" Nicole's voice cracked as she spoke.

Emma looked back at her, saw the tears forming in her eyes and the way her hands shook at her side.

"I thought that's what you came for," Emma said. "What you wanted to hear."

Nicole shook her head. "I'm not sorry."

"I don't understand," Emma said, frowning. Her heart and mind warred with each other, battling over different interpretations of Nicole's words.

"I left him." Nicole wiped at her eyes.

Emma blinked. Left him? "But why?"

Nicole stifled a cry. "Oh God, don't you know? Maybe you really are sorry for what happened between us."

Emma's heart hammered in her chest. "I'm not," she said. "I mean, I am. I mean, I don't know what I mean."

Nicole's eyes pleaded with her.

Emma stood up, fighting the urge to wrap her arms around Nicole, to kiss away the sadness in her expression. "I never wanted to hurt you, Nicole. I love you." There, she'd said it. She forced herself not to regret her admission. Nicole studied her. Emma stood motionless, unwilling to acknowledge the fear she felt inside.

"Do you really love me?" Nicole whispered.

Emma took a step closer. "Yes, I do."

Nicole's hands covered her face, and Emma heard the muffled sobs as Nicole's shoulders shook. Emma bounced from foot to foot, unsure of what to do next. The sounds of Nicole's quiet crying made up Emma's mind. Finally, her heart and mind agreed. She couldn't bear to watch Nicole cry. Emma closed the space between them and lifted a trembling hand to stroke Nicole's brown hair.

"Please don't cry," she said. "I don't know what I've done wrong."

Nicole's tears subsided. She brushed away the remnants as she looked into Emma's eyes and smiled softly.

"Nothing, Love," she said. "You've done nothing wrong." Nicole's hands sought out hers. "I've been so confused, so lost without you these past few days."

Emma leaned forward until their foreheads touched. "So have I. I've missed you so much."

Nicole lifted a hand, caressing Emma's cheek. Emma let her eyes drift shut.

"I'm sorry I upset you," Emma said

"Shh." Nicole rested her finger on Emma's lips. "I should be apologizing, Love. I should never have run away like that."

Emma tried to speak, but Nicole replaced her finger with her lips, placing a tentative kiss on Emma's lips. Nicole leaned back again to speak. "You made me feel something I've never felt before." She cupped Emma's face in her hands.

Emma felt as if her whole body tingled at once when those words echoed inside her. She pulled Nicole closer, kissing her deeply. The heat and rush of desire swelled inside her, a feeling she never thought to have again with this beautiful British woman.

Nicole shifted until her lips brushed Emma's ear as she whispered, "Take me to bed."

"Are you sure?" Emma steeled herself for rejection, but none came.

"Please. I need this. I need you." Nicole's hands drifted down Emma's back, pulling her in closer. She felt the warm press of Nicole's body on hers and heat throbbed between her thighs. Her legs moved of their own will, bringing Nicole with her to the unmade bed. Emma knelt on her bed, still holding Nicole's hand. She looked up, searching for signs of hesitation. She saw only Nicole's dark, dilated pupils and her moist red lips.

Nicole knelt beside her on the bed. "I'm not sure what to do."

Emma smiled. "Just do whatever feels right."

Warm air from the window blew across them as they slowly explored each other. Emma leaned in and trailed a line of soft kisses down Nicole's cheek and neck, ending at the open collar of Nicole's v-neck top. She heard a quiet sigh as Nicole pressed herself closer. Emma lifted her head and felt hot breath as Nicole's lips sought hers. Her body rose with passion, her hands slipping under Nicole's blouse and feeling the heated flesh under her palms.

Emma's breath caught as Nicole ran her fingers along her bare legs. She was amazed that all her attention could be focused on one electric sensation as Nicole traced her fingers up Emma's thighs until she hit the edge of her shorts. Emma caressed Nicole's arms. She kissed along the neckline of Nicole's top and then softly brought her hand up to feel the curve of Nicole's covered breast. Nicole gasped, causing Emma to pause. She looked up into Nicole's face.

"Please," Nicole whispered. "Don't stop."

With trembling hands, Emma pulled off Nicole's top, exposing an intricate lace bra covering full, sensuous breasts. She touched the outline of the bra as she drank in the beauty before her. Nicole reached back and undid the clasp. She hesitated a moment, and Emma saw a glimmer of shyness take over her lover.

"May I?" Emma asked, her voice deep and shaky.

Nicole nodded, her face flushed.

With one hand on each strap, Emma eased the bra down Nicole's shoulders, exposing round breasts and delicious pink nipples. She let out a long slow breath as Nicole tossed aside the bra. Emma gently pushed Nicole back onto the pillows, and then she kissed the smooth skin between Nicole's soft breasts. She traced her tongue around Nicole's belly button, then back up to feel the soft curve of Nicole's breast against her cheek.

Her hair cascaded over Nicole as she lowered herself on top of her lover, sliding her legs between Nicole's. She drew an erect nipple into her mouth and suckled. Nicole moaned and squirmed beneath her, pushing herself harder onto Emma's thigh. Emma lifted herself up. Watching Nicole for signs of acceptance, she worked open the button and zipper on Nicole's jeans.

Nicole lifted Emma's hand aside and, in one swift motion, pulled off her jeans and white lace panties, kicking off her sandals in the process. She lay back on the bed, her lithe body shining with perspiration from the humid day. Emma stared at the beautiful mound of light brown pubic hair between Nicole's thighs. She wanted to sink into it, bury herself in its scent and wetness.

"You're beautiful," she murmured as she slid down Nicole's body. She let her long hair caress Nicole's body as she kissed Nicole's thigh. She gently cupped Nicole's pubic mound, feeling Nicole's hips rise to meet her hand. Emma felt her own need throbbing as she let one finger slide lightly along Nicole's wetness. Nicole gasped. Emma stroked up and down with more pressure, while Nicole's hips reached for her, quivering.

Emma slid down further. She pulled back her own long hair and then took one long lick of Nicole's wetness as she slid her finger inside her lover. Nicole let out a long deep moan, her hips trembling in her arousal. Emma felt how close Nicole was as she licked and teased, drawing her finger in and out to the rhythm set by Nicole's thrusting hips. She felt her own moisture dampening her shorts as her desire rose with Nicole's.

Nicole's hands clutched the sheets on either side of her as short high gasps escaped her lips. Emma pushed deeper, with each rise of Nicole's hips, keeping pace with her tongue until she felt the final thrust of Nicole's hips against her hand, felt Nicole tighten around her finger as her body clenched in the final act of orgasm.

A loud, low groan signaled Nicole's completion as she collapsed against the crumpled sheets. Emma rested against her thigh a moment, rocking her own need on Nicole's leg. She withdrew her finger reluctantly.

"Come up here," Nicole whispered.

Emma shifted so she lay beside her lover, enjoying the glistening perspiration that covered Nicole's naked body. Nicole kissed her, gently at first, and then more deeply, urging Emma's lips to part for her exploring tongue. Emma's body felt electrified wherever Nicole's body touched her.

Nicole's hands drifted under her top. "I believe you're over-dressed for the occasion, Love."

Emma pushed herself up as Nicole lifted her shirt and pulled it up over her head. As she brushed her cheeks against Emma's exposed breasts, Nicole's brown hair tickled Emma's chest. Nicole caressed the curve and rise of Emma's breasts, brushing across her hardened nipples. Emma closed her eyes as the heat from Nicole's touch sent jolts of arousal shooting down between her thighs.

Nicole tugged at Emma's shorts. "Buttonflies?"

Emma smiled. "Do you need some help with that?"

"No, I can do it. At least this part."

Emma sensed Nicole's shyness returning. Her lover's shaking hands fumbled on the buttons. "Let me help," she said, working the buttons on her own shorts.

Nicole slid her hands under Emma's waistband and pushed shorts and panties down below Emma's knees, and then stopped. Emma waited, her legs shaking. Nicole sat back, her gaze riveted on Emma's body. Emma felt a growing sense of panic.

"Nicole?"

Nicole looked up at her. "You're so beautiful."

Emma pushed the rest of her clothes off, kicking them to the floor. Her cheeks flushed under the heat of Nicole's penetrating stare. Finally, Nicole spoke again. "What should I do?" she asked.

Emma lay back down. "Lay down with me."

Nicole lay beside her, curving her body to Emma's. She bent her head to kiss the space between Emma's breasts. Emma moaned when Nicole's tongue licked her nipple, then gasped when Nicole suckled, feeding Emma's hot desire. She moved Nicole's hand lower. "I want you to touch me."

Nicole's trembling fingers stroked along Emma's inner thighs. Emma moved her legs wider as she focused on the sensation of Nicole touching her thighs and lower abdomen. Her hips swayed, yearning for Nicole's touch. Then Nicole's fingers brushed along Emma's outer folds, sending thrills through her. Nicole's fingers dipped into her wetness, and Emma moaned.

Nicole stroked slowly in circles. "Is this all right?" she asked.

Emma's hands pressed on Nicole's back, pulling her closer. "Oh yes," she said.

Nicole's mouth returned to Emma's breast as her fingers worked in slow circles. Emma gasped, her hips pushing against Nicole's hand. She felt herself grow moister, slicker, as Nicole dipped into her wetness and returned to slow, languorous circles around her pulsing need.

"Harder, please," Emma begged.

Nicole's fingers pushed more firmly, driving Emma's excitement to new heights. Her body quivered as Nicole's rhythm matched her rising passion. Nicole lifted her head and kissed her lips hard. Emma thrust one last time against Nicole's hand as an orgasm shot through every part of her body.

She fell back on the bed, sweating and panting in Nicole's arms. Nicole lay beside her, her head resting on Emma's shoulder. The hot afternoon breeze filtered over their intertwined, sweating bodies until they both drifted into a peaceful sleep.

Chapter
Sixteen

EMMA WOKE UP when someone on the street blasted their car horn. The diffuse light that cast its glow across her bed sheets did nothing to help her recognize the time of day. Nicole still lay nestled in the crook of her arm, her warm breath blowing softly across Emma's chest. Emma's stomach rumbled. Nicole shifted and stretched beside her.

"What time is it?" Nicole asked, blinking.

Emma checked her clock. "It's only three o'clock."

Nicole settled back against her as Emma's stomach protested its empty state again.

"Feeling hungry?" Nicole teased.

"Hmm. Haven't eaten well this week," Emma confessed.

Nicole rose on an elbow. "Because of me?"

Emma cringed at Nicole's sad expression. She brushed her hand along her lover's cheek. "It doesn't matter. You're here now."

Nicole leaned into Emma's palm. "I love you."

Emma pulled her closer, covering her mouth with a long, passionate kiss. "I love you, too," she said after they separated.

Emma's stomach interrupted their moment. Nicole laughed.

"Maybe we should get something for that rebellious tummy of yours," Nicole suggested.

Emma sat up. "All right." She looked at Nicole, not wanting to have to cover that gorgeous body just yet. "Any chance I can entice you into the shower first?"

Nicole's face flushed. "Don't you have a roommate?"

Emma rolled over Nicole and tiptoed to the door. She listened awhile, and then opened the door a crack. "Seems we're all alone," she said as she sat back on the bed. "So, a nice shower and then the hunt for food?" Nicole sat up in bed, pulling the sheet up to her waist. Emma saw the shy expression on her lover's face and guessed its origin.

"Could I see it?" she asked, stroking Nicole's leg under the sheet.

"It's ugly."

Emma leaned over and kissed her. "You're beautiful, everything about you is beautiful." She slowly lowered the sheet. When Nicole didn't protest, she pulled it all the way off and ran her hand up Nicole's lean leg. She traced one finger along the white scar that stretched along Nicole's upper thigh.

"I can't really feel anything there," Nicole said.

"Nerve damage?"

Nicole nodded.

Emma lowered herself and traced small kisses around the outside of the scar where she hoped Nicole could feel it. "I love you," she said.

Nicole smiled. "A shower, then?"

"Hmm, yes, please." Emma got up and wrapped a towel around herself. She pulled out her blue cotton robe, and Nicole slipped into it, tying the robe around her slim waist. Emma peeked out to check once more, and then they skipped into the bathroom and locked the door. Emma turned on the water while Nicole let the robe slip to the tile floor. Emma's breath caught once again, seeing Nicole's naked body before her. They stepped into the steamy shower together, the water beating down between them. Nicole ran her hands along Emma's side and back, threatening to re-ignite their earlier passion. When Nicole's stomach growled in answer to Emma's, they both giggled.

"Maybe we should stick to washing," Emma suggested.

Nicole found the soap and lathered her hands. "Turn around," she said.

Emma faced the shower wall as Nicole ran her soapy hands along Emma's back, spending extra time massaging Emma's backside before continuing on to her legs. Emma pressed her hands against the shower wall, praying her knees wouldn't give out as Nicole drew her hands around to Emma's front in slow sensual circles. Emma's breathing came in short gasps as Nicole re-soaped her hands. Then pressing herself against Emma's back, she ran her slippery hands along Emma's abdomen, chest, and along the curves of her breasts. She spent just a moment teasing Emma's nipples before letting go for Emma to rinse off.

Emma regained her balance as the water washed away the soap, but not the sensations of Nicole's hands on her body. Emma switched positions with Nicole. She soaped up her hands, but when Nicole made to turn her back, Emma stopped her. "I like to start with the front," she said with a smile.

Emma let her hands slide along Nicole's arms and sides, and then she slid her hands down Nicole's chest and cupped her breasts. Nicole's intake of breath was cut short when Emma leaned in to kiss her. Sliding her hands around Nicole's back, she pulled her lover closer. Nicole moaned softly, "This is a bit more than just washing, Love."

"Complaining?" Emma asked.

"Oh no, definitely not complaining."

They held each other under the hot spray of the shower, kissing faces and necks, nibbling a shoulder, licking droplets of water.

Emma pulled back. "Still have places to clean," she said with a grin. Her next exploration went along Nicole's back, then down her legs. She knelt and slid her hands between Nicole's silky thighs, feeling the water cascade over her face while she longed to taste her lover once again.

A prolonged stomach growl from Nicole made her smile instead. "Okay," she said. "I take the hint."

"Sorry, Love," Nicole said with a laugh, pulling her up and greeting her with a long wet kiss. They stayed in each other's arms while the rest of the soap swirled down the drain. Reluctantly, Emma turned off the water. She stepped out of the shower and passed Nicole a dry towel, grabbing another one for herself. Emma offered to dry Nicole's body for her.

"I don't think I could stay standing if you did," Nicole said.

Emma shrugged. "Can't blame a girl for trying."

When they were both dry, Nicole wrapped herself in Emma's robe again, and Emma draped a towel around herself as she opened the bathroom door to let Nicole out first. A wave of steam followed them out. Nicole froze, and Emma looked around her to see Jasmine sitting at the kitchen table, a wide grin on her face.

"Awful lot of giggling going on in that shower, Ladies," Jasmine said, eyeing them both up and down.

Emma watched Nicole's face turn bright red. "Nice timing, Jasmine," she said.

"Hey, I thought four hours would be enough for you two, but I guess I underestimated the allure of all things British."

Nicole ducked her head into Emma's shoulder, stifling a laugh.

"I hope you two are hungry," Jasmine said. "I brought home a ton of Chinese food."

"Mind if we get dressed first?" Emma said, leading Nicole back to her bedroom.

"Don't feel the need to get all formal on my account," Jasmine replied as Emma shut her bedroom door. Moments later they emerged, dressed and ready to eat. Jasmine set out plates and served up chow mein, fried rice, and pork strips for herself. Emma and Nicole chose their own dinner from broccoli with beef, shrimp and snow peas, and some unrecognizable egg dish.

"So," Jasmine said over a mouthful of rice. "I want to hear all about it."

Nicole blushed furiously.

"She means all about Adam and the wedding," Emma said.

Jasmine shrugged. "I'm not squeamish. You can tell me all about the last four hours if you prefer."

"No, thank you." Nicole said, finally finding her voice.

"Okay, then the wedding, or lack of a wedding."

Jasmine's eager face waited for Nicole to begin. Emma tried to hide her own growing interest as Nicole explained breaking down and confessing her feelings to her mother Thursday evening.

"Talking to my mum just made me realize that I couldn't go through with it, the wedding," she said. "I didn't love Adam anymore. I'm not sure I ever really did. He was just convenient, you know?"

Emma nodded, though she didn't fully understand. But she didn't want to interrupt Nicole's story.

Nicole reached out and took Emma's hand. "I realized it was you that I wanted a future with. When I'm with you, I feel like I can be myself. And you make me feel special, like I'm more important to you than anything or anyone else."

"You are," Emma said, wrapping her arm around her lover.

"I didn't know how my parents would react when I confessed that I was in love with a woman," Nicole said.

"What did they say?" Emma asked.

"My dad didn't say much," Nicole said. "But he leaves most of the emotional chats to my mother." Nicole smiled, looking at Emma. "She wants to meet you."

Emma swallowed hard. Meeting Nicole's parents after all that had happened seemed a frightening notion at the moment.

"So," Jasmine interrupted. "Who told Pam, and who told Adam?"

"I went to see Adam last night. My mum dealt with his mother directly. It was hard enough for me to talk to Adam." Nicole rested her head on Emma's shoulder. "I'd rather not go into the full details," she continued. "Suffice it to say it was a difficult day, the hardest of my life."

Emma squeezed her lover's hand.

"Oh, and my mother did use some choice language when she talked to Adam's mum. I don't think I've ever heard such words coming from my mum before." Nicole smiled.

"Such as?" Jasmine prodded.

"Oh, something to the effect of 'Bugger off, you and your son's political future,' and 'Obstinate old cow! You weren't paying for any of this anyway.'"

"Oh, I wish I could have been the fly on that wall," Jasmine said as she cleared away her plate. "So, now what?"

Emma felt a tremor run through Nicole. She looked at her lover and saw doubt and fear reflected in Nicole's eyes.

Nicole lowered her eyes. "I'm to go back to England this week. My mum wants me to come home for the summer."

Emma felt her heart lurch. Nicole would be gone all summer? Her face paled as she looked to Nicole for reassurance, for some indication that this wasn't her way of saying good-bye. Her heartbeat echoed in her ears as she waited in silence. Nicole played with Emma's fingertips for a moment, and then looked up. Emma saw the same questioning expression in Nicole's face.

Nicole cupped Emma's hand in her own. "I'm going back to Oxford for the summer."

Emma nodded, fighting to hold back tears that threatened to spill at the thought of Nicole being so far from her.

Nicole lifted Emma's face when she'd looked down. "Will you come with me?" she asked, so softly Emma mistrusted her hearing.

"What?" Emma asked.

"To England, Love. Will you come with me, for the summer?"

Emma felt as if she floated on top of a gentle ocean wave. "You mean to your parents'?"

Nicole nodded. "We live outside Oxford, in the Thames valley. I can't say we'd have much to occupy our time compared to this area."

Emma's mind flashed with what they could do to occupy the hours in the quiet English countryside. Her cheeks flushed. "Yes," she said. "I'd love to come to England with you."

Then she wondered where they would be staying and her eyes grew wide. "Will we be staying with your parents?" she squeaked.

"Yes," Nicole said over the sound of Jasmine's laughter. "And," she added with emphasis, "They know all about you, and they know I love you." Nicole pulled Emma's hand to cover her heart. "I love you, and I want you with me. That's all that matters to them, and to me."

"I love you, too," Emma sighed. Two months of making love to Nicole would not be enough. Two lifetimes wouldn't be enough, she thought. She whispered a silent prayer of thanks to whatever power had brought them together, and would keep them together for what she hoped would be forever.

Butch Girls Can Fix Anything

by Paula Offutt

Kelly Walker can fix anything — except herself. Grace Owens seeks a stable community of friends for herself and her daughter. Lucy Owens wants help with her fourth-grade math. As their stories unfold in the fictional town of High Pond, N.C., each must deal with her own version of trust, risks, and what makes someone strong.

ISBN 978-1-932300-74-1

And Playing the Role of Herself

by K. E. Lane

Actress Caidance Harris is living her dreams after landing a leading role among the star-studded, veteran cast of *9th Precinct*, a hot new police drama shot on location in glitzy LA. Her sometimes-costar Robyn Ward is magnetic, glamorous, and devastatingly beautiful, the quintessential A-List celebrity on the fast-track to super-stardom. When the two meet on the set of *9th Precinct*, Caid is instantly infatuated but settles for friendship, positive that Robyn is both unavailable and uninterested. Soon Caid sees that all is not as it appears, but can she take a chance and risk her heart when the outcome is so uncertain?

The leading ladies and supporting cast of this debut novel by newcomer K. E. Lane will charm you, entertain you, and leave you with a smile on your face, eager for Ms. Lane's next offering.

ISBN 978-1-932300-72-7

FORTHCOMING TITLES
from Yellow Rose Books

Breaking Jaie

by Renee Bess

Jaie Baxter, an African-American Ph.D candidate at Philadelphia's Allerton University, is determined to win a prestigious writing grant. In order to win the Adamson Grant, Jaie initially plans to take advantage of one of the competition's judges, Jennifer Renfrew, who is also a University official. Jennifer has spent the past ten years alone following the murder of her lover, Patricia Adamson, in whose honor the grant is named. Jennifer is at first susceptible to Jaie's flirtation, but is later vengeful when she discovers the real reason for Jaie's sudden romantic interest in her. A lunch with an old cop friend reveals that Jaie may very well have ties to Adamson's death.

Jaie is confronted with painful memories as she prepares an autobiographical essay for the grant application. She recalls the emotional trauma of her older brother's death, the murder of a police detective, her dismissal from her "dream" high school, and her victimization at the hands of hateful homophobic students. She remembers her constant struggles with her mother's alcohol-fueled jealousies and physical abuse she had to endure. This wake-up call causes her to look at her life in new ways.

But Jaie is not the only student applying for the grant. Terez Overton, a wealthy Boston woman, is Jaie's chief competitor. Jaie is drawn to the New Englander immediately but is also unnerved by her. She has no clue that Terez is trying to decide whether she wants to accept an opportunity to write an investigative article about an unsolved murder. Writing that article could put her budding relationship with Jaie in jeopardy.

And just when the angst of old memories and the uncertainty of her future with Terez are complicating Jaie's life, her manipulative ex, Seneca Wilson, returns to Philadelphia to reclaim Jaie using emotional blackmail. Senecas actions serve to wound and break Jaie in many ways. Will Seneca drive the final wedge between Jaie and Terez? Who will win the Adamson grant? And what did Jaie have to do with the death of Patricia Adamson?

Coming August 2007

Family Values

by Vicki Stevenson

Devastated by the collapse of her long-term relationship, Alice Cruz decides to begin life anew. She moves to a small town, rents an apartment, and establishes a career in real estate. But when she tries to liquidate some of her investments for a down payment on a house, she discovers that she has been victimized by a con artist.

Local resident Tyler Sorensen has a track record of countless affairs without any emotional involvement. Known for her sexy good looks, easygoing kindness, and unique approach to problems, Tyler is asked by a mutual friend to figure out how Alice can recover her money.

While Tyler's elaborate plan progresses and members of her LGBT family work toward the solution, they discover that the con game involves more people and far higher stakes than they had imagined. As the family encounters unexpected obstacles, Tyler and Alice struggle with a growing emotional connection deeper than either woman has ever experienced.

Coming August 2007

OTHER YELLOW ROSE PUBLICATIONS

Sandra Barret	Lavender Secrets	978-1-932300-73-4
Georgia Beers	Thy Neighbor's Wife	1-932300-15-5
Carrie Brennan	Curve	1-932300-41-4
Carrie Carr	Destiny's Bridge	1-932300-11-2
Carrie Carr	Faith's Crossing	1-932300-12-0
Carrie Carr	Hope's Path	1-932300-40-6
Carrie Carr	Love's Journey	978-1-932300-65-9
Carrie Carr	Something to Be Thankful For	1-932300-04-X
Carrie Carr	Diving Into the Turn	978-1-932300-54-3
Linda Crist	Galveston 1900: Swept Away	1-932300-44-9
Linda Crist	The Bluest Eyes in Texas	978-1-932300-48-2
Jennifer Fulton	Passion Bay	1-932300-25-2
Jennifer Fulton	Saving Grace	1-932300-26-0
Jennifer Fulton	The Sacred Shore	1-932300-35-X
Jennifer Fulton	A Guarded Heart	1-932300-37-6
Jennifer Fulton	Dark Dreamer	1-932300-46-5
Anna Furtado	The Heart's Desire	1-932300-32-5
Lois Glenn	Scarlet E	978-1-932300-75-8
Gabrielle Goldsby	The Caretaker's Daughter	1-932300-18-X
Melissa Good	Eye of the Storm	1-932300-13-9
Melissa Good	Thicker Than Water	1-932300-24-4
Melissa Good	Terrors of the High Seas	1-932300-45-7
Melissa Good	Tropical Storm	978-1-932300-60-4
Maya Indigal	Until Soon	1-932300-31-7
Lori L. Lake	Different Dress	1-932300-08-2
Lori L. Lake	Ricochet In Time	1-932300-17-1
K. E. Lane	And, Playing the Role of Herself	978-1-932300-72-7
J. Y Morgan	Learning To Trust	978-1-932300-59-8
A. K. Naten	Turning Tides	978-1-932300-47-5
Meghan O'Brien	Infinite Loop	1-932300-42-2
Paula Offutt	Butch Girls Can Fix Anything	978-1-932300-74-1
Sharon Smith	Into The Dark	1-932300-38-4
Surtees and Dunne	True Colours	978-1-932300-52-9
Surtees and Dunne	Many Roads to Travel	978-1-932300-55-0
Cate Swannell	Heart's Passage	1-932300-09-0
Cate Swannell	No Ocean Deep	1-932300-36-8
L. A. Tucker	The Light Fantastic	1-932300-14-7

About the Author:

Sandra Barret grew up in New England, where she spent more years than she cares to mention as a software programmer. She lives on a small horse farm with her partner, two children, and more pets than are probably legal to own. She's an avid reader of lesbian SF, fantasy, horror, and romance.

Web site: www.sandrabarret.com

Printed in the United States
68012LVS00008B/166-171

9 781932 300734